INTO
THE
DEEP

SAMANTHA YOUNG

Other Contemporary Novels by Samantha Young

On Dublin Street Series:
On Dublin Street
Down London Road
Until Fountain Bridge (a novella)

Young Adult Urban Fantasy titles by Samantha Young

The Tale of Lunarmorte Trilogy:
Moon Spell
River Cast
Blood Solstice

Warriors of Ankh Trilogy:
Blood Will Tell
Blood Past
Shades of Blood

Fire Spirits Series:
Smokeless Fire
Scorched Skies
Borrowed Ember
Darkness, Kindled

Other titles by Samantha Young

Slumber (The Fade #1)
Drip Drop Teardrop, a novella

Dedication

For Whitney, Henny, Liza and Steph, my American roommates.
You made my first year at the University of Edinburgh so fun. I had
the best time with you guys. Thanks for the memories. And the funny photos.
Those are definitely keepers...

Chapter One

Edinburgh, September 2012

"Did you go food shopping yet? Is the food expensive? Do you understand what half of it is?"

I swallowed my laughter. "Mom, I'm in Scotland, not the Amazon."

"I know but they eat things we wouldn't dare eat."

She sounded so horrified I couldn't help my dry retort. "They're not cannibals."

A spray of soda shot past my eyeline and I twisted to see my best friend Claudia choking on Diet Coke as she listened to my side of the conversation. We were sitting in the kitchen of our student apartment, our butts on the comfortable, but still weird, waiting room chairs that had been supplied in our common room/kitchen. Our backs were to the wide floor-to-ceiling window that looked out over the courtyard of our building, the sun hitting the glass and prickling our skin with its heat. Everything about the room was clean, fresh, and hardwearing. The accommodation was basic but it was warm and safe and a million times better than I'd been led to believe it would be.

"So dramatic, Charley. I'm just saying, the food is a little different," Mom continued. "I want to make sure you're eating right."

Whether I was in Edinburgh or back home in Indiana, my mom always wanted to make sure I was eating right. This was because I couldn't cook. Delia Redford was an awesome cook and baker, as was her oldest daughter, Andrea, so she took the fact that her youngest (that would be me) couldn't so much as boil pasta without screwing it up as a personal failure on her part. Luckily for me, I could read and work an oven so frozen dinners kept me from starvation.

"Mom, they eat pretty much what we eat mostly because … you know … they're people."

"Except their chocolate is better," Claudia muttered, nibbling on a bar of Dairy Milk.

I frowned at her. "That's a matter of opinion."

"What's a matter of opinion?" Mom asked curiously. "Is Claudia there? Is she eating right?"

My lips twitched. "Mom wants to know if you're eating right?"

Claudia nodded and mumbled around a mouthful of chocolate. "Never better." She waved her fingers and swallowed, "Hi, Delia Mom!"

Mom laughed. "Tell her I say hi back."

"Mom says hi back."

"Your father told me to tell you that the two of you have to check in every day."

I grimaced. "You didn't make Andie check in every day when she was in Dublin."

"We didn't have to *make* Andie check in every day. You, however, have always got so much going on it's a wonder we hear from you at all."

"Well, it's not like I'm smoking crack, Mom. I'm studying and organizing sh—stuff."

Her tone turned sharp. "Were you going to say shit?"

"Would I, a grown woman of twenty years old, dare to curse in front of my mother?"

She harrumphed.

I sighed. "Mom, we're not calling you every day. It's too expensive. And I don't have time to Skype with you every day. I'll send emails when I can during the week and we'll set up a Skype chat once a week, okay?"

"You don't have to make it sound like a chore."

"Momma, I love you. It's not a chore. I am going to miss you too … but I've been gone two days. Please give me a *chance* to miss you."

At her soft chuckle, I relaxed. "I'm just worried. You're my baby and Claud is my adopted baby."

"We'll be fine. But we've got to go. It's induction week and Claudia and I have some things we need to do before classes start. I'll email you soon."

"But you didn't answer my question about food."

"We went food shopping. Our fridge, our freezer, and our cupboards are packed full."

"With what?"

"Food, Mom."

"What kind of food?"

I threw an exasperated "help me" look at Claudia and she instantly cried out in mock pain.

"What was that?"

"Got to go, Mom. Claudia is going into sugar shock." I hung up and grinned at my laughing friend. "I should switch it off before she calls back."

We jumped as the phone buzzed in my hand but when I looked down, it read, "Andie Calling."

"I cannot catch a break. Hello," I answered.

"Hello to you too," Andie said. "You've been gone two days. You don't write, you don't call …"

"I just got off the phone with Mom two seconds ago."

"Right. How'd that go? Did she give you the food chat?"

"Did you get that too?"

"When I did my study abroad? Yeah. I think she thinks non-Americans aren't from Planet Earth and that they somehow subsist on weird alien food that our bodies can't process."

"Yeah, I'm getting that."

"So? Do you like Edinburgh?"

"So far. It is weird being so far from home, but it's a beautiful city."

"How's Claudia?"

"Enjoying the chocolate."

"It's not as good as ours."

"That's what I said!"

"You're both wrong," Claudia interjected as she got up to put her chocolate wrappers in the trash. "Now can you tell your sister you'll call her back? If we stay here any longer, I'm going to smash your phone."

"I heard," Andie said. I could practically hear her rolling her eyes. "I need to get to work anyway. It's early here, remember. It's early and the first thing I do is phone my baby sister to see how she is and it's an expensive long-distance call but does she care?"

I laughed. "I care. I do. I just don't have time to fully appreciate it. Claudia has an abnormal hatred for our perfectly nice apartment and I brought her back here for lunch. I'm pretty sure she's going to break out in hives."

"Well, we wouldn't want that. Speak soon, Supergirl."

"Later." I switched off the phone and gave Claudia a look. "That was rude."

"This," she gestured to the room, "is not an apartment. It's a common room with a hallway outside that leads to five identical rooms with fire doors that lock."

"There's also a bathroom that locks. I'd call that an improvement upon most student accommodations."

"You're funny."

"And you're spoiled."

Claudia narrowed her eyes. "I miss our apartment. It's bright and airy. We have a balcony. Plus, there are only two of us living there."

I'd heard this ever since Claudia laid eyes on the new place, so I ignored it and led her out of the kitchen, stopping at my bedroom door to make sure it was locked.

Back home we were juniors at Purdue in Indianapolis, and since Claudia's parents were loaded, we lived in a nice apartment in West Lafayette, about a ten-minute drive from campus. There was no way I'd be able to afford anything like it if it weren't for Claud. I joked that she was spoiled, but I only meant it in a material sense. Yeah, she was used to nice things but her life was a rich kid's cliché—absentee parents who couldn't give a crap what she did. They threw money at her instead of love and expected her to be grateful. Instead of letting it eat away at her, Claudia embraced the people who showed her real affection and offered fierce loyalty in return.

We'd met freshman year and hit it off. I liked her and not because of her money, and she liked me because she said I was the most honest person she'd ever met. When I took Claudia home for Thanksgiving, meeting my family cemented our friendship. My mom and dad treated her like their kid and fussed over her (which she secretly loved). Even Andie bestowed overbearing elder sisterly condescension upon her (which Claudia also secretly loved).

I didn't come from money. We lived in a small town called Lanton, just a little over two hours northwest of Indianapolis. My dad owned the local garage and my mom owned a florist. We did okay. The only reason they could afford to send their daughters to good schools and even offer them a chance on a placement abroad was because of my mom's aunt Cecilia. Cecilia had married a very wealthy pharmaceuticals guy and when he died, she got all his money. Now, Cecilia liked to spend that money, so by the time she died, she didn't have a whole lot left. She had, however, always doted on Andie and me, and had put some cake away in a trust fund for our education.

As to Claudia's grumbling over the apartment, I was guessing it was just a front for her nerves. We were excited but a little scared of being in a foreign country by ourselves for the school year, but where I admitted it and moved on, Claudia found something to bitch about so she didn't have to think about her anxiety.

Because we were older students but would be taking some freshman classes, we were housed with three British students who were our age but only just starting college. Our roommates had met and bonded a full day before we arrived, so Claud and I would have to work a little bit harder to establish a friendship with them. Hopefully, we'd get around to that. For now, we were still trying to get organized before classes, determined to get to know the city as quickly as possible.

"It'll get better once we're settled and meet more people," I promised Claudia as we stepped out of the apartment. "There are a couple of people from Purdue living across the courtyard. We could get to know them."

"If we didn't get to know them over there, why would we here?"

"Well, that's a spiffy attitude."

"Spiffy? Really?"

I laughed to myself as we walked down the stairs, but that laughter cut off abruptly as we hit the second floor. Claudia didn't ask me what I was doing. In fact, there was utter silence behind me, so I guessed she was drooling too.

In the middle of the landing, sticking a photocopied poster high on the wall, stood a seriously hot guy. His shirt had ridden up as he raised his arms above his head, flashing us a glimpse of golden skin and great abs. The shirt encased the perfect V torso, and his ratty jeans encased the perfect ass. A hot tribal tattoo covered one roped forearm and as he caught sight of us out of the corner of his eye, I mentally sighed. His grin was awesome—slightly crooked, definitely flirtatious, and belly-whoosh-worthy. It was a great match to his beautiful light gray eyes, chiseled jawline covered in sexy scruff, and thick, messy, dark blond hair that was just dying for female fingers to get a hold of it.

"Hey, guys," he greeted us in a rough voice, his American accent welcome and familiar.

Claudia pushed gently passed me and walked casually toward him. I smiled at the sway in her hips as she approached him. So did he, his eyes glued to that sway.

My friend was gorgeous. And gorgeous in that unbelievably classy, this-girl-is-used-to-the-finer-things-in-life way. A lot of guys back home were intimidated by her, and if they weren't, they assumed she was something she wasn't and treated her like a vapid socialite who'd be more impressed with the size of their trust fund than if they could make her laugh. So, unfortunately, despite being exceptionally pretty, Claudia was lonely in the romance department.

I watched hot, tattooed, rebel-without-a-cause eye her with appreciation. Claudia had long dark hair and exotic coloring inherited from her Portuguese mother, as well as a tiny waist, long legs, boobs, and ass. She was the kind of girl other girls loved to hate.

She wore designer skinny jeans, Lacoste tennis shoes, and a cute white Ralph Lauren blouse with capped sleeves and a nipped-in waist, and looked as though she was on the way to the country club. I saw immediately that our poster-hanging hottie found this amusing.

Claudia tilted her chin toward his handiwork. "There's a party?"

"Yeah." He smiled down at her and his grin widened as I neared. "I'm hanging these for a friend who lives here, next stairwell over. You guys should definitely come. I'm Beck, by the way."

"Claudia." She nodded at me. "This is my friend, Charley."

"Hey, Charley." Beck's flirtatious grin remained fixed on his face as he perused me from top to bottom. Unlike Claudia, I was wearing clothes that would get me thrown out of the country club—my favorite, ass-hugging skinny jeans with the hole in the knee, the denim baby soft from having been run through the wash a million times, complemented by an oversized vest with "Library Nerd" scrawled across the chest. I'd dyed my long blond hair to platinum three years ago because I thought it made my hazel eyes more interesting. I had it pulled back into a messy ponytail and was wearing my usual plethora of silver—two long necklaces, three rings on one hand, two on the other, and a jangle of silver and leather bracelets on both wrists.

Claudia wanted to clean me up. I wanted to grunge her down.

I nodded back at him, my cheeks warming at the appreciative gleam in his eye. The guy was smoldering, and I was pretty sure if I licked my finger and pressed it to his skin, steam would rise with a satisfactory hiss. Still, I'd done the whole bad-boy thing in high school and I was definitely over it. I shot Claudia a look that mentally relayed she should go in for the kill.

She smirked and turned to look at the poster. I followed her gaze.

"Um," Claudia turned to Beck, frowning, "does your friend know he misspelled 'snacks'?"

Beck snorted. "Babe, it says 'FREE BOOZE' on the poster. Do you think anyone else will read the next fucking line?"

"He's got you there," I murmured.

She ignored me. "Don't you care? You're putting the posters up. If people see that, they'll think you're the moron who spelled 'snacks' wrong."

Beck shrugged and stepped around us to head up to our floor. "Not a problem since I don't give a fuck what people think."

"Sounds enlightening," Claudia turned on her heel, following him with a grin that would've melted a lesser man. "You want to teach me that kind of enlightenment? I'd make time."

I watched as Beck faltered a little on the first step, as if surprised by her coquettish question. He quickly covered it by giving her another sexy once-over and then smiled into her eyes. "See you at the party, babe."

"We'll be there," Claudia answered. She grabbed my hand, jerking me down the stairs with her. As soon as we burst out of the concrete stairwell and into the warm courtyard, Claudia leaned against a bike railing. "I think I could orgasm just looking at him," she moaned, turning to stare longingly back up at the building.

I wrinkled my nose. "Oversharing again."

"Come on. Dip that boy in a cold lake and he'll turn it into a hot springs."

"You are such a cheeseball," I laughed, pulling on her wrist and dragging her out onto Guthrie Street. We lived just off the Cowgate, the east end of the Grassmarket, which we discovered with all its pubs and a club nearby was kind of a hotspot. Our bedrooms faced over the Cowgate, so both Claud and I had invested in foam earplugs so we could sleep at night.

Our accommodation was only a couple of streets away from the main campus, the landscape sloping up toward the University of Edinburgh. We headed that way, needing to collect our student ID cards from the information center. The ID was kind of important— you needed it to get in and out of the library, as well as the student union venues.

"I agree he's hot but I don't do bad boys anymore." I ignored the familiar ache in my chest and locked my jaw in an effort to appear unaffected. "And I didn't think you did bad boys ever?"

"I'm seriously making an exception for Beck." Claudia's eyes fluttered closed on another moan. "Beck. Even his freaking name is hot."

"Well, my mother would hate him. He said 'fuck' twice within a matter of seconds."

"I'd fuck him twice in a matter of seconds."

Shocked laughter escaped my lips.

"I'm not kidding."

And when I looked at her face, I realized she wasn't. I instantly sobered. "Please do not do anything you'll regret."

She waved off my concern. "I'm not stupid. If he wants in my pants, he has to earn it." She rubbed her hands together gleefully. "And I am going to have so much fun making him earn it."

I didn't particularly enjoy the idea of attending a party where I'd be left to socialize alone as my best friend attempted to wrap Beck around her finger. But ... she was Claudia and I loved her and I'd never seen her so instantly excited over a guy before. I'd suck it up for her. "Then I guess we're really going to that party tonight. Maybe we should invite our roomies?"

"What are their names again?"

I searched my brain, knowing the answers were in there somewhere. "Maggie, Gemma, and Lisa. Right?"

"I thought it was Maggie, Jemima and Lauren."

"Jemima? I would remember if her name was Jemima."

"We are awful roommates."

"We are. I'm going to organize some kind of get-together for us all."

Her eyes glittered. "Ooh, can we invite Beck?"

Crap. She was definitely a goner.

"Maybe I should've worn a dress," Claudia muttered for the fiftieth time as we walked up stairwell one to apartment three. We could hear the music throbbing from within and we'd already passed a couple of drunken freshman out in the courtyard.

I sighed, squeezing back against the wall to let an annoyed-looking guy hurry down the stairs and outside. "I told you a dress would be too much. This is just like any other student party, Claud, not a formal."

As soon as we hit floor one, she knew I was right. The door to apartment three was thrown open and there were students milling around outside drinking out of red plastic cups. A couple of girls smiled at us and the guys gave us "the nod" as we passed to wander inside. Everyone was dressed casual and I was glad I'd talked Claud into jeans and a tank top.

"This place is much bigger than ours," I commented as we gazed around the crowded common room and kitchen.

"There are more rooms," Claudia explained, pointing down the hall to our left. I noticed at the end it turned a corner. I counted five doors on the one side, and guessed Claud was right and that hidden corridor housed more.

"You came." Beck appeared like magic in front of us, holding out two beers. "Nice to see you again, ladies."

Looking much the same as he had that afternoon—except perhaps hotter—Beck's presence seemed to paralyze us for a second as neither of us said a word.

He grinned cockily as if he knew what kind of reaction he elicited in the opposite sex and shook the beers at us. "You want?"

I reached for one of the bottles. "Thanks. Good showing." I gestured to the busy party.

"I told you... put 'free booze' on a poster and voila." He smiled at Claudia as she finally came out of her stupor to take the beer. His eyes flickered back to me and my chest. "Nice shirt."

My vintage Pearl Jam T-shirt, faded, worn, a little snug, but as soon as I saw it in the thrift store, I had to have it. Thankfully, the fact that it was snug just made it hot. It wasn't the first time a guy had complimented me on it and I still couldn't decide if it was because it was vintage Pearl Jam or if it was because it was tight across my breasts.

Probably a little of the first and a lot of the second.

"Thanks," I muttered and "accidentally" hit my elbow off Claudia's arm as I looked around the room.

She took my hint.

"So, Beck," she stepped closer to him, "you here on the study abroad program for the semester or the year like us?"

"The year," I heard him say as I pretended to be more interested in the room at large than in the conversation between him and my best friend. "I came from Northwestern. What about you guys?"

"Not that far from you, actually. Purdue."

"I think a couple of the guys who live here are from there. You know them? Alan and Joey? We met them first night here."

I turned back now, taking another swig of my beer and shaking my head as Claudia answered, "Nope. Do you live here too?"

"Nah, I'm along the street at College Wynd with my buddy Jake."

I instantly flinched at the name, my heart kicking up speed as it always did when I heard it. Thankfully, neither of the two of them noticed and as they chatted, I breathed slowly in and out, forcing myself to relax. It had been three and a half years and just the thought of him tightened my chest.

When I came back to myself, I noticed Claudia shooting me surreptitious "get lost" looks. I pointed the neck of my beer bottle behind them. "I'm going to go … see if I recognize anyone."

I knew by the twitch of Beck's lips that neither Claudia nor I had been subtle, but I wasn't the one trying to impress him. I wandered through the throng, heading into the center of the room where a large table had been turned into a beer pong court, a tournament already underway. Mind-numbingly bored at the thought of it, I turned to head toward the kitchen where people were leaning on counters and chatting to one another. I squeezed past a short guy whose face was practically in my boobs.

"Nice shirt." He grinned up at me.

What did I tell you? It was a magic shirt. I muttered a thank-you and headed toward the kitchen.

"Charley!"

I blinked at the sound of my name being shrieked across the room and my eyes widened as I saw my roommate Maggie waving excitedly to me from the kitchen. Surprised by her exuberant reaction to my presence, I threw her a somewhat bewildered smile and headed over.

"Hey, Maggie."

"You came, you wonderful girl, you. Come give me some love!" She threw her arms around me and I muffled an *oof* against her thick, red hair as we collided. She was pretty drunk and slurring a little, but that didn't stop her English accent from being *awesome*. She shoved me forcefully back. "Is Claudia here too?"

"Yeah, she's talking to some guy we met this afternoon."

Maggie nodded, her pretty eyes bloodshot. "I lost Gemma and Laura. I don't know where they went but I met these guys." She turned to a medium-built guy with curly blond hair and baby blue eyes. With him were a tall, skinny guy with cool rimless glasses, tattooed arms, and a lip ring, and a short, curvy girl with bright purple hair. "This is Matt, Lowe, and Rowena."

I lifted my beer in greeting. "Hey, I'm Charley."

Lowe, the tall, skinny guy, raised his beer and I noted his fingernails were covered in chipped black nail polish. "Cool shirt."

"You're American too?"

"From Northwestern."

"Purdue."

His gaze suddenly sharpened with deeper interest. As his eyes traveled up and down my body, I noticed rather belatedly that he wasn't skinny. He was lean, but muscular ... and he was cute. Really cute. "A Boilermaker. We're practically neighbors." *Very, very* cute.

He was also another bad-boy Beck. In fact, I'd bet they were friends. "If your neighbor has to travel a few hours to get to your house for Bundt cake, then sure, we're neighbors."

Lowe smiled as Matt and Rowena chuckled.

Maggie just looked confused. In an effort to change the subject, she asked, "Did you see the poster, then, for the party?"

"Yeah. And Beck invited us."

Lowe scowled. "You met Beck?"

I looked back over my shoulder through the crowds and pointed to him. He and Claudia were still speaking but she seemed to be frowning at whatever he was saying. "He's talking to my friend Claudia."

My focus drifted as I moved to turn back to the group and I caught a profile in the crowd that made the blood rush in my ears. I froze, my eyes taking in the familiar jawline and straight Roman nose. Familiar lips kissed an unfamiliar forehead.

It couldn't be him.

My heart sped up as I watched the profile turn. A more than familiar beautiful smile hit full force and winded me.

For what felt like forever, I drank in the sight of Jacob Caplin—the first boy I'd ever loved.

I hadn't seen him in three and a half years.

And there he was, tall and built, looking more clean-cut than he used to in a long-sleeved thermal and black jeans. His dark hair was shorter than he used to wear it but it suited his handsome, angular face. I didn't even want to look into his dark eyes because I knew it would only usher me into an even bigger world of pain than I already found myself in. That pain intensified as I followed the arm he had wrapped around a dark-haired girl buried into his side, her hand resting on his chest. I was tall at five eight; she was taller. Curvier. Much, much prettier. With her long, dark hair and olive skin, she looked perfect against him.

I hated her.

I hated him.

Three and a half years and it hadn't stopped hurting.

"Charley! Hullo, Charley!" Maggie shrieked drunkenly and I watched as my name hit Jake's ears. I noted the way he tensed, my fingers trembling around my beer bottle.

His eyes shot up from his group and tore through the crowd across the room. His chest jerked as his gaze collided with mine and his arm fell away from the girl cuddled into him. His lips parted as shock slackened his handsome features and I watched him mouth my name.

Everyone disappeared around me as we locked eyes for the first time in years. The music dulled to a throb, the conversation to a muffled buzz, and all I could hear was my heartbeat. I wanted to get out of there. I wanted to get as far from him as possible, but as he pushed past his questioning friends and headed toward me, I found myself glued to the spot, my cheeks flushing with emotion as he came to a stop before me.

"Jake," Lowe uttered a warm greeting.

Jake nodded his chin at him in a familiar way that caused another streak of pain to score across my chest. "Lowe." His eyes quickly moved from his friend to me and the pain burst into a burning flame. I'd loved Jake's eyes. A lush dark brown, they were so intelligent and warm, so deep, I thought I would happily spend the rest of my life getting lost in them.

I was young.

I was an idiot.

"Charley," he breathed in his low, rich voice that could still send a delicious and very unwanted shiver down my spine. "I can't believe it's you." He ran a shaky hand through his hair, waiting for me to say something. Anything.

I wanted to be cool. Unaffected. Indifferent.

Unfortunately, I was not any of those things. Instead I handed my beer to a confused Maggie and brushed past him without saying a word.

He still wore the same cologne, cologne I'd bought him. Cologne that smelled so great on him, I'd spent a good portion of our time together nuzzling my nose into his neck.

That memory hurt too.

Hurrying down the hall, I saw Claudia talking to some guy I hadn't met. I didn't have time to wonder what had happened to Beck because I heard Jake yell my name. Claudia looked up at the sound of it and her eyes widened when she saw my face.

"I'm leaving," I told her tightly as I passed. She immediately fell into step behind me.

I raced down the stairs and across the courtyard, throwing myself into our stairwell and shutting it quickly behind Claud.

"What the hell is going on?" Her eyes were bright with concern as I pushed past her and ran up the stairs.

It wasn't until we were in my bedroom with the door locked that I whirled around to face her, my whole body shaking as the pain I'd been trying to hold in exploded out of me. Claudia caught me, holding me tight and murmuring soothing words in my ear as I sobbed an explanation into her hair.

Chapter Two

Indiana, September 2008

"We're so going to get in trouble for this," I muttered, staring around at the gathering of my class, their faces flickering in and out of the light cast by the bonfire I knew I'd have to keep a careful eye on.

I'd come home from spending the summer with my cousins in Florida to discover my friends Lacey and Rose had colluded with my ex-boyfriend Alex. They'd put together a welcome home party for me in the woods at the edge of Alex's parents' property on the outskirts of town. A huge old gazebo sat surrounded by crumbling concrete seats overwhelmed with weeds. Right now the gazebo was littered with underage drinkers, beer cans, firewood, and a music dock.

Lacey shoved me playfully. "Who cares? Let's just enjoy it. I doubt they'll bust us. Tomorrow's Labor Day—they're too preoccupied with the festival to care what we're up to." She handed me a beer.

"You didn't need to do this."

Rose nodded. "I suggested we throw a party before going back to school. It was Alex who suggested we make it your party."

Lacey snorted. "Could he be more obvious?"

I followed her gaze to where Alex was standing with a sophomore girl, but he didn't appear to be listening to her as he watched our little group. "He knows we're not going there again. We dated for three months before summer and it didn't work out."

"Yeah for you." Rose sighed sadly. "He's still hung up on you. And he's so cute, Charley. And he plays football. That's hot."

"Alex is nice and all, but he's not for me."

Alex was perfectly nice, in fact, but during the three months we dated, I kept waiting for that *something* to hit me. When we kissed, it was just ... nice. And since kissing was nice but nothing more, I didn't really want to do anything else with him, which made me seem frigid. Anyway, we were too different. He was all about football and keeping up appearances for his family. That was important for him, considering his mom was the mayor.

To be honest, I didn't know what Alex saw in me. I'm sure his mother thought the same thing. My sister Andrea would've been perfect for him if they'd been the same age. She was prim and proper and immaculate from head to toe. I, on the other hand, always had my nose in some project, I was obsessed with music, I dressed where my mood took me, and I said it like it was.

The only thing Mayor Roster had ever found appropriate about me was my sister. I think it was the only thing that gave her hope— that maybe one day I'd suddenly transform into a mini version of Andie.

"Forget Alex." Lacey turned to me, her eyes bright in the firelight. "I've decided Jake Caplin is perfect for you."

"Ah, the mysterious Jake," I chuckled.

All summer I'd been treated to excited phone calls from my friends. First they relayed the news that a new family had moved to Lanton. This was news because Mr. Caplin was opening a law office that had thrown Brackett & Sons, the already existing law office, into a tizzy. It was also news because the Caplins had two boys—

Jacob, a junior, and Lukas, a freshman. Both, apparently, seriously cute.

They'd also made quite a name for themselves over the summer. Or at least Jake had. He'd quickly found friends, seemingly able to move from group to group according to Lacey. He hung out with the musicians, the nerds, and the stoners, but also had a lot of fun with the jocks. And, more importantly, Lacey said, he'd already slept with a bunch of junior and senior girls. Rumor had it he'd also slept with Stacy Sullivan, a hot senior who worked at Hub's, a popular diner on Main Street. This was news because Stacy only dated guys in college. Having sex with Stacy made Jake a bit of a legend among our classmates.

But all of it just made me question why the hell Lacey would want me to hook up with him.

"Oh my God, he's here." Lacey said breathlessly as if Batman had just walked into the party.

I twisted my head to follow her gaze and found myself staring past the fire and into the dark eyes of Jake Caplin.

I felt his look seize hold of me and I swear to God, my breath hitched in my throat.

He was beautiful.

I didn't know how to describe him any other way. And as he moved through the crowd, eyes on me, my friends whispering in disbelief that he was coming over, I decided then that I didn't care about rumor. There was something about the way his tall, built body moved—confident and strong but also somehow wild and untamed. I watched his mouth curl up at the corners in a half-smile and I read a million things in his expression. A million stories, a million jokes, a million dreams …

Deep down, I somehow knew that Jake Caplin would never, ever bore me. It sounded crazy—I know it did because we'd never even exchanged a word, but I just *knew*.

"So, you're the mysterious girl who's been gone all summer." He stopped right in front of me, casual, beer in hand. I tipped my head back to meet his gaze, my body tingling. It suddenly occurred to me that someone as beautiful as Jake must have girls throwing themselves all over him all the time. I read it in his cocky confidence. I read it in the ease with which he spoke to me, a complete stranger, when there were guys I'd known my whole life who stuttered when they tried to flirt.

"And you're the mysterious newbie," I answered with a shrug.

He smiled at my response and held out a hand. "Jake."

Reaching out tentatively, I let him take my hand, ignoring the curl of tension in my lower belly as our skin touched. "Charley."

"I know. You're famous. Supergirl." He grinned wickedly and I shot my friends a dirty look. I couldn't believe they'd told him that story.

No, in fact, I could believe it.

Two years ago I'd gone into town with Lacey and Rose. We were coming out of Hub's when we heard my sister Andie shouting. It was so unlike her that we stopped to spectate. Andie was a senior at the time and she and her long-term boyfriend Pete had been having problems. That day those problems had escalated so much that my sister—who was the epitome of public decorum—started to shout at him in the town square. He'd shouted back as she walked away, and Andie had stupidly stopped in the middle of the street to turn and shout a response.

I saw Mr. Finnegan's SUV come roaring around the corner, and I also noted he was too busy fiddling with something on his dashboard to notice my sister. I didn't even think. I tore across the street and shoved her out of the way, just in time for Finnegan to realize what was happening and hit the brakes. Unfortunately, he found the brakes too late and he still hit me. The impact wasn't hard enough to do serious, serious damage, but I ended up with concussion, a few fractured ribs, and a broken fibula.

I'd been laid up for a while. Enough time for the town to hail me as a local hero and everyone, including my sister, to affectionately nickname me "Supergirl."

"I hate living in a small town," I grumbled, taking another pull of my beer.

Jake laughed, a deep, rich sound that tugged my eyes instantly back to his. My heart started racing hard again as we stared at each other. "Don't sweat it. If you're going to adopt a nickname, I could think of worse ones, and definitely not a better reason to have one."

"We're going to get more beer," Lacey announced cheerily and not so very subtly grabbed Rose's hand and dragged her away, giving Jake and me privacy.

I grimaced at how obvious they were. "Sorry."

"Don't be." Jake stepped a little closer. "I've been looking forward to meeting you."

I tipped my head, my expression knowing. "Oh, I've heard you've met lots of people already."

He fought a smile. "You shouldn't listen to gossip."

"Especially when it's true?"

He laughed now, shaking his head. "I was just being friendly. Getting to know the new town. It's not easy moving to such a small place after living in Chicago. Everything seems to move faster there and faster here causes shock."

"Yeah, I can imagine it's a huge change." I frowned and leaned against the post behind me. "Why did you move here?"

Jake blew out a breath between his lips and shrugged. "My mom and dad are from small towns, they missed it. My dad was pretty successful in Chicago and my mom liked her life there. However, my kid brother, Lukas, got mugged coming home from school one night when he missed the bus. They pulled a knife but didn't hurt him. Still, it freaked my mom and dad out so much, they upped stakes."

I nodded. "You know bad things happen everywhere."

"You get a lot of muggings in Lanton, do you?"

"Only when things are slow. I like to shake things up a little."

Jake threw his head back and laughed, his eyes glittering warmly. "Ski mask and all?"

I shook my head. "Bandit eye strip, a banana, and a black trash bag."

He chuckled. "Let me guess—the banana works three-fold: a 'gun,' a snack to keep your mugger energy up, and then the slippery peel is a great tool in your escape."

I widened my eyes in mock surprise. "Dude, you got this down. Want to be a bandit with me?" I didn't mean it to sound flirtatious, but it totally did.

Jake's gaze turned even warmer and he ducked his head a little to murmur, "Definitely."

Flushing and unable to keep the smile off my face, I dropped my gaze from his, a little overwhelmed by the intensity of the spark between us.

"So you and Alex, huh?"

My eyes immediately shot up and I saw Jake looking over his shoulder to where Alex stood watching us, not appearing too happy at all. It definitely didn't help that his best friend Brett Thomson was sneering at us and although I couldn't hear what was being said it was apparent Brett was making comments about us that were upsetting Alex. I'd never understood why a nice guy like Alex was friends with Brett. Brett, unfortunately, hadn't fallen far from the bad-apple tree. His dad, Trenton Thomas, was a car salesman. On the surface he was charming and self-effacing. Some people liked him. But a lot of people knew him for what he really was—a misogynist, a bully, and a petulant toddler all rolled into one. I'd witnessed the way the elder Thomas treated his son and wife when I'd been at Brett's house while dating Alex. I wanted to punch him in the nuts. My mom and dad had gone to high school with him and said he'd always been an ass. Lucky Brett had inherited all those wonderful qualities from his dear papa.

I waited until I had Jake's attention again before I replied softly, "He's a good guy, but we broke up before the summer and that's not going to change."

"Well, by the look on his face right now, he wants it to change. We were kind of friends before this … I'm guessing by that death stare, just talking to you has changed that."

I sighed, annoyed. "Sorry. His family is kind of a big deal, and Alex is a little territorial. He'll move on."

"I don't know." Jake's expression grew serious. "Is it possible to move on from a girl like you?"

I laughed softly. "Nice line."

Jake smiled, running a hand through his messy dark hair. "I'm not sure that was a line."

"Oh, it was a line. So was that. You're very good at the flirting thing. Very confident for your age."

"I don't know about that. I've never really had to wor—"

"Work at it," I finished for him, quirking my eyebrow at him. "Confident or arrogant …"

His laughing eyes narrowed on me. "You think you're pretty smart."

"No. I *know* I'm pretty smart."

"Now who's arrogant?"

I chuckled but shrugged. "Well, I have reason to be. I'm awesome."

"Fuck." Jake was grinning again and he placed a hand above my head on the post and leaned in. "I really want to kiss you right now."

Heat suffused me, the butterflies in my stomach going absolutely crazy at the thought of it, but I somehow managed to control myself. "I don't know you well enough for that."

"I disagree," he leaned closer, his intent clear. "Five minutes with you and I feel like I've known you forever."

"Jake."

He stopped, his expression changing at the sound of his name on my lips. I didn't know what that expression meant, but it made me want to melt into him. I forced myself not to.

"I'm not going to kiss you."

A spark of intensity lit up his gorgeous dark eyes. "Are you going to make me work for it?"

I nodded and straightened up from the post, bringing our bodies so close I could almost feel him against me. "If I don't believe I'm worth the effort, why the hell would you?" With a small shrug, I slipped past him and headed toward my friends who were gaping at me, obviously eager to know what was going on. I didn't get the chance to tell them because Jake fell quickly into step beside me.

We hung out with my friends for the rest of the night, exchanging barbs, enjoying the frisson of electricity that sparked and pulled between us. We enjoyed it, but we didn't encourage it. *Jake* didn't encourage it. There was no more talk of kissing me, but I knew as my dad arrived to bust up the party, dragging me and Lacey and Rose back to his car, that Jake Caplin was intending to make the effort.

I knew because as I walked away, he watched me the entire time. He watched me like he wanted to watch me forever.

I knew this because I was looking back at him thinking the exact same thing.

Chapter Three

Edinburgh, September 2012

My eyes felt swollen as I pried them open at the sound of the knock on my bedroom door. I felt crunchiness in the corners and on my lashes. Salt from my tears. Grounding them out, I tumbled from my bed, catching myself on the desk that was squished in close in the narrow space. My room was long but not wide, which gave me a slight space problem. It was also taking me a while to get used to sleeping in a twin again.

"Charley, it's Maggie. You there?"

"Coming," I mumbled, flinching at the sight of myself in my mirror.

I looked like hell.

After I cried in Claudia's arms the night before, I told her that the guy chasing us out of the party was Jake. She knew all about Jake. She knew Jake was the reason I was a failure at relationships.

My body still ached with tension as I was reminded of the reality of the situation.

Jake was here. In Edinburgh. At college. In the same city as me.

It was too painful to contemplate this early in the morning.

I pulled my door open a fraction and Maggie's eyes widened a little at my current state. "You have a visitor."

My eyes narrowed. "Who?"

"Beck."

Beck was here to see me? Why? I sighed heavily. "Tell him I'll be right out." I closed the door and turned back to find my jeans. I shimmied out of my pajama shorts, pulled on jeans and a hoodie, and scraped my hair back in a ponytail. The truth was I didn't give a crap if I looked like shit. Beck was hot, yes, but I had no intention of going *there*. Especially not when Claudia had a crush on him.

Upon opening my door to step out, I found myself forcefully shoved back inside by my best friend. Claudia flipped the lock in a hurry and then slammed her back against the door. Her gaze drifted over me and she paled. "You cannot go out there like that."

"It's just Beck," I grumbled.

Claudia shook her head. "Lying redhead alert."

I guessed she was alluding to Maggie but had no clue what she meant. My expression said so.

She sighed. "It's not Beck. It's Jake."

I sucked in a breath at the news. "Why would the redhead lie?"

"He probably asked her to lie."

"Either that or she saw the drama between us last night. She knew I wouldn't go out if I knew it was him." My heart pounded in my chest. "I'm not going out there."

"Not looking like that."

I ignored my friend's look of disgust and threw myself on my bed. "Not ever. Tell him to go."

Thankfully, Claudia didn't argue with me. She disappeared for a few minutes and when she returned, she came right over to crawl onto the bed beside me. "He's gone. He looked like I'd just told him Santa wasn't real."

"Do you feel sorry for him?" I wasn't sure if *I* did or not.

Claudia shook her head. "I don't know what to feel. I don't know him. All I know is what he did to you. I also know it was pretty bad what he went through and, you know, it can take time to get over these things. Maybe he just wants to apologize."

I turned my head, wishing like hell the knifelike pain in my chest would just disappear already. "I don't know if I have it in me to listen to that apology. It took me a while to get over it, and now he's back in my face again, reminding me of everything ..."

We lay in silence for a while until eventually I turned my head on the duvet to stare at Claudia's stunning profile. "What happened last night with Beck?"

Claud's lip curled and I couldn't quite read what that expression meant even as she replied, "He said I'm a good girl and he doesn't mess with good girls because he wasn't a one-woman kind of guy."

My eyes widened. "He said that?"

"Mmm-hmm. He said he likes me. Wants to be friends."

"At least he's honest, I guess. Are you going to be friends with him?"

Claudia shrugged. "Sure, why not. I don't do manwhores, no matter how hot they are, but he's fun. Friends. Whatever."

"Are you sure my eyes aren't puffy anymore?" I asked, ducking my head as we walked up the cobbled lane toward the college.

"No puffiness or redness in sight. You look hot. You always look hot," Claudia said a little absentmindedly.

"Are you nervous about seeing Beck again?"

"Nervous? Why on earth would I be nervous?"

I ignored her and kept following Maggie, Gemma, and Laura. They'd heard we were going to the student union to hang out with Beck and they'd invited themselves along. Beck was a popular draw.

Claudia had come into the kitchen at dinner to tell me she'd just spoken with Beck and he'd invited us to hang out at the student union. At first, I was wary. It turned out Beck and Jake were best friends at Northwestern, so Beck had called Claudia to ask if I was okay. Apparently, Jake had told him our whole story. Claudia hadn't told him anything about my reaction to seeing Jake but she said she wasn't sure if we were free. Beck had caught the hint and assured her that Jake wouldn't be there.

The student union had a number of locations across the university, but the one we were headed to was Teviot. Teviot was housed in a beautiful, old, Gothic-style building on the main campus at Bristo Square. It had a nightclub inside, a couple of different bars including this really cool Library Bar Claud and I had checked out the day we got our IDs.

Beck had texted Claud to let us know they were in the Teviot Lounge bar. We followed our roommates up the stairs and into a crowded space that had the typical look of a British pub. Everywhere was dark wood, low lights, comfortable seating, and hardwood, hardwearing furniture. The smell of stale beer was a little overwhelming but it was a given in a bar with carpeted floors. We squeezed past the students milling around the doors, and I followed Claudia as she checked out the room for our newest friend.

She grabbed my hand. "He's over there."

I couldn't see him yet, but I followed her as she pulled me through the crowd. We came to a stop at a table around the corner from the bar. Beck was standing with Matt, while Lowe, Rowena, and some guy I didn't recognize sat at a small table next to them.

We'd lost our roommates and for a second, I pondered looking for them. They *had* specifically come with us to see Beck. Then again, they were twenty years old ... they didn't need a tour guide or a babysitter.

"Charley, Claudia, glad you could come," Beck greeted us. "Let me get you a beer."

He disappeared before we could say yay or nay and Matt, the blond from the party, smiled at us. "We met last night," he nodded to me and then turned to Claud, "but I definitely would remember meeting you, and we definitely did not." Matt's grin widened.

She smiled politely back. "I'm Claudia."

"Claudia, this is Lowe." Lowe winked at her and then lifted his beer in greeting to me. "Rowena." She gave us a friendly wave. "And our buddy, Denver. It was his party last night. Poor guy got stuck in different accommodation from us."

Denver had messy dark hair that fell to his chin. He wore a lot of silver jewelry, a tight Black Sabbath shirt, and a pair of black skinny jeans and motorcycle boots. Matt seemed to be the odd one out, but still, there was something about the group...

"Are you guys in a band?"

Matt grinned. "Yeah. We play a lot in Evanston."

"We have a few gigs lined up here," Lowe added, his gaze fixed on me.

I was impressed. "How did you manage to swing that so quickly?"

Lowe shrugged. "We sent out demos to a couple of pubs and bars before we got here. Arranged some dates. We have to rent a drum kit, which is a bummer, but it would be an even bigger bummer to be here for a year and not play one fucking gig."

"What are you guys called?" Claudia asked, seeming interested, which surprised me since she wasn't big into music unless it was classical or country.

"The Stolen." Beck appeared behind us with two beers. I thought that was impressively fast considering the line at the bar.

No doubt he charmed his way through the crowd. "We're indie rock."

"I told them people will love them here," Rowena piped up with a big smile.

"Oh my God, you're Scottish," I replied, somewhat stupidly.

"Aye."

Feeling like an idiot, I tried to explain my "duh" moment. "I just thought you were American with you being with the guys and …" I drifted off, actually not sure why I'd assumed she was American.

She shook her head. "I live across the hall fae Denver. Ma flatmates are aliens. Denver saved me fae them."

"She's our token Scot," Denver joked, throwing his arm around her shoulder. "We're keeping her around for the accent. It does help, though, that the girl knows good music."

Rowena looked perfectly happy tucked into his side and I wondered absentmindedly if she was more than his token Scot.

We all fell easily into conversation, Matt hogging Claudia's attention, his gaze almost stunned as they talked. He was captivated and I instantly felt bad for him because I knew Claudia didn't feel the same. When Claudia liked a guy, she was pretty obvious about it. Beck could attest to that—Beck, who, I noticed, was watching Claudia with an intensity that surprised me for someone who apparently wasn't into her. He finally caught me studying him and he grinned, his expression teasing as he stepped near me.

"So," he leaned his head down close to mine, "I know your friend is a good girl, but I still haven't made up my mind about you."

I didn't know if he was coming onto me or just making conversation, but I thought I better lay it out for him anyway. "I don't *do* bad boys."

His eyes narrowed. "*Anymore.*"

31

My gaze sharpened at his insinuation and Beck shrugged. "Jake's like a brother. He tells me everything."

I looked away, my heartbeat picking up at the mention of him. Trying for nonchalant, I took a swig of beer. If I was to go by Beck's next comment, I'd obviously failed.

"Look, the guy feels like shit about the way he treated you. You should give him a chance to say it."

Making a face that I'm sure screamed "bitter," I turned back to Beck. "He knows where I live. He's known for three and a half years and he's had that whole time to apologize."

Beck sighed, every ounce of bad boy melting out of him as he told me solemnly, "It took Jake a long time to get over what happened. When he finally started to breathe again, he realized how much he'd fucked it up with you ... but it was already done. It was too late." He made a helpless gesture. "I could go on for hours, but it's not my place. Just give the guy a chance to explain, okay?"

Everything he said reminded me of the pain and anger in Jake's eyes. The blame and guilt. He'd aimed it at the wrong person but that didn't mean he wasn't entitled to those feelings. I knew that. It just made the whole situation between us that much harder. However, I didn't know if I could be in the same room with him and be okay. I chewed on it, my eyes slipping away from Beck's to gaze around the room. They didn't get very far.

Standing in the crowd around the bar was Jake and the brunette he'd been with last night. That sharp pain in my chest resurfaced as I watched Jake cradle the nape of her neck in his strong hand and hold her as he spoke to her.

He used to hold me in that exact same way, except he always had to duck his head a little to meet my eyes. Although I teased him about his alpha-male handling of me, I'd secretly loved it. I always imagined he'd held me by the nape because he wanted my entire focus on him. It was at once protective and sexual.

And I'd thought it was only for me.

I felt Beck move closer as I watched them. I tilted my jaw a little in his direction without taking my eyes off Jake. "He definitely looks like he's over the whole thing now."

"Melissa's a good girl," Beck replied, drawing my attention back to him. He watched Jake for a minute and then turned to me with a sad shrug. "She's helped him a lot. He deserves that kind of happiness. Don't you think? After everything ... he deserves a good girl to stand by him."

He had a good girl who stood by him, I thought angrily, my eyes flashing before the pain overtook.

Beck must've caught that pain because he instantly flinched and cursed under his breath. I felt his fingers graze my cheek gently. "Charley, ignore me. That was the wrong thing to say. I know that. Jake knows that. But ... actually, you know what ..." He shook his head. "I don't know about any of it from your side, so I'm just going to shut the fuck up." He chucked my chin affectionately and turned back to the group, throwing out some off-the-cuff remark to Matt who sent him a death glare for mocking him in front of Claudia.

I could only stand there, frozen by the knowledge that not only was Jake Caplin here at the same college as me, but he was also here with another girl he'd fallen in love with.

To hell with that.

Throwing back the last of my beer, I dropped it on the nearest table and without a word to Claudia or anyone, I turned on my heel, letting my hair fall over my cheek in the hopes that Jake wouldn't recognize me as I passed. I hurried out of the lounge and down the staircase, thinking I was home free as I hit the concrete stairs outside, gulping in the cool summer air.

"Charley!"

Jake's voice caught me as I walked onto the square.

"Charley!"

Chapter Four

Indiana, September 2008

"Charley!"

My stomach did that weird flippy thing at the sound of Jake's voice nearing me, but I didn't slow down. I turned my head a little, hearing his footsteps pound against the running track as he raced after me. He caught up and I gave him a small smile as he turned in front of me and started running backward. Luckily, I wasn't running very fast, or he might've found himself on his ass. "Hey, Jake."

He rolled his eyes. "'Hey, Jake', she says casually as if I haven't just embarrassed myself chasing after her."

And he wasn't just talking about running down the school track after me. The last three weeks Jake had been paying me so much attention, the entire school was talking about it. In fact, I wouldn't be surprised if the entire town was talking, as my mom had even mentioned it at dinner the other night. So far Jake had asked me out twice—I'd said *no* the first time (considering it was only two days after the party) and *maybe* last time. It was last week and we'd spent enough time around each other for me to know that my hormone-riddled teenage body didn't just want him. *All* of me did.

"Do you care what anyone else thinks?" I slid him a sly smile knowing he did not. Since he'd started pursuing me, I'd heard that he'd been catching a lot of crap from Brett and his goons. I was glad to hear that Alex had nothing to do with it. Still, it was irritating. It hadn't seemed to have put Jake off, though. I got the impression Jake wasn't the kind of guy who backed down from anyone.

Jake's lips twitched. "You're killing me right now. That smirk, the hair, the sweat, those shorts …"

"The sweat?" I wrinkled my nose, suddenly feeling very unattractive.

He shrugged, a devilish gleam in his eyes. "Sweat makes me think of the things we could do together to get sweaty. Good and sweaty."

I flushed. "You're terrible."

"I'm awesome," he corrected me, repeating my words from the first night we'd met. Suddenly he stopped, his arm reaching out to catch me as I passed. I found myself being swung around and held tight against him, a surprised gasp escaping my lips as my hands fluttered against his chest.

My skin flushed hotter than it already was from running as I tilted my head back to stare up into his face. "What are you doing?"

His arm tightened around me. "It's been three weeks since we met and I still haven't gotten you alone. I'm not cool with that. Life is too damn short. So, Charlotte Julianne Redford, will you go out on a date with me already?"

I fidgeted as I tried to catch my breath. My hand slid across his chest as I did, coming to a rest just above his heart. To my surprise, I felt it pounding against my palm as hard as mine was. I looked up into his eyes. "Why?" I didn't know if I was asking about his racing heartbeat or why he'd chosen me to relentlessly pursue.

Jake's other arm came around my waist and he pressed me even deeper into him so my arms had to slide up around his neck. He bent his head, his eyes flaring as my breasts brushed his chest. Our mouths rested close to one another as he answered softly, "My mom came down on me last year for moving too fast with girls, breaking hearts, for not taking girls seriously. I told her I never made any promises and she told me it was about time I did. My dad heard and told her to lay off, that I was young, but that one day I'd meet a girl who would knock me flat on my ass." He grinned, his nose brushing mine. "Well, he was right, and it happened sooner than I thought it would. You've knocked me on my ass, Charley. I think it might have something to do with the fact that you make me laugh a lot and you're really smart. And really hot. Really, really hot," he murmured against my mouth. "All I know is that you probably deserve better than me, but I'm too selfish to let you. I'm into you, and I want you to be so into me, you don't even care that I'm not good enough for you."

I teased my lip with my teeth, his confession firing up my blood and spreading this beautiful ache across my chest and into my stomach. "If this is a line, I'll kick you in the nuts, Jacob Caplin."

He made a face. "It's not a line. *I* don't need a line."

"You are so unbelievably arrogant."

"I know." He chuckled and smoothed a hand up my spine. I shivered as it caressed my back and then slipped under my ponytail. His hand cupped my nape and gripped me gently, tipping my head back so I was looking him directly in the eye. "I need you to keep me on my ass so my ego doesn't become a major problem. Please, Charley ... go out with me."

Teasing him, I didn't say anything for at least ten seconds, which felt like an awful long time. I felt his fingers flex with tension and slowly I smiled. As I did, he relaxed against me and I nodded. "Yeah, okay. I'll go out with you."

"You did not drive a pickup in Chicago." I smiled widely as Jake led me by the hand to his truck.

He'd been the perfect gentleman, coming to the house to meet my mom and dad before taking me out on a date. My mom thought he was fantastic, I could tell, but my dad was wary. He'd heard the stories about Jake and wasn't too keen on Casanova taking his daughter out on a date.

Jake smiled back at me as he pulled open the passenger door of the Ford. "It was a bribe from my dad. I've always wanted one, don't ask me why." He shrugged. "It eased the pain of moving to bumble-fuck Indiana."

I got in, huffing at the insult to my town. "So you're telling me I'm going out with a spoiled brat."

He laughed and shut the door. When he got into the driver's side, he smirked. "Just so you know, I've worked every summer but this one as a car valet for my uncle. I saved it all and put it toward this. My dad didn't want me to sell my car for the pickup, but he eased up on me as a bribe to keep me sweet on the move." His smiled turned cocky. "If I'd known you were waiting for me, I wouldn't have needed the bribe to keep me sweet."

I rolled my eyes. "Okay, Mr. Smooth, so you're not spoiled, but try to refrain from insulting my town."

He tried to swallow his smile and failed. "You got it. My sincerest apology."

We were quiet as we drove out of my neighborhood and toward Main Street. When we passed the high school and turned onto the road that would lead us out to the highway, I shot Jake a curious look. "Where are we going?"

He didn't answer. Instead he turned off onto Brenton Fields and pulled the truck to a stop in the middle of the open. There was nothing around us but grass, trees in the distance, and a starry sky above. Jake grinned at me again and got out of the truck, leaving his MP3 player playing through the radio, the truck's headlights on. He helped me out and holding my hand led me to the truck's rear. I stood, my belly still fluttering with girlish excitement as I watched Jake spread out a blanket on the truck bed and pull a cooler out of the corner. He took out some sandwiches, cookies, chips, and two bottles of water.

"Dinner awaits." He held out his hand. I laughed as he pulled me onto the bed.

I was glad I'd brought a sweater. We were nearing October and the temperature drop was more noticeable at night.

Still laughing, I bit into my peanut butter sandwich.

Jake smirked at me. "What?"

"Nothing," I giggled now, which made him grin even harder. "I just think you might've watched too many movies set in small-town America in the fifties. We don't really do the date in the back of a pickup thing. We usually hang out in each other's rooms surrounded by modern technology."

He clamped a hand over his chest as if I'd shot him. "I'm crushed. And here I thought this shit was romantic."

I laughed harder. "This shit is romantic." I stifled my giggling and gave him a genuine smile. "Thank you."

Jake nodded in return and settled back against the truck. "You know, you're not like other girls our age."

I quirked an eyebrow in interest. "I'm not?"

"Nope. I find it incredibly hot how cool you are."

"I think that's what they call a paradox, my friend."

"I mean … you're not into drama or gossip or mindless, stupid stuff that doesn't matter. I watch you with your friends and if one of them starts drama for no reason, you walk away or ignore it while the rest of them fan the flames. When they gossip about someone, you roll your eyes, and if it's mean gossip, you tell them to grow up. Not a lot of sixteen-year-old girls have the balls to do that. Not a lot of fourteen-year-old girls have the balls to throw themselves in front of an SUV to save their sister, either."

I groaned. "Oh God, don't buy into that, Jake. Anyone else would've done the same."

"No." My eyes sharpened on him at the gravity in his voice. "No, they wouldn't."

I squirmed a little under his intense regard. "Jake ..." I sighed, lowering my sandwich and staring at anything but him, "for all my cracks about being awesome ... I don't want you to build this idea of me in your head ... an idea that I can't live up to. I'm just Charley. An ordinary girl from Lanton, Indiana."

"I don't agree with you."

My chest felt too full, my whole body tense with whatever heaviness was settling around our picnic on his truck bed. We'd only been on our date for twenty minutes, for goodness' sake, and already we were in Seriousville.

"Charley, look at me."

I did as he asked and found the breath leaving my body again at the look in his eyes.

"This shouldn't be possible," he whispered, "but somehow, it's happening. You're something special to me, and I can only hope that I'm something special to you."

"I barely know you," My brain murmured logic; my heart screamed its opposite.

Jake shook his head slowly. "I don't know if that's true."

We were silent a while, eating our sandwiches and listening to the radio.

Finally, not able to contain it, though I knew it was insane, I whispered, "You're something special to me."

Jake turned his head, his eyes glittering in the dark. "Yeah?"

I ducked my head, embarrassed. "We haven't even kissed yet."

"It's going to be epic."

"What if it's not?"

Jake threw his head back and laughed. "Are you this pessimistic about everything?"

"No. I'm just asking a question."

"Trust me. It'll be epic."

I took a drink of water, eyeing him carefully. I swallowed and wiped my lips dry. "This overconfidence of yours could definitely become a problem."

"It's not a problem. You love it."

"No, I love cheese fries, chocolate milkshakes, The Killers, Metric, Lucky jeans, my mom and dad and Andrea."

Jake chuckled. "In that order?"

I narrowed my eyes playfully. "Maybe. What do you love?"

"Gio's Pizza: the best pizza in Chicago, Reese's peanut butter cups, the White Sox, Pearl Jam, Silversun Pickups, Bob Dylan, The Smiths, my pickup, my mom and dad and maybe Luke too."

I nodded and then asked casually, "Have you named your pickup yet?"

"Nah, but I was thinking The Vedder."

My eyebrows puckered together in confusion. "Why?"

Jake flinched like I'd shot him. "After Eddie Vedder. Lead singer of Pearl Jam?"

I shrugged. "Sorry. I've never listened to their stuff."

Yup, this time my words *had* shot him. Jake shook his head. "No, no, no. Okay, no. I'm not dating a girl who has not listened to Pearl Jam. You can borrow my CDs."

I laughed. "It's cool. If you feel that strongly about it, I'll download their albums."

"Uh, one, there are a lot, and two, it's Pearl Jam. You have to listen to them on CD."

I tried not to laugh again, my lips twitching with the urge. "Okay."

"Never listened to Pearl Jam," he muttered, incredulous.

Choking on laughter, I replied, "It's not a punishable crime."

"That's a shame. I could find a very creative way to punish you."

I blushed and threw a napkin at him. "You have a filthy mind, Mr. Caplin."

He grunted. "Of course I do. I'm sixteen years old." He pushed the picnic up the blanket and I watched warily, wondering where he was going with this. In the end all he did was stretch out on his back, arms behind his head as he gave me an inviting smile. Casually, I lay down beside him, feeling the heat of his body as if it were pressed against mine. I'd left space between us so he wouldn't get any funny ideas.

While we stared up at the stars, it occurred to me that we were lying there in this perfectly comfortable silence I'd never felt with anyone before.

"Just call it 'Eddie.'"

Jake snorted. "What?"

"'The Vedder' doesn't trip off the tongue. Eddie's simpler."

"You want me to call my pickup 'Eddie'?"

"It's just a suggestion."

"He's not the dog from *Frasier*. He's a pickup."

"Call him 'Ford' then."

"He's not a businessman with a stick up his ass."

Now it was my turn to snort. "Zorro?"

"I get the feeling you're not taking this seriously."

"No, I am. Naming a truck is very important. I was going for masculine. Powerful."

"And you came up with Zorro?"

"The Hulk? Batman? The Batmobile?"

"I'm not even humoring you on those."

"Alan? Bob?"

"You're so lucky you're cute."

"Ozzy? Lennon? Morrison? Joplin?"

"Charley …"

"Hendrix."

Jake stilled next to me and I felt his gaze on my face as he turned to stare at me. "I like that," he murmured softly.

I turned my head to meet his eyes and smiled. "Hendrix?"

"Yeah, it's cool."

I smoothed a hand down the bed of the truck and announced into the night, "I hereby christen thee Hendrix."

Suddenly my hand was caught in Jake's and my eyes drifted back up to his as he rubbed his thumb across my knuckles. "You named my truck," he murmured.

"You can un-name it," I muttered back unsurely.

Jake shook his head. "We're in too deep for that, baby."

My hand tightened in his and he felt it. His fingers flexed and he threaded them through mine. "I'm not too sure about the deep. I breathe better in the shallow."

"Not true," he whispered. "You hate the shallow."

I finally let go of the breath I was holding and turned my head to gaze back up at the starry sky. Keeping hold of my hand, Jake asked me what my favorite color was.

"Green."

"Me too," he replied quietly. "But I like black too."

"Is black a color?"

"As opposed to a shade?"

"Yeah."

"Does it matter?"

"I guess not."

"What's your favorite song?"

And so began three hours of questioning back and forth. By the end of the date, I think Jake Caplin knew more about me than I even knew about myself.

As Hendrix pulled up to my house, the murmurings of butterflies in my stomach turned into a full-blown riot. This was it. This was the kissing part.

But Jake didn't lean in for a kiss. Instead he moved around the truck to help me out. He took my hand and I followed him up to my porch. Quieted by my anticipation, I let Jake turn me and clasp me by the nape of the neck again. He pulled me in close and ducked his head to hold my gaze. "You're going out with me next Friday."

I blinked, coming out of my anticipatory fog. "You're not even asking now?"

Jake shook his head solemnly. "I can't take the chance you'll say no."

Okay, he had to stop with the perfect words before I melted into goo. I smiled up at him, my hazel eyes full of flirt. "Ask me."

Jake took a deep breath and gave my nape a squeeze. "Charley … will you go out with me next Friday?"

I shrugged casually. "Sure, why not."

Chuckling, Jake drew me close and pressed a sweet kiss to my forehead. When he pulled back, he winked and let me go. "See you at school on Monday."

I nodded, standing there in a state of bewilderment as he walked away, got in Hendrix, and drove off. Without kissing me.

Huh.

Confused, I turned on my heel and walked inside. Mom and Dad were sitting in the living room pretending to watch television, covering up the fact that they'd definitely been spying on us.

"How'd it go?" Dad asked, his voice tight, as if he really didn't want to know but needed to.

"You'll be glad to know that Jake was the perfect gentleman." *Did I sound glum when I said that?*

"Good," Dad grunted.

"Are you going out again?" Mom asked.

I nodded. "He asked me out next Friday."

"Oh, Christ," Dad muttered.

Mom laughed. I rolled my eyes and headed into the kitchen for a glass of orange juice, my heart still pounding from the adrenaline Jake's presence had released inside me. It almost cracked a rib when I felt my phone vibrate in my pocket.

My face split into a huge goofy grin at the message.

I'm going to kiss you when you least expect it. And it WILL be epic.

Butterflies back in full force, I quickly texted him back. *I trust you.*

Chapter Five

Edinburgh, September 2012

Slowly, I glanced over my shoulder. Seeing the anguish on Jake's face, I turned to him despite myself. "What do you want, Jake?" I asked.

He took the steps down to me, his long legs eating them up quicker than mine had. Before I knew it, he was right there in front of me again and I was right back where I'd been last night when he approached me. I clenched my jaw to stop myself from saying something awful. He didn't deserve awful but I wasn't sure he deserved forgiveness, either. I was too confused. Part of me still felt for Jake and all he'd been through, and the other part hated him for breaking all the promises he'd made me.

From the moment we'd met, he'd dragged me into the deep, swearing to me he was in there with me. It was a lie. He'd waded back out to the shallows and left me to drown. Worse, he'd found a new deep elsewhere with some other girl.

Jake cleared his throat, bringing me back to the present. "I have a lot of things I need to say, Charley. I know you don't owe me anything ..." his eyes darkened to black, "but you need to hear this. After last night, I know you need to hear this."

"I don't need anything from you. I grew up. I'm over it."

"I know, but clearly you still haven't forgiven me. Last night proved that."

"It was shock. I was enjoying myself and then suddenly, *you* were there."

Jake winced. "Okay. Well, I'm not asking you to get over that shock. I'm just asking for a coffee so we can sit and talk."

Remembering how relentless Jake could be when he wanted something, I gave him a sharp nod. "Tomorrow. The Library Bar. Twelve o'clock. I'll give you five minutes." I whirled around to walk away from him, but his voice stopped me again.

"You don't have to run away because of me. Come back inside, finish your drink."

I inwardly cursed at his audacity and looked back at him over my shoulder. "I'm not running away because of you. I finished my drink so I left. But I can see you're still an arrogant asshole." I moved off with long strides, desperate to get away from him.

"I'll take that as a good sign!" he shouted across the square.

I lifted my fist in the air and shot my middle finger up at him.

"That too!"

I grunted and sped up. The last thing I needed was Jake to be Jake.

I thought Claudia would say I was crazy for agreeing to meet Jake, but instead she thought it was a good idea for me to clear the air with him. I didn't know if that was because she liked hanging out with Beck and didn't want to stop, or because she'd decided maybe she liked Jake a little after spending time with him at Teviot. She'd texted me when she realized I'd left, but I told her to stay. After

Beck dropped her back at the apartment, she informed me, a little tipsy, that Jake and Melissa had joined the band for drinks.

Apparently, Melissa had been quiet for most of the night and Jake appeared to spend half his time reassuring her. His ex-girlfriend showing up in Edinburgh probably had put a little kink in their romantic study abroad, but I couldn't give a shit.

Not true, actually. Part of me really did feel for Melissa. In fact, part of me wanted to run straight to her to warn her to get the hell out of there before Jake Caplin ripped her heart out.

Claudia didn't see Jake the Heartbreaker, however. She cautiously told me that Jake was charming and friendly and acted like everything was cool. The only moment of tension at the table came when Lowe asked about me. Claudia had said I was tired and Lowe had responded by telling her to ask me to wear my Pearl Jam T-shirt next time I came out with them.

"This will be good," Claudia said confidently as she walked me to the door. "Clear the air before classes start so you can focus on enjoying your time here."

I wished I was as confident as she was. Instead I walked into Teviot with my chest vibrating and my stomach churning. I didn't want to dress up for him because I thought that would be pretty obvious, but I also stupidly wanted to look hot enough to annoy him. I wore my best black skinny jeans, short black ankle boots with a little heel, and a green Harley Davidson T-shirt that was a little short in the hem and snug across the bust. I topped it with my jewelry and let my hair spill down my back in its usual waves. Jake once told me I had sex hair all day, every day, and it used to drive him nuts. My petty hope was that everything about me now would drive him nuts. If I had to suffer through my attraction to him, it would certainly help a little if he had to suffer too.

I got a couple of nods from guys as I passed and decided I'd done well today with my outfit. Yay. In the Library Bar, my eyes met the bartender first. He was cute in that I'm-deliberately-scruffy-so-you'll-think-I-don't-care-but-I-really-do kind of way. He wasn't really my type, but I smiled to be polite when he gave me a nod. Turning, I found Jake sitting along the right side of the room in an open booth. He was scowling at the bartender.

Ignoring the flutter in my stomach, I walked casually toward him, but my confidence slipped a little when Jake's eyes found me. I felt his gaze sizzle through every nerve ending as he took me in from head to foot. A muscle ticked in his jaw and he moved back against the leather booth as if suddenly restless to get out of there.

"Jake," I greeted him flatly and slid into the opposite bench.

"Charley." He lifted a hand to get the bartender's attention and the guy came over to take our orders for coffee, his heated focus making things awkward. I was almost relieved when he left.

An uncomfortable silence—something Jake and I had never had to cope with before—fell between us as we waited. Finally when the coffees came, Jake took a sip and then started talking. "Your hair is much lighter. It looks good."

Although affected by the compliment, I pretended I wasn't and stared blankly back at him.

He switched tactics. "I know I fucked up hugely."

I put my coffee mug back on the saucer and sighed as if I didn't have time for this crap. "Is that why I came here, Jake? To listen to you state the obvious?"

"I'm trying here. You used to admire honesty. Have you changed?"

I narrowed my eyes at him. "I'm meaner now. A lesson I learned from you."

Dropping his elbows on the table so he could lean closer, Jake gazed at me soulfully. "I was a dick to you. I can't take that back. But I can apologize. I can try to explain."

Giving him a small nod, I encouraged him to go on.

"I was lost somewhere else inside my head when it happened, Charley. I couldn't see past that to anything or anyone. I was angry that it got that out of control and I blamed myself. You got caught up in it."

"I never turned my back on you. I don't understand why you blamed *me*."

His brows puckered and he closed his eyes, as if in pain. "I didn't blame you. I said things I didn't even mean. All I wanted was to get out of there and put the whole thing behind me. By the time I looked back, it was too late. I couldn't change what I'd done to you. I couldn't change what I'd destroyed. I thought it was better to just let you move on. We were just kids, Charley."

He said it like our age meant anything. He said it like others had said it to me when he left, as though because I was only sixteen, my relationship hadn't been real—that I hadn't fallen hard and deep. To have Jake agree with them hurt like a mother. "Move on from me? Or from there?"

"From there. From you too. You were a part of it, as much as I didn't want you to be."

On that, I disagreed. "Then it's a good thing you didn't come back, if that's the way you still see it."

"Charley, all I remember now about you is the good stuff. I let all that other shit go." His eyelashes lowered over his eyes as he stared down into his coffee. "You were the best friend I ever had. I miss you. I've always missed you and regretted how I left it. But at the party … the way you looked at me," his breath caught, "that was hard. I'd somehow convinced myself that you would be indifferent about …it all. You quickly dissuaded me of that."

His heartfelt apology and admission that he'd missed me both hurt and soothed me. I relaxed a little against my seat, cradling the mug in my hands for the comforting heat it provided. "I know it wasn't easy for you and your family, Jake. I know that's the biggest understatement of the century ...I tried, though, I tried to understand, and as much as I want to, I can't excuse what you did to me because of what happened. That doesn't mean your apology doesn't help. It does. Thank you."

Jake smiled softly and I felt that smile right in my gut. I flicked my gaze away quickly, pretending to scan the room. "I want us to be friends."

His words brought my surprised gaze back. "What?"

He shrugged. "We're both here for the year. We were great friends once ..."

I suddenly found it a little difficult to breathe and I quickly stood, putting money on the table beside my coffee. "Look, Jake, I'm sorry I reacted that way to you at the party, and I promise that from now on, if I see you around I'll be polite. You don't deserve any more shit in your life. But it's been a while. We're different people now. Let's just leave it at that." Before he could reply, I walked away, waving back at the flirtatious bartender as if walking away from Jake Caplin wasn't one of the things I hated doing most in the world.

"We're going where?" I drew to a halt at the gates of the courtyard. It was past nine on Friday night and the Cowgate and Grassmarket were already buzzing with music and people. I was wearing my jeans and the Pearl Jam T-shirt because Claudia insisted I should—her words from a couple days ago came back to haunt me at the same time she finally told me what our plans were for the evening.

"Beck stopped by to invite us to listen to the band play their first gig. It's this little bar just down the street."

"Since when are you and Beck so chummy?" I asked as a delay tactic. I needed to come up with a reason not to go.

"I told you he wants to be friends and when he's not being a manwhore, he's pretty cool. I see no problem in hanging out with him and his band."

"Uh ... Jake's the problem."

"Jake's not in the band."

I was going to wring her neck. "I know that, Claud. But you also know he's their friend and he'll be there. With her."

She grabbed my hand and gave it a sympathetic squeeze. "Babe, the best thing you can do is pretend that you're over it. No one will think you're faking it. You're smart and you're hot and they know you could get anybody. There's no reason for them to think you're hung up on Jake."

"Although sweet, you're completely biased." I groaned in frustration. "I just don't know if I can be around him and Melissa."

Claudia shrugged. "Then find someone to take your mind off them. Beck told me Lowe thinks you're smokin' hot."

I gestured to my shirt. "The Pearl Jam shirt. He's going to think I'm into him."

"Why wouldn't you be? Lowe is cute."

I raised my eyebrow. "He's also a bad boy."

"So? You're not looking to marry the guy. You're just looking for a distraction."

"You know I don't sleep around."

"Who says you need to sleep with him?"

"You have an answer for everything, don't you?"

My friend got serious all of a sudden, her grip turning almost painful. "I thought you were over this guy. Then we get here and he's here too, and I realized that you are not over him. I don't think, even when you weren't thinking about him, you've ever gotten over him. I think this is the perfect opportunity for you to finally put him behind you."

In the end, I knew she was right. I'd been holding onto the seventeen-year-old Jake I'd been in love with. He didn't exist anymore. If I spent some time around twenty-year-old Jake who was in love with Melissa, then maybe that would finally sink in. I gave in and let Claudia lead the way.

She wasn't wrong. The guys were playing at a bar called Milk, tucked in the corner between two sets of buildings built onto a steep slope. A narrow lane took pedestrians from the Cowgate up onto the part of the city that would lead to The Royal Mile. For the last few days, Claudia and I had been nursing hangovers from time spent with our roommates and neighbors, and we'd used the time to get better acquainted with the city that was to be ours for the next nine months. We'd wandered all over Old Town, stopping by the grave of the famous canine Grey Friars Bobby, and the nearby café The Elephant House where J.K. Rowling was said to have written some of Harry Potter in the back room that overlooked Edinburgh Castle. Claud and I had then headed toward New Town to check out the stores on Princes Street and George Street. And of course, we'd backtracked after that to Edinburgh Castle. Its lure was too great. Perched upon volcanic rock, lording over the modern city like a medieval king, Claud and I had both gotten neck pain from staring up at it as we walked down Princes Street. Fascinated, we'd wandered all the way back up to The Royal Mile and up the cobbled streets to the castle. Our legs ached from walking so much, but it surprisingly helped with the hangovers. I was thinking we'd need to slow down our partying, though. Being able to legally drink in a bar was a novelty, but I wanted to depart Scotland with a fully functioning liver.

Claudia led me into Milk and at first, we were really confused. The packed room was tiny and closed in with its dull lights, brick walls, and large bar area taking up most of the space. A leather bench ran the length of the opposing wall, tables and chairs pushed up against them.

"Are you sure this is the right place?" I asked, not able to see Jake or Beck or anyone recognizable.

Frowning, Claudia pulled out her cell and flicked through her messages. Her brow cleared and she grabbed my wrist, pulling me through the crowded bar with a polite *excuse-me* here and there. At the end of the room, hidden by the bar, an arched wall led into another larger room. Tables and chairs took up most of the floor and at the opposite end of the room was a small stage where Matt fiddled with a drum kit and Lowe with his guitar and amp.

The place was crowded.

"Claudia!"

We looked over at a table near the stage to see Beck standing, waving us over with a grin. Cutting through the tables, my legs started to tremble as I caught sight of Jake and Melissa sitting in the seats closest to the stage. My eyes quickly jumped from them to Rowena sitting next to Jake and Denver. There were a couple of empty seats at the end of the table and I was relieved that I'd get to sit far enough away from the happy couple to breathe.

I was surprised by the way Beck greeted Claudia. It wasn't the kiss to her cheek—Claudia returned that comfortably and the whole thing suggested they were as platonic as they claimed. However, my eyes drifted down as Claudia stood on tiptoe so Beck didn't have to bend so far, and I watched with confusion as Beck's hand gripped Claudia's hip and then caressed it as he reluctantly let her go.

Claudia didn't seem to notice, but I knew her well enough to know that she was pretending. There was a slight flush on the crests of her cheeks. Still, Beck had said he wouldn't sleep with her, so Claudia told me she had shoved her attraction to him to the back of her mind and was enjoying his friendship.

Only problem was I wasn't so sure Beck wasn't having a hard time with his decision to not sleep with her. This was only the second time I'd seen them hang out and even as he greeted me, his eyes flickered quickly back to Claudia as she greeted everyone.

"Love the shirt," Denver commented as I took a seat next to him. Claudia sat on my left and Beck sat down next to her.

Claudia laughed because she knew all about my magic shirt. I grinned at Denver. "Thanks."

I couldn't help it. My gaze moved to Jake and Melissa at the end of the table. He was staring at my shirt, a little crease between his brow, and I shifted uncomfortably, my eyes moving to Melissa. Her chair was tucked into Jake's and they sat intimately close so no one could mistake they weren't together. Our eyes met and I gave her a small smile, one she returned a little tremulously.

She was probably wondering why Jake was glaring at my T-shirt. I could explain it to her, but that would be awkward. Jake introduced me to Pearl Jam and was delighted when I fell in love with Eddie Vedder's voice, their sound, and their stories. The T-shirt was a reminder that, if even only in the smallest way, he'd had an effect on the person I'd become.

"She's back and she's wearing the T-shirt." Lowe's voice brought my head up as he strolled over to us. He squeezed Claudia's shoulder as he passed. "I owe you."

I knew what he meant and only managed to stop myself from scowling. When he drew to a halt by my chair and held his arms out to me, silently asking for a hug, his bad-boy charm worked and I felt the urge to scowl disappear. I stood up and laughed Lowe off like his flirting was no big deal. We hugged and my skin flushed for a different reason as I felt the hard muscle of his back under his light T-shirt. Grinning, I looked up into his blue eyes and decided Claudia was right: Lowe was hot and he thought I was hot. That was flattering and distracting and just what I needed.

"Denver, take a shot of me and Charley together," Lowe nodded at his friend and pulled me into his side, his arm tight around my shoulders.

Denver frowned. "Why?"

"Because my brother gave me shit about spending money on this study abroad. I want to post this picture on his Facebook page to make a point that I made the right choice."

"Oh, God," I groaned. "I hope your lyrics are better than that line."

When the group chuckled, I grinned over at them, the smile faltering on my lips when I saw Jake staring off to the other side of the room, his eyes dark. The moment between Lowe and me rewound in my head and I felt my heart stutter in realization.

It was exactly the kind of thing Jake would've said to me back in the day and exactly the kind of cheeky response I'd have given him.

I was about to pull away from Lowe, not wanting this distraction to turn into another Jake situation, but Denver had his camera phone out and Lowe was pulling me back into his side. His fingertips were calloused from playing the guitar and as they coasted around to cup my hip, he brushed under my T-shirt, eliciting a shiver I knew he felt and enjoyed because his grin widened. I made a face at him and he laughed so boyishly, I couldn't help but laugh back. Later, I'd discover that was the shot Denver took, because Lowe *did* put it on Facebook and tagged it after friending me. It was a great photograph, us laughing into each other's faces, holding onto one another like we'd known each other our whole lives. As soon as I saw it, it made me uncomfortable and flustered.

Lowe disappeared to the bar to get Claudia and me a drink. When he returned, Claud moved down a chair so Lowe could sit with me. Matt eventually came over to the table and sat down by

Jake, and Beck announced that the band was supposed to be on soon.

Once conversation had started up, Lowe put his arm behind my chair and leaned into me. My gaze automatically dipped to his lip ring and a curious thought flashed in my eyes before I could stop it. I knew Lowe caught it because his teeth grazed the ring a second before he smiled.

"Was that a naughty thought, Charlotte?" he murmured, eyes twinkling.

I shook my head casually to cover my embarrassment. "Just wondering if it was painful?"

"Not as painful as the tat on my ribs."

Knowing exactly what he wanted my response to be, my lips twitched. "I'm not asking you to take your shirt off."

"Damn. I've got a live one." He smiled and then dipped his head closer to mine. "Is it weird? Seeing Jake again?"

I arched an eyebrow at him, not particularly happy to learn they'd obviously been talking about me.

Lowe just shrugged. "We've been friends since freshman year. I knew something was up so he told me about you guys. It's a shit situation."

"It was a long time ago."

"So you're a free agent, then?"

I wondered for a second if there was a code amongst guy friends about pursuing ex-girlfriends. Clearly not, according to Lowe. I sighed. "I'm not his, if that's what you mean." Funny, but that was the first time I'd said it aloud since we broke up. I was no longer surprised by how much it hurt.

"Are you anybody's?"

"I don't think we're ever anybody's, and to believe otherwise will get you hurt."

SAMANTHA YOUNG

Lowe tipped his head in thought, his eyes strangely serious. "I think you'll like my lyrics."

"I can't wait to hear you guys."

"I warn you once you do, you'll become a groupie."

Laughing, I shook my head. "Sorry, I've never been a follower."

"I think that's a challenge."

"No, it's a fact. Take it as a challenge if you like, but you'll find it a Sisyphean task."

Lowe laughed so hard he drew everyone's eyes. His were glittering. "Classics major?"

My lips twitched. "Psychology."

That made him laugh even harder. "Really?"

"Nah. Criminal law."

"You're shitting me?"

"Nope." I smiled around my beer, glad for Lowe and his distraction from Jake. My smile almost faltered when I caught Jake's eyes, but he just gave me a tight smile and leaned his head to the side to listen to whatever Melissa was saying. Ignoring the sudden churning in my gut, I glanced over at Claudia to find her grinning happily at me, her gaze darting to Lowe pointedly. She gave me a wink, which I ignored, and laughed, turning back to Beck.

"Why are you studying law?"

"She wants to be a cop."

This came from Jake and my head jerked to him in surprise. He was staring at me with that frown line between his eyebrows again. I hated that his answer was like a free kick to my heart. Claudia, sensing I was lost as to how to respond, answered for me. "Actually, Charley's parents hated the idea of her being a cop so much that she compromised with a pre-law degree so she can apply to law school."

Something sharpened in Jake's expression as he returned his attention to me. Although I doubted anyone else understood it, I certainly did. Back when we were "us", I'd discussed my parents' unease at my career choice with Jake. Every time I found myself caving to them, Jake was there to bolster my resolve. In actuality I hadn't given up on being a cop. I was compromising until I could convince my parents it was what I really wanted to do with my life. It had always been important to me to have their full support in everything I did, and I was growing more worried every day that I might not be able to persuade them to see things my way. I didn't know how the story of my career was going to end if they didn't jump on board soon.

To Jake it would seem like I'd given in to them completely, and that my change of heart was another thing that could be traced to his lack of presence in my life. I didn't know how that made him feel, but I could tell it made him feel *something*.

"Claudia is pre-law too," I turned to Lowe. That's how we'd met.

"Why law school?" Beck asked her, grinning like he didn't quite understand her.

"Because when I closed my eyes and ran my finger down the undergrad programs, it stopped on criminal law."

And she wasn't joking.

Beck almost choked on his beer, shaking his head at her like she was crazy.

This started off the rounds of "what's your major?" I think every group of new college friends got this off their chests quickly so they never had to utter those banal words ever again. Jake, Beck, and Lowe were industrial engineering undergrads, Denver was doing applied mathematics, Rowena was studying English, and Melissa and Matt were history undergrads.

The guys were teasing Rowena about her major and she was taking it all in good spirit when a bearded guy came up to the band and told them it was time for their set.

Lowe winked at me as he got up. I wished him good luck. He nodded and walked off confidently, the short chain on his jeans swinging as he hopped onto the stage. Claudia shimmied closer to me with an excited smile as the guys readied themselves. The entire time I diligently ignored Jake and Melissa.

Almost simultaneously, Lowe and Beck lifted their guitar straps over their heads, followed by Denver who was their bassist, and Matt seated himself behind the drums. Only Denver and Lowe stood near mics, and Lowe's was center stage.

I glanced around at the crowded bar and noted a lot of people about our age. Nearly half were girls who looked like cartoon lionesses, staring at Beck and Lowe like they were juicy, talking zebra steaks.

I smirked and turned back to them as the first guitar riff pulsed through the room. As Lowe began singing in a smooth, deep voice—so sexy, I'd happily replace my vibrator with it—I fell into the band's sound. Lowe was right. I loved his lyrics. They were real, no fairy-tale bullshit, but they were also a contradiction, like he knew what he'd experienced but he couldn't help still feel maybe there was the possibility of more out there. I'd always thought it was brave of musicians to put their souls on a track. That was even clearer to me now that I actually knew the band, and I had to admit, I was impressed.

A couple of songs into their set, Lowe sang about "being lost in the shallows" and as soon as the lyrics were out of his mouth, my gaze instantly flicked to Jake.

My breath got caught in a painful ball in my throat as my eyes met his.

He wasn't watching the band. He was watching me.

I shuttered my gaze, ignoring the rushing of blood in my ears, and turned back to concentrate on the band. I couldn't, though.

Not even Lowe's hot voice could distract me from Jake and the memory of us.

I squirmed uncomfortably for the rest of the set, almost grateful when Lowe murmured into the mic, "You've been listening to The Stolen. Thanks, and have a good night." He smiled over at me as the crowd erupted into applause and whistles, and I smiled back, almost begging him with that look to come over and once again take my mind off Jake Caplin.

Chapter Six

Indiana, October 2008

"So," Mrs. Tate, our English teacher, switched off the television. "Now that you've all supposedly read the book and we've watched the film, I can ask what you think. We've not got a lot of time left, so just briefly. First thoughts?"

I looked around, waiting for a classmate to let their opinion be known. Most of the guys appeared to have fallen asleep watching the movie. Except Jake. I caught his eye as I turned my head to the right. He'd asked Nikki Wells to move from the seat across from me in the next aisle and of course she'd said yes, grinning up at him like he was the Second Coming.

I'd been on three dates with Jake, and we hung out a lot at school. Everyone thought we were together, but I still wasn't sure. Despite the mysterious feeling of deep connection between us, I didn't know quite how to take it that the biggest player in our class hadn't seen fit to kiss me yet. Friday night he'd taken me out and not made so much as a move. Now, Monday morning, I'd seen what appeared to be him flirting with a senior girl at his locker. I'd walked right by him with barely a nod.

I was starting to worry the assholery of Brett Thomas and his goons was getting to Jake. They still hadn't let up, and it wasn't just about me. Jake's dad, Logan, had caused some controversy opening up his law firm and poaching clients from Ed Brackett—Brett's uncle. Ed was a fairly quiet and reserved guy, the complete opposite of his brother-in-law, so any difficulties Jake's dad was having originated with Trenton Thomas. Rumor had it he was making "idle threats" to anyone who was thinking about taking their business from Ed to Logan Caplin.

Most of the time I loved Lanton, but sometimes I really hated living in such a small town.

I felt bad for Jake's dad and I hated that Brett was being such a pain in Jake's ass, but that didn't excuse him from befuddling the hell out of me, so when Jake winked at me, I raised one very unimpressed eyebrow.

"Charlotte?" Mrs. Tate's dry tone brought my gaze to her. She looked pointedly at Jake and then back to me. "Any thoughts?"

How about … you've known me my whole life so why do you never call me Charley?

"Well?"

I sighed and leaned back in my chair. "Honestly, I found the whole thing a little angst-ridden for my liking."

My classmates tittered and Mrs. Tate frowned. "You found Jane Austen *angst-ridden*?"

Apparently Tate thought I was wrong. Oh, well. "There are a lot of misunderstandings that could've been cleared up if they'd just talked to one another. The whole thing with Edward and Elinor was exhausting. If he'd just admitted he loved her and broke off his stupid secret engagement to whatshername, Elinor wouldn't have had to go through all the emotional crap she went through. I mean, she's very gracious and all, but she spent a good part of that novel pining for a man and she didn't even know if he felt the same way about her. Edward was a nice guy, but he needed a swift kick to the behind."

Mrs. Tate crossed her arms, unimpressed. "Charlotte, we're talking about an entirely different time period, culture, and class system. I think the situation is a lot more complicated than that."

Okay, so maybe I was projecting.

The bell rang before I could respond and chairs immediately scraped back as the students hurried to get the hell out.

I was stuffing my books in my bag when a shadow fell over my desk. Glancing up sharply, my eyes met Jake's determined gaze. "What is it?" I frowned, recognizing mischief there. "What are you doing?"

"Clearing up an obvious misunderstanding."

"What are—"

I didn't even get the rest of the question out before Jake pulled me up out of my seat, wrapped a tight hand around my nape, and crushed my mouth beneath his.

Shock soon gave way to sheer delight as his talented mouth moved over mine. I sighed and his tongue slipped past my lips and tangled gently with mine. My fingers curled around his T-shirt as the taste and smell of him overwhelmed me. My skin was hot from the deep, wet kiss, and my body screamed "wow!"

Who knew a kiss could be like that?

The whooping and whistling finally wrenched me out of my fog and I remembered with burning cheeks that there were still kids in the classroom. I pushed gently against Jake and he released me, our faces close as we fought to catch our breath. He squeezed my neck again and grinned at me. "Epic."

I laughed, embarrassed but thrilled. He didn't need to know that though. "Cheesy."

"Epic."

"Okay, that's enough." Mrs. Tate came into my eyeline and I flushed harder. "Jake, let Charley go."

I blinked at her use of my nickname but as Jake moved away, I saw that he had caused a miracle. Mrs. Tate was fighting a smile. She thought he was charming.

With no more show, the students slowly filtered out of the class. Jake pulled on his backpack and held out a hand to me, a cocky smile wide across his face. "Coming?"

I took his hand.

"Jacob, if you kiss another student in my class again, I will give you detention," Mrs. Tate warned softly, her lips curled up at the corner.

Jake pulled me closer as we walked by her. "Won't happen again, Mrs. T."

Mrs. T? It was decided. Jacob Caplin could probably get away with murder.

Out in the hall, I could see news had traveled fast about Jake's little classroom exhibition. All eyes were on us as he walked me to my locker. Before I could open it, Jake maneuvered me so I had my back to it and he leaned into me, his arms above my head, caging me in.

"So our first kiss was very, very public," I murmured, unable to tear my eyes from his warm ones.

Jake smiled. "I told you I'd do it when you least expected it."

"I am going to take your promises a lot more seriously from now on."

"Good." He touched his mouth to mine, a shivery brush that had the same effect as his deep one had. My breathing shallowed and I felt a whole lot of lusty thoughts that I wished I wasn't feeling in public. I was so glad I wasn't a dude.

"Hey, Jake!"

Without moving his body, Jake twisted his head over his shoulder at Amanda Reyes. She'd stopped beside us, even though our body language made it clear we were having a private moment.

Amanda was in my class but we'd never been close friends. She didn't really have a group of friends, more like acquaintances. She was quiet usually, so her stopping to talk to Jake, her cheeks flushed bright at the sight of him, should've been a surprise. But it wasn't. Anytime she passed us, she said hi to him.

"Hey." Jake nodded back and then instantly turned to me, the polite indifference in his expression melting as his eyes roamed my face.

I watched Amanda's shoulders slump as she walked away.

My focus returned to Jake as his mouth lowered toward mine again. "She has a thing for you."

"All I care about is that you have a thing for me," Jake whispered against my lips.

I chuckled but as he pressed his whole body closer to mine, my smile died and I found myself uttering thickly, "I might have a thing for you."

His groan vibrated down my throat as he kissed me and then reluctantly pulled back. He pushed away and stared down at me, a frown between his brows. "Shit. Now I'm addicted." He took a step away and I laughed.

"Are you running away from me?"

He leaned in a little so only I'd hear. "It's either that or I walk around with a permanent ..." His eyes flickered down and my gaze followed to his crotch. I made a face as I got his meaning and turned away to open my locker.

"You're filthy," I told him halfheartedly.

His hand appeared on my locker, the heat of his chest searing into my back, and I shivered again as his lips brushed my ear. "You love it."

And then he was gone and I was left hyperventilating against my locker.

After a few moments, I managed to pull myself together. I'd just switched out my books when I turned and crashed into Brett.

Awesome.

Brett stared at me, his features taut, his eyes hard. It was not a good look on him, but it was a familiar one. "He's playing with you."

Knowing exactly what this was, I sighed heavily and walked around him. Unfortunately, Brett fell into step beside me as I strode down the hall toward my next class.

"He's slept with every girl in our class, Charley. He's just using you."

"Well, that's a gross exaggeration," I replied dryly. "I assure you it's only half."

"You think this is a joke," Brett snapped. "This guy is going to seriously hurt you."

I turned around and started walking backward away from him. "I'm Supergirl, remember? I don't get hurt."

His face screwed up. "You're acting like a slut and an idiot."

"And you're an asshole," I replied cheerily and spun around, ignoring my gossiping classmates as I headed for class.

As soon as I took my seat, my cell buzzed and I looked at it as everyone settled in. It was from Jake.

You called Brett an asshole? Everything okay?

Jeez, news really did travel fast in this school. **Dude killed my erection. I retaliated. Xoxo**

Ten seconds later: **LMAO.** And two seconds after that: **I'm so into you.**

I smiled, probably looking like the idiot Brett had just accused me of being. **Good xoxo**

Chapter Seven

Edinburgh, September 2012

"Who? What? Who? How?" Andie's hazel eyes, identical to mine, were wide as she stared into the camera.

That was pretty much the reaction I'd been expecting when I told her via Skype that Jake was in Edinburgh.

"You heard me," I replied, gazing past her to her office. Light spilled in from a window somewhere, reminding me I was five hours ahead. It was almost midnight in Scotland but Andie was always so busy with grad school and her internship that we could only talk on her schedule. I didn't mind. I *really* wanted to talk to her.

"Jake, your ex-boyfriend Jake? The Jake who knew that you were always planning to spend your third year studying abroad at the University of Edinburgh?"

And that was exactly why I *really* wanted to talk to my big sister.

She knew mostly everything about my relationship with Jake, not because she'd been there to witness it (she'd only met him once during her Christmas break home from Dublin), but because I'd told her probably every little detail. This meant she knew that Jake was privy to all my thoughts and feelings and plans and dreams.

I'd talked to Jake a million times about studying in Edinburgh because Andie was always calling home from Dublin talking about what an amazing time she was having. I wanted to study in Europe too, and while Ireland struck my sister's fancy, for me, it was Scotland. Jake had said he wanted to come with me.

"Yes."

"So," Andie scrunched up her nose as she ran her hand through her hair, a habit we shared and a tell that we were trying to work something out, "he obviously came to Edinburgh because he knew you'd be there. Why? To apologize? To get you back?"

And this more specifically was why I wanted to talk to Andie. It was the question I'd been too scared and confused to ask, so I wanted someone else to ask it because I knew if they did, it would make me feel less crazy for thinking it. I still felt crazy. Because of Melissa. "He did apologize. But he's here with his friends and … his girlfriend."

"He brought another girl? What!" Andie slammed her hands on the desk and leaned closer into the camera so her nose and mouth looked huge. "He knew you'd be there, that little …"

I sat back and let Andie have her rant, expelling all the questions and anger I too was feeling. When she was done, she sat back, exhaling.

"Uh, everything okay in here?" a masculine voice I knew well asked from off camera.

Andie twisted her head around to stare in the direction of the voice and her face got soft. "Yeah, baby, I'm just raging on behalf of Supergirl."

"What happened?"

"Boy problems."

"Thanks," I mumbled sarcastically. That made it seem so trivial.

"Do I need to kick someone's ass?" The voice got closer and then Rick's handsome face appeared beside Andie's. "You okay, Charley?"

"Hey, Rick, good to see you." I wasn't lying. My sister's fiancé was the shit. He was ten years older than Andie and a Chicago police detective. They met a year ago when Andie's friend's car got stolen and Andie had driven her to the precinct. To Andie's friend's annoyance, Detective Rick Pertrard, who'd overheard the complaint to the officer on duty, had taken an immediate shine to the damsel-in-distress's friend and not the damsel herself. He'd asked for Andie's number and the rest was history. They moved in together after only six months and got engaged two months after that. I loved the changes I saw in my sister. She was far less concerned with being perfect all the time, and she'd definitely loosened up.

As for me, I kept trying to make Rick my mentor but since my parents still weren't happy with the cop idea, he was fighting me on it, more concerned with being a good son-in-law than encouraging me down a career path he knew would piss off my parents. That sucked, but he was still the shit.

"You too, sweetheart, but I repeat: are you okay?"

"I'm fine."

He frowned and looked at Andie. "Then what's with the raging?"

"She's not fine. She's very far from fine but she's Charley, so she's fine."

Rick's gaze flickered between us. "As long as you understand each other, I guess." He kissed her cheek and waved goodbye to me before heading out of shot.

Andie turned as soon as he was gone. "So what's your plan?"

I shrugged. "No plan. It looks like we might have to be around each other because Claudia is hanging out with Jake's best friend. A lot. I need to suck it up."

"Charley, despite what I just said to Rick, this is me you're talking to. I came home from Dublin to find my baby sister a wreck. What happened with Jake changed you and I never got my old Charley back, so you can say you're fine to everyone else, but not to me. Okay?"

Her words automatically called on the lump in my throat and I looked away from the screen, fighting tears. I failed and swiped at them. "I'm not doing this again," I told her harshly. "I already sobbed my guts out to Claudia after the party."

"Good."

I looked at my sister as if I'd just discovered she was the devil incarnate. "What?" I snapped.

"I know you think tears make you less badass but screw that. You can't bottle that stuff up. I know everyone told you to get over him, that he was just puppy love, but your family—never. We never said it because we never believed that. You were young but it was real, and I wanted to hunt him down and kill him for breaking your heart. A heart, I might add, that has never quite been the same since. Look at you and Alex."

"I'm not talking about Alex," I groaned.

Andie held up her hands in surrender. "Okay, we won't talk about Alex. But I will say that I think you are crazy if you spend time with Jake. It would be crazy anyway, but even crazier because he's there with his girlfriend."

I nodded glumly. "You're right."

"Of course I'm right. I'm a psychiatrist."

"You're not a psychiatrist yet."

"I know. Only two more years." She grimaced. "God ... I don't think I'm going to make it."

I thought of the next nine months and spending it avoiding Jake and the knifelike feeling in my chest every time I saw him. "I know what you mean."

It was almost the end of week one of classes and I was already feeling the weight. Papers were due, tutorial materials were needed. I would actually have to do school work while I was here. The induction week in a foreign city had kind of lulled me into a false sense that I was on vacation.

With classes up and running, Claudia and I had agreed to put our heads down and get organized. We could go back to having fun once we were settled into our academics.

Settling in for me would usually mean my brain was too cluttered with thoughts on classes to be able to concentrate on anything else, but not this time. I hated to admit it, but Jake Caplin was taking up way more of my thoughts than I'd like.

While running my finger along the books in the reserve section of the university library in search of material I needed for an upcoming tutorial, I heard his voice right beside my ear. I jumped, thinking I'd actually conjured him.

"Jesus," Jake cried out softly, dodging my flailing arm.

I glared up at him, my hand now pressed to my chest as I tried to get my heart rate to normalize. "Are you trying to kill me?"

"I'm sorry. I didn't know the words 'Hey, Charley' were considered lethal."

"They are if you sneak up behind me and practically whisper them in my ear. It's creepy. Creepiness often precedes death."

"I'll keep that in mind," he replied in a strangled voice.

"You do that." I turned back to the bookshelf so I didn't have to look at his gorgeous face, which happened to need a shave. When Jake needed a shave, he looked beyond hot. It was so unfair.

I felt his head dip close to mine. "Whatcha looking for?"

"The equation for time travel. Some guy just gave me permanent heart failure and I'd like to go back in time and change today so that I'm lying on a beach in Guam being waited on by a hottie named Han with heavy footsteps and an aversion to whispering."

Jake chuckled and I felt the deep sound in every one of my erogenous zones. "Still a smart-ass, I see," he said.

I looked up at him and ignored the fact that he was wearing another tight-fitting, long-sleeved shirt and that he obviously worked out. His shoulders and biceps were broader than they used to be and I realized belatedly that even his face was a little different. It was sharper, harder, the softness of youth having melted away.

He was quite possibly more beautiful than he used to be. Wonderful.

My gaze shifted past him and I shrugged casually. "Some things change. Some things don't."

"You have and you haven't."

His comment brought my eyes back to his. I frowned. "What do you mean?"

It was now Jake's turn to shrug. "You're still a smart-ass, still cocky, but you're quieter about it, more reserved. You're not ... you don't seem as open to people as you used to be."

Finding myself in dangerous territory, I deflected his observation with sarcasm. "I was never open to people, but I live in a small town and was given little choice in the matter."

Jake ignored the sarcasm. "Come grab a coffee with me."

I felt an uncomfortable flip in my chest. "Now?"

"Yeah. There's a café across the main forum of the library. It's two seconds away. We're here. It's there. We could be drinking coffee or juice or soda, milk even, or tea, or you know they have food there too ..."

"Jake Caplin, are you rambling?"

He nodded, his warm eyes alight with humor. "I'm rambling. I'm a rambler now."

Crossing my arms over my chest, I tilted my head with an arrogant smile. "Are you nervous around me?"

His mouth curled up at the corner and he gave me a little nod. "I'm nervous you'll say no. Our last coffee didn't go so well."

I hadn't thought it had gone poorly. I made a face. "Didn't it?"

"You walked out after taking three sips."

"I was making a statement."

Jake shrugged, all humor suddenly gone from his expression. "Well, I didn't like it. I don't want you to repeat that statement."

I knew by the rapid fluttering in my chest that agreeing to have coffee with Jake was a bad idea. Andie would also think it was a bad idea. However, the whoosh in my belly—a consequence of Jake's intense focus on me and worry that I'd reject his friendship—was something I hadn't felt since we'd been together. It was a sudden reminder how addictive the belly whoosh I got from Jake's attention was.

And I found myself giving in to temptation. "I could do coffee."

His slow smile caused another big whoosh and I told my belly to get a grip as I walked out. I followed Jake across the crowded main entrance of the library, a forum that students had turned into a hangout, and we let ourselves into the perplex security gates to the library café. The place was packed, so I found us a spot to sit near brightly colored bean cushions while he got us coffee.

Five minutes later I looked up and watched him coming toward me with the tray in his hands. The belly whoosh went to war with the ache of the loss of him in my chest. I forgot how much I loved the way his tall body moved. The pleasure of watching him was so familiar.

It amazed me that the residual feelings from our eight months together felt like an album of memories compiled over years.

Taking a seat across from me, Jake smiled. "So, it looks like we're going to be seeing a lot of each other over the next few months. I think we should try to get past the weirdness."

What a conversation opener. "Straight to the point."

"The Charley I knew was a straight-talker. Has that changed too?"

I blew over my hot coffee and replied before taking a sip, "What do *you* think?"

Jake snorted. "I'm thinking that hasn't changed."

We drank from our mugs, silence falling between us. I knew Jake was waiting for me to lead the way, telling me that the ball was in my court and he was happy to go along with whatever I wanted. In the interest of keeping our new group sweet, I put my mug down and relaxed back into my chair. "How are your mom and dad?"

Relief visibly traveled through Jake's body and he too relaxed. "They're good. We moved back to Chicago and Dad got his old job back. Mom was happy to be back with all her old friends. They're doing a lot better. What about your family?"

"They're okay. Dad's busier than ever at work but Mom's store hit troubles. The basement has some really dangerous mold growing in there, so she's had to close down while they deal with that. It's expensive in a lot of ways but you know Mom, you can't keep her down. She's working from the house. It's driving Dad nuts."

Jacob's eyes brightened and he nodded. "I'll bet. What about Andie?"

I smiled now as I thought of Rick. I was so happy my sister had found the right guy. "She's great. Living in Chicago. Postgrad psych, doing her internship, and she's engaged to a rugged police detective."

"Who you've bribed into being your mentor," Jake guessed drolly.

I felt another pang in my chest at the reminder of how well he knew me. I shrugged it off as if it wasn't a big deal he knew all the simple stuff about me that made me *me*. "I tried. He's too concerned with impressing Mom and Dad to commit, but I'll wear him down."

Jake gave a huff a laughter. "I have no doubt."

Brushing off the moment, I asked about his brother Lukas.

Jake instantly grinned. "Oh, he says hi."

"Tell him I say hi back." It occurred to me Jake must've mentioned he'd run into me, and I wondered if his whole family knew. I also wondered how they felt about that.

"He said to say that he saw the picture of you and Lowe on Facebook and you're looking, and I quote, 'hotter than ever.'"

Remembering Lukas's crush on me, I laughed. "He hasn't changed. He was worse than you. I imagine he's breaking hearts all over a college campus as we speak."

"Well, yeah, but he tells me he's met 'the one.' He slept with her first week in and she's an even bigger player than he is and doesn't feel like settling down with the first freshman she banged. So Lukas's game plan is to outplay her in some weird, modern mating ritual."

Laughter bubbled between my lips as I attempted to ignore the fact that I had a new ache from missing Lukas too. In my intense pain over losing Jake, I'd almost forgotten how much I cared about his little brother.

We yammered on for a while about family and then somehow, the conversation got turned around to my dating life.

"Am I in a relationship?" I repeated Jake's quiet question and then slowly shook my head. "No. I *was* back in freshman year. Since then, though, I've not really been looking for anything serious. I'm just focused on college and my friends."

Jake nodded thoughtfully and then asked, "What happened to the guy from freshman year? Were you together long?"

"About ten months."

This appeared to surprise Jake, and not in a good way. I still knew him well enough to know that the flicker of hardness in his dark eyes meant he didn't like something. I pushed it aside. "That's a while," he finally responded, taking a long sip of his cooling coffee.

"Yeah." I didn't say anything else because I didn't want to talk about it. Especially not with Jake. "So," I drew in a deep breath, hating that my stomach churned just at the mere thought of my question, "how long have you and Melissa been together?"

He stared at me a moment, perhaps trying to gauge if I could really handle the answer to my question. He put his empty coffee mug down and sat back. "We were friends first. We met sophomore year at the study abroad meeting, actually. Our friends started hanging out and uh, Melissa wanted to date but ... um, well, we finally got there at the end of sophomore year so that takes us to six months of actual dating."

"She's beautiful. And she seems really nice, Jake," I said. And I meant it. I didn't like it, but I meant it.

Jake's expression softened. "I almost forgot how kind you are."

"Our history is not her fault."

Our eyes locked and the air around us grew so thick and hot, it felt like even my skin couldn't breathe. I stood up, exhaling heavily, like I'd just come out of an oppressive sauna after being trapped inside for days. "I've got to go. I need to hit the gym."

"You work out?"

I nodded, watching as he unfolded himself from the chair and stood to tower over me. "I still haven't given up on the idea of applying to the police academy after college, and I think a cop should be in good shape."

"Of course. I work out too. We should go together."

I opened my mouth to say no but as soon as I looked up into his warm, eager eyes, I melted. "Okay."

I was such an idiot.

Chapter Eight

Indiana, Halloween 2008

Seconds after I threw the door open and saw Jake standing there, I burst out laughing, delighted at what he was wearing. "You didn't!"

He grinned back at me. "You said you were going as a cop."

I giggled as he reached out and wrapped an arm around my waist, pulling me against his body so he could duck his head and kiss me. My hands automatically wrapped around his neck and my lips parted to let his tongue dance with mine. We came up for air at the sound of a throat clearing. I tensed as I turned to find my dad in the doorway, glaring at Jake.

"Have her back by ten."

Uh, I didn't think so. "Dad, we're going to Hub's after the dance. A whole group of us."

Dad's mouth pressed tight as I begged him with my eyes. "Fine," he sighed heavily. "Eleven."

I was going to protest this as well, but Jake squeezed my waist to silence me and answered respectfully, "Eleven it is, Mr. Redford."

Dad gave him a wary nod before his eyes flickered back to me. He took in my costume and grimaced. Feeling another argument coming on, I pulled out of Jake's arms and gave my dad a quick kiss on the cheek. "Tell Mom I said goodnight."

My dad's expression softened and he brushed my jaw affectionately. "Have a good time, sweetheart." His focus sharpened on Jake. "But not too good a time."

"Dad, I'm going with Jake ... I'll have an awful time."

Jake grunted behind me but I made Dad smile, so it was worth it. I said another goodbye and then Dad closed the door behind us. Jake held my hand as we walked to his truck.

"So, if you're going to have such an awful time with me ... why are we going?" Jake teased.

Glancing up at him from under my lashes, I checked him out in his tight, black, long-sleeved top, black jeans, black boots, and the black cloth with eyeholes cut out tied around his upper face. "I said that to loosen up my dad. If I told him the truth, he'd lock me up until I'm thirty." I got into Hendrix as he held the door open.

"And what's the truth?" he asked and then hurried to get into the driver's side.

"That I'm even more smitten with my boyfriend since he dressed up as a robber to go with my cop costume."

Jake chuckled. "Smitten?"

"It's a good word."

"It's a little tame."

"It's too early in the night for anything racier."

He quirked an eyebrow. "But you were thinking something racy?"

"Let's just say I like your costume. A lot."

As Jake slowed at a red light, he turned to look at me, his eyes drifting down my body and back up again. "I like your costume a lot too."

After speaking to Lacey and Rose about costumes for the Halloween dance, I knew my cop costume was nowhere near as revealing as what they planned to wear, but my girlie cop costume was tight, so tight my dad nearly had an apoplectic fit. There was a point I didn't think he'd let me out the door, but my mom managed to talk him around. I didn't see what the problem was—I wasn't showing any cleavage or leg. Okay, so maybe the pants fit like a second skin and I was wearing a padded bra under the snug blue shirt, but other than that, it was perfectly acceptable attire.

"Lukas is dressed like a robber too."

I smiled. "Why?"

"Because it was an easy costume."

"That's really why you chose it, right?"

"Nope." He smiled boyishly. "I chose it to increase the possibility of you using those cuffs on me later."

Sometimes I wondered if he was trying to fluster me when he said stuff like that, but he really should know better by now. I patted the cuffs clipped to my belt. "Well, if you play your cards right ..."

Unfortunately, Jake was hard to catch off guard. Rather than choke and get all turned on like any normal sixteen-year-old boy would, he just smiled like I amused him. "Baby, we ever really use cuffs, I won't be the one in them."

Now I was the one making strangled noises. "Jake!"

"What?"

"We're sixteen!"

He laughed as he pulled into the school parking lot. "So?"

"It's one thing to joke about it but another to actually ... you're like a thirty-year-old trapped in a teenage boy's body."

"Wow." Jake stopped the engine and turned to me. "I did it. I finally got you ruffled. Over handcuffs." He winked at me. "I'll keep that in mind." He got out of the truck before I could punch him in the arm.

I got out after him. "You're not funny."

"I'm hilarious." He pulled me into his side, letting go of my hand so he could wrap his arm around my waist.

Approaching school we saw a bunch of freshman hanging out at the main entrance. A tall kid dressed head to toe in black turned and I recognized him instantly. Lukas. Jake and I had been dating for almost two months and had each been to the other's house for dinner. This meant I'd spent some time with his brother only to discover that Lukas was a younger version of Jake, brimming over with cocky charm and charisma.

As we drew to a stop in front of him, Lukas gave me a body scan as he whistled. "Looking hot, Charlotte."

"Luke, eyes up or I'll detach your retinas," Jake warned.

Lukas grinned mischievously. "Not my fault your girlfriend is hot."

"Lukas, stop checking me out. It's weird. You're a fetus."

Looking affronted, Lukas held his hands to his chest. "Moi? I'll have you know I've been sweeping women off their feet since I was five. I have a wealth of experience, baby. Ditch the old guy and I'll show you the time of your life."

"You need to stop spending time with your brother." I glanced up at Jake, glaring at him. "He needs to stop spending time with you."

Jake's body shook against mine as he laughed quietly. "This," he gestured to Lukas, "has nothing to do with me. If this is how I act, shoot me, shoot me now."

"Pfft." Lukas made a face. "You wish you had my game."

Jake closed his eyes as if in pain. "It hurts, it physically hurts."

I laughed and tugged on Jake's waist. "C'mon. Let's leave the player to play."

Throwing me a wink scarily like the one Jake had given me in the car, Lukas turned back to his friends and my boyfriend led me into the dance. Lacey and Rose hurried over as we strolled into the darkened gymnasium, avoiding black and orange streamers, string, and fake webs. A paper spider fluttered into my face, almost scratching my cornea. I batted it away, tripping over Jake's foot.

"Someone overdid it on the decorations," I grumbled as Jake righted me.

"What are you wearing?" Lacey screeched and I turned in Jake's arms with wide eyes.

"Ow!" I shook my ear out pointedly.

Lacey winced. "Sorry. But what are you wearing?"

"My cop costume. I told you."

"But ... I thought it would be like a skirt version. A short skirt version." She gestured meaningfully to her and Rose's costumes. Lacey was wearing a sexy vampire outfit, her dress a good few inches above her knees, while Rose was wearing a very short sexy nurse costume. Both were also showing off a lot of cleavage. It was a wonder they'd gotten past the chaperones, but as I studied the room, I saw there were quite a few sexy outfits and a lot of uncomfortable-looking male teachers. "The tight pants are hot, I'll grant you, but a skirt would've been hotter."

"I think she looks great," Jake interjected.

Lacey rolled her eyes. "Of course you do." She grabbed Rose's hand and dragged her away. Rose, who hadn't even gotten the chance to say hi, gave me a weak wave and followed Lacey through the crowd.

"Hey, Jake," a senior girl cooed as she walked past. She was wearing the same sexy nurse costume as Rose.

"Hey," he gave her a small nod but turned back to me.

I raised an eyebrow at him. "You are good."

"Good, how?"

"She just gave you 'the nod' while wearing a naughty nurse costume and you barely batted an eyelash. I appreciate the effort that must've taken." I squeezed his hand.

Jake didn't laugh, however. Instead he ducked his head, his lips grazing my ear as he replied, "I've got the most beautiful girl in the room on my arm. Why would I look elsewhere?"

I shivered and leaned closer into him as he grazed his lips across my neck.

"Dance with me?"

I nodded my throat clogged with emotion and the sharp realization that it took very little for Jake to turn me on. When I'd been dating Alex, I'd barely felt a thing. It was like Jake had flipped the switch on my hormones.

Dancing with my cheek on Jake's shoulder, my body enfolded against his, I saw Alex across the room. He had his jock friends around him and they all seemed to be having a good time, but Alex was staring a little forlornly at me and Jake, hitting my guilt button big time. He'd gotten more and more distant these last two months and Brett had become an even bigger douchebag, making snide remarks to me and Jake in class and out. We were doing a good job of ignoring it, knowing Brett was deliberately trying to provoke Jake into a fight. Jake wasn't easily provoked, especially since it was him I was making out with on a daily basis. The only time he'd gotten close to losing it was when Brett had made some sexual remarks about me. I'd had to pull Jake away and take him into the library to cool off.

Jake's family still hadn't been having the easiest time of it in Lanton. Whether it was Trenton or Brett or a loyal sheep from either posse, someone had been making prank calls to the Caplin house, Logan's car tires had been slashed at Hub's, and worse, Jake's mom's cat had gone missing five days ago. We didn't know if it was foul play but my mom said she wouldn't put anything past Trenton Thomas.

It wasn't a surprise to me that an hour later when Jake wandered off to the punch table to get us a couple of drinks, I saw

Brett corner Lukas and his friend in the back of the gymnasium. I narrowed my eyes, not liking the sight of Brett and Damien Nixon towering over the freshmen. Where the hell was Alex? He was usually the one that reined in their behavior.

When Brett shoved Lukas and Lukas got in his face, my stomach churned.

Brett was really a big enough asshole to target Jake's little brother?

I jerked my head around to make sure Jake hadn't seen it yet and was relieved to find Amanda Reyes talking to him, keeping him distracted. Anger fueling me, I strode toward Brett ready to kick his ass, only to be abruptly stopped by Alex.

He did not look amused.

"Don't, Charley. I'll handle Brett." He turned on his heel, followed by two more of his buddies, both of them seniors and on the football team. Lukas saw them coming and I saw a flicker of fear in his eyes that I hated. He clearly thought Alex was there to create more hassle. I was so relieved when Alex grabbed Brett by the neck, dominating him. Whatever he said made Brett blanch and nod. Alex let him go and Brett's face darkened with humiliation. He nodded at Damien and they backed away from Lukas.

While Brett and Damien followed the seniors to the other side of the room, Alex made his way back to me.

"Thank you," I said as soon as he reached me.

Alex nodded. "I told Brett to back off. I'm not happy with him lately. I'll try to keep him off your back." His eyes softened. "You know I don't want to cause you trouble, Charley."

"I know that. And I really appreciate you helping out Lukas."

"No problem. Maybe save me a dance later?"

I felt heat at my back and then Jake asked, "What's going on?"

I looked up at him over my shoulder and smiled a little weakly. "Nothing."

SAMANTHA YOUNG

When Jake's eyes hardened, the atmosphere between us thickened. Sensing it, Alex gave him a tough guy chin nod and shot me an appreciative look before heading across the gym to his friends.

"I know when you're lying, Charley."

"It was nothing. Brett was giving Lukas a hard time. I was going over there to sort it out but Alex saw it happening and dealt with it."

Watching the muscle tick in Jake's jaw, I realized maybe honesty in this instance might not have been the best policy.

"That's it. I'm done with this shit. He and I are having it out."

Definitely not the best policy.

"No." I grabbed his arms, pulling him closer to me. "Alex warned him off and he's his teammate, so he has sway over him. He's also friends with the seniors and if Alex asks them to, the seniors on the team won't have Brett's back. And if they don't have his back, Brett is effed."

Jake ducked his head to meet my gaze as he cupped the back of my neck. "It shouldn't be up to Alex to deal with someone who is hassling my girl and bullying my brother."

"Jake, you know Brett is looking for an excuse to fight you. Don't give it to him. That's drama we don't need."

His grip on me tightened. "You suggesting I'd get hurt in a fight with Brett?"

Giving him my "what the fuck?" face, I answered, "Did I say that? Were those the words that came out of my mouth?"

He stared at me a moment before shaking his head. "Whatever, smart-ass." Jake sighed but my body relaxed as I realized he was giving in. He released his hold on my nape only to place his hands on my hips. .

"Where are our drinks?"

He shrugged. "I kind of left them when I saw you talking to Alex."

Of course he did.

Sensing my annoyance at his obvious jealousy, he pulled me closer. "I like your costume."

"You already said that."

"I meant it."

He kissed me.

My irritation melted and I sank against him, opening my mouth and kissing him back, deepening it. I loved the way his fingers tightened on my hips, almost bruising as they flexed with need.

"Ahem."

A loud clearing of the throat once again drew us apart and I pulled back to stare at a smirking Lacey. "We're bored and Alex is having a party at the gazebo again. You coming?"

That sounded just wonderful. Not. "We'll catch up with you."

Satisfied, Lacey and Rose took off.

Looking back at Jake, I found him scowling at me. "We'll catch up with you?"

I shrugged. "If I said we weren't going, she would've argued with me until I'd have no choice but to slay her." I wrapped my fist around my invisible stake and demonstrated by hitting it softly against his heart. "My little white lie got rid of Vampyra peacefully instead."

Jake's expression cleared and he smiled as he wrapped both hands around my fist and drew my body against his. "What are we doing, then?"

I answered immediately, "Brenton Fields."

Jake had to wait for Brett to leave the dance before he'd leave Lukas alone there. Mr. Caplin was picking Lukas up, so at least we didn't need to worry about him getting home. We drove out of town and pulled into our usual spot. Jake left the radio and the lights on, spread out a blanket in Hendrix's bed, and pulled me up onto it.

We lay side by side, staring up at the stars, but it wasn't long until I was shivering in my not-so-warm costume.

I snuggled into Jake's side and he immediately draped an arm around me so I could rest my head against his chest.

"If you're cold, we can leave," he murmured softly against my hair.

No way. If I was cold, I could think of a far better way to deal with that problem. Feeling the familiar tingling only Jake seemed to incite, I turned my head a little and whispered, "Do you think the girls you slept with are sluts?"

Jake tensed under me. At first I didn't think he was going to answer, but then he finally replied, "Firstly, with me it's more that I started out young than that I've slept with lots of girls. Me and my friends back in Chicago... we moved fast with this stuff, but there haven't been as many girls as people say. Okay? And secondly, no. Why would you think that?"

"Because they were obviously eager and they gave it up easy. And you didn't give them the time of day afterward. *I* don't think they're sluts. I think if boys can do it, girls should be able to too. But I don't know how *you* feel about it. I mean, I made you work for a kiss and here you are."

His chest rumbled underneath my cheek as he chuckled. "I'm here because you crack me up. You never bore me. You surprise me. That's why. Not because you made me work for it." He caressed my arm softly as he asked, "Where is this coming from?"

Butterflies suddenly appeared, their wings fluttering against my stomach in anticipation. "I just ... you've been taking things slow with me and I don't know if ... I wasn't sure if you would think I was a slut if I said I wanted to speed things up a bit."

He sucked in a sharp breath. "I don't think a girl is a slut for wanting sex, Charley. That would make *me* a slut, and frankly, I'm a little offended by the word," he teased, his voice hoarse from my meaning. When I didn't say anything, Jake trailed his fingers down my waist and he asked thickly, "Speed things up how?"

Wanting to face him when I said this, I pulled up, one hand flat against the truck bed, the other still resting on his chest. "I don't think I'm ready for sex … but I do want more from you."

Jake's eyes darkened, his lids lowering slightly as his gaze dipped to my mouth. "More how?"

I bent my head, bringing my lips close to his. "What comes before sex?"

"A lot."

I tipped my head to the side, smiling to cover the fact that I was nervous. I was nervous, but I was also sure. "Then show me a lot."

The words registered with Jake two seconds before he rolled me under him, his mouth hard on mine. My arms slid around him and I opened my legs to let him fall deeper against me. At the feel of Jake's erection nudging between my legs, I gasped into his mouth and my fingers tightened in his hair. His groan reverberated through me and I tilted my hips, liking the waves of pleasure rocking through me as he rubbed against me there.

When his hand coasted up my waist and cupped my breast through my bra, I jerked a little with surprise. I'd never let Alex close enough to do anything like this. I'd never wanted it. But with Jake, I'd started to fantasize about it.

Having him touch me in real life was a million times better.

Jake broke our kiss. "I want to touch you." He pulled gently at a button in my shirt, his hesitancy a question. I nodded, my eyes fixated on his face and the intensity of his expression. All that focus, all that need was for me.

It made me feel strangely powerful and in control.

Shivering but not with cold this time, I waited impatiently as Jake popped the buttons on my shirt, gently spreading it open so I was naked except for my bra. To my shock my nipples hardened under his perusal, something that had never happened to me before. That hard tightness was like a tease and my hips undulated under Jake in a silent plea for more.

He sucked in his breath and put pressure on my left hip with his palm. "Baby, calm. You keep doing that and I'm going to lose it."

I tensed, suddenly unsure. "I'm sorry."

"Don't be sorry," he whispered hoarsely and then kissed me softly. "Don't ever be sorry." He coasted his hand over my naked belly. "Can I see you?"

Knowing exactly what he meant, I took a breath. I wanted this, I did, but it didn't mean I wasn't worried about how attractive he'd find me naked. Licking my dry lips, I nodded again and reached up to undo the front clasp on my bra.

Tentatively, Jake brushed the fabric apart and the cold air blew over my naked breasts, my nipples pebbling into impossibly hard points. I felt Jake swell even thicker between my legs.

"Fuck," he muttered as he cupped me carefully, his touch worshipping. "You're so beautiful."

I arched into his hand, wanting more, wanting pressure ... or something. "Jake," I squirmed, wishing I knew what it was I was asking for so I could tell him.

It didn't matter since it seemed Jake was a good guesser.

He crushed his mouth over mine, his kiss hungry and wet, and he squeezed my breasts gently, sending a lightning rod of feeling straight to my core. I cried out into his mouth, lifting my hips again, pushing against his hard-on, wanting pressure *there*.

Jake growled, his lips moving from my mouth and trailing down my neck and chest until he reached my right nipple. He blew his hot breath over it and it puckered up for him. "Yes," I breathed and then sighed as he took it into his mouth, sucking it so hard, the tight pleasure between my legs became almost unbearable.

"Jake," I clutched at his hair, "Jake, please."

His head came up and his features were taut, his breathing heavier, shallow, as he braced up on his arms, his hands at either side of my head. He thrust suddenly and his erection pushed up against me. At my pleasured gasp, Jake began to roll his hips, rubbing harder but torturously slowly. "You ever had an orgasm, baby?" he asked quietly, his voice so full of sex, I barely recognized it.

"What?" I gasped again, trying to catch my breath.

"You ever make yourself come?"

My cheeks heated and I shook my head. "No."

"Can I make you come?"

"Do you even have to ask?" I moaned.

Jake found this amusing. I didn't. I was too impatient to discover whatever it was my body was reaching for.

He stopped moving against me and I instantly frowned. "What are you doing?"

In answer, Jake reached for the top button on my pants. Thankfully, I'd taken off the belt with the cuffs before I'd gotten onto the truck bed so we had no obstacles slowing us down.

"Is this okay?" he asked softly, unbuttoning my pants. I had to admit I liked that he kept checking to make sure I was all right.

"Yeah, baby," I whispered back and saw his eyes flare at the endearment. It was the first time I'd said it.

He kissed me as his fingers tugged on my zipper, the sound abnormally loud in the quiet night. My hips jerked at the touch of his fingers above the line of my panties and I could feel Jake

SAMANTHA YOUNG

hesitate. He began to pull away so I clutched his neck and kissed him harder. As our tongues tangled, the kiss deeper than any we'd shared before, Jake's hand slipped under my panties and his fingers pressed against me, coming to rest on my clit.

The feeling made me cry out. Our mouths parted as I looked up into his eyes in shock.

He lowered his forehead against mine, his eyes closed, and he began to move his fingers over my clit. The coil of tension in my belly tightened and I whimpered.

"That's it," he murmured against my mouth, "baby, that's it."

I pushed against his fingers, my own digging into his waist as I clutched him tight and let him build my body up to something wonderful.

Not much time passed before the coil snapped and lights flared behind my eyes as I arched my back and fell apart, my body shuddering against him as I experienced my first-ever orgasm.

It was a whole new world.

Coming back down to earth, I tried to catch my breath as my heart pounded against my ribs. The blood rushed in my ears, drowning out all other sound.

Jake kissed me, a butterfly brush against my lips, then my jaw, then my collarbone, and then my breasts. Lazily, because my body felt all jellified and languid, I ran my fingers through his hair as he played with my breasts and licked at my nipples, sending beautiful aftershocks and shivers through me.

"Thank you," I whispered and Jake's head immediately shot up.

He shook his head, his expression impassioned. "No, baby ... thank you."

Loving that and wanting to repay it, I shoved against him and the move so surprised Jake, it allowed me to roll him on his back.

As I moved over him, my breasts seemed to hypnotize him and he immediately reached up to cup them in his hands.

I closed my eyes in pleasure as his thumbs brushed over my nipples and it took me a minute to shake myself out of the spell he kept putting me under. "No," I murmured, pulling back. "It's your turn."

"Charley," his voice cracked with need, "you don't have to. Tonight was for you. We don't have to do everything at once."

"But I want to see you."

Jake closed his eyes as if he was in pain. "You're going to kill me."

I smiled and leaned over to whisper over his lips, "But what a way to go."

He reached up to cup my cheek in his hand, his expression seeming somewhat awed. "You're amazing, you know that, right?"

His words seeped into my chest and curled around the ache of feeling that lived in there, that ache that belonged to him and him alone. "You make me feel amazing, Jake. You make me feel like I can be just who I am. I've never trusted anyone the way I trust you."

Abruptly, Jake sat up and wrapped his arms around my waist, pulling me hard against his chest. "I feel the same way about you."

"Good." I nibbled his lower lip and then smiled against his mouth. "Can I see you?" I repeated his words back to him. Jake nodded slowly.

His arms loosened so I could move from his lap to his thighs. Cockiness seeming to return, Jake casually leaned back on the palms of his hands and stared at me as if to say, "Well?"

I narrowed my eyes on him, which made him smile.

My faux frown disappeared, melting under his charm. I smiled back and then looked down at his lap where his erection strained against his jeans. Suddenly feeling a little dry-mouthed again, it came as no surprise to me when my hands trembled as I reached out to unzip him.

Jake noticed. "Baby, we don't have to do this tonight."

"I want to," I promised him. I attributed the trembling to not wanting to disappoint him, but I shoved that thought away as soon as I looked deep into Jake's eyes. I trusted myself when I was with him. I trusted him with me. He would never make me feel bad about myself.

Slipping my hand under Jake's boxer briefs, his abs jerked at my touch. My heart was back to thudding like crazy as I encircled my hand around his hot, silken but throbbing erection.

I squeezed it gently, testing the waters, and Jake groaned. Spurred on by the sexy strain in his features and dark heat in his eyes, I tugged him out into the cold air and stared.

So that was what it looked like. Wow.

His reddish-purple mushroom-headed hard-on was so big, I instantly wondered how this thing was going to eventually fit inside me. My mind wandered briefly and my stomach flipped with nerves, but the sound of Jake's scratchy voice asking me to stroke him pulled me back to the present.

As I watched Jake watch me, his hips jerked to meet my strokes and his cheeks colored with heightened passion. His breathing grew more and more shallow and he began to pant. Witnessing his arousal and knowing I was the cause of it was almost as good as what he'd done to me. It turned out I had nothing to worry about regarding getting this stuff right. I caught on quickly, and honestly, Jake seemed easily pleased.

When he came in a sticky mess all over my hand, my eyes grew so big, Jake was still amused about it when he took me home. I endured his teasing, though, knowing I'd find some way to pay him back.

Later, before I got out of the car, my palms already sweating at the thought of seeing my parents and hoping that they didn't notice the lack of innocence in my eyes, Jake tugged me close and kissed me. I also then hoped my parents weren't spying on us because the way Jake kissed me ... well ... it was filled with knowing. It was sexual. It was possessive. It was different from any kiss that had come before it because our relationship had changed.

We were truly intimate now.

A thrill coursed through me as I pulled back from him and smiled.

It should've scared me how crazy I was about this boy, but it didn't, because I had the comforting knowledge that Jake Caplin was just as crazy about me.

Chapter Nine

Edinburgh, Halloween 2012

The month of October sped by. When I didn't have my head buried in my laptop and fogged with energy drinks, I was hanging out with Claudia, sometimes our roommates, crashing mini-parties in the apartments in our block, or hanging out with The Stolen and attending whatever gigs they'd managed to line up. Things with Jake were better, especially when it was just the two of us. I had coffee with him at least once a week and we went to the gym together three times a week. There was still that distance between us, but we could banter back and forth to cover it. Whenever the entire group was there, however, it was a little strained, mostly because of Melissa's presence.

During those times the rest of the group did their best to distract me—whether I was watching the bizarre friendship between Claudia and Beck that was so thick with sexual chemistry, we were all waiting for the entire thing to explode, or whether I was flirting with Lowe or watching Lowe flirt with someone else, or cracking up at the socially awkward crap that Matt said. Beck and Lowe were constantly hooking up with girls, which definitely didn't bother me and didn't *appear* to bother Claudia, so it caused no awkwardness. I did often wonder if Beck was trying to get a reaction out of Claud, though. There was something in the way he studied her when he thought she wasn't aware of his regard.

I wasn't interfering. My own romantic life was a mess. I had no right to delve into anyone else's.

"I can't believe I let you talk me into this. This is not me. Not to mention the fact that I have a paper due in three days and I've only written fifty words." I turned from the mirror in Claudia's room, my arms akimbo, my legs splayed. It was an unfortunate choice of body language considering my costume and Claudia immediately burst into laughter.

I was dressed as Supergirl.

Claudia was Wonder Woman.

The outfits were ridiculous and showed off a lot more skin than either of us was used to. It occurred to me that she might be trying to make a point to *someone* and I'd gotten dragged into the whole thing so she would have me to share in the mortification of it all. Still ... I eyed her red and gold bustier and star-spangled blue hot pants and decided the belly top, miniskirt, and cape I was wearing could be worse.

"We can't go out like this," I groaned, glancing back at the mirror. "If I become a cop and pictures of me dressed like this get out, I'll never live it down."

Claudia grimaced. "Is that all you think about? We're twenty years old and we're hot. Halloween is the one night of the year we can feel free to show boobs and leg. And our outfits are cute. More to the point, we need this. The guys are great and all, but we've been hanging out with them for nearly six weeks. While they rack up a bunch of temporary romances between them, we've been dry. Until now. Tonight is for us."

"We promised the guys we'd go to their gig."

My friend shrugged. "We'll go for a little while. Then we hit the party." She gave me a sharp look. "It'll be good for you to hang out with someone who is not Lowe or Jake. Especially not Jake. I can't imagine how Melissa feels about you two spending time together." Claud narrowed her eyes. "I'm guessing Jake hasn't told her. She's been too cool with you. Either that, or she's a really good actress. She hasn't looked at you like she wants to kill you. Not once."

"That's because Melissa is *nice*."

Claudia snorted. "You make nice sound like a bad thing."

"It's not a bad thing. We're just so different. I don't see how Jake could've loved me when he's in love with someone so completely my opposite." I winced as soon as I said it out loud. It had been on my mind the last few weeks, niggling in my gut. Melissa and I were so different, I was beginning to think that it couldn't have been possible for Jake to be in love with me. My memories, though … well, they liked to argue with that toxic thought.

"You're nice too, Charley. Melissa's just really quiet and reserved."

"And I'm loud and obnoxious?"

"No," Claudia laughed. "You're confident and you're a smart-ass."

I scowled. "I wish people would stop calling me that."

"Then stop being a smartass."

I wrinkled my nose at her and turned back to my reflection. "I feel naked."

Claudia came up beside me and rested her chin on my shoulder, her grin gleeful. "Aaron is going to die when he sees you." She lifted her head and smoothed a hand over her hair. "Zach is going to die when he sees me."

A few days ago Claudia and I were in the Library Bar at Teviot when these two guys sitting across from us started chatting. They were both from southern England and had very cool, very hot accents. They were smart and funny and cute and a lot of flirting had flown across the aisle of tables. It turned out they were senior undergrads and lived in one of the swankier apartments beside the main campus, just up from The Meadows—the park located behind the university.

Luckily, I thought Aaron was funny and Claudia thought Zach was charming and vice versa, so there was no fighting over who was interested in whom. The guys invited us to their Halloween party and before I could say anything, Claudia accepted for the both us, taking down their cell numbers too. In a way, I would've been much more comfortable with the whole Supergirl costume if we were heading directly to their party. It was stopping off at Milk on the way that was making me nervous.

And I had every right to be nervous.

We turned up at the bar and none of the guys were in costume—not even a little bit. Neither were Rowena or Melissa.

We walked across the bar, attempting to ignore the grins and catcalls from strange guys and girls, and I fought to keep my cheeks from burning. Claudia giggled at the glare I shot her way. She made the most of the scene we were creating by putting her arm around my waist and a little more wiggle in her hips.

The mischievous twinkle in her eyes loosened me up a little and I chuckled, letting her squeeze me close. As I tried my best to pretend I felt as sassy as I looked, the whistles brought Denver's head up from talking to Rowena. His eyes widened as he took in the sight of us. I lip-read the words, "Holy fuck," as they spilled out of his mouth, and that brought all of the band's heads around, including Jake and Melissa.

I did my absolute best to avoid eye contact with Jake and instead took in the open-mouthed gaga expressions on the guys' faces. It was pretty funny. Sometimes guys were just so easy.

"Santa finally got my letter," Beck said as the image of Claudia in her Wonder Woman costume burned into his retinas.

"We need to send the fat man a case of beer," Lowe added, his own gaze on my legs.

"I won't be needing my porn tonight," Matt informed us.

"Oh, Matt," Claudia and I groaned as Beck slapped him across the head.

"What?" Matt cried, rubbing his head. "That's a compliment."

"It's fucking gross." Lowe grinned, shaking his head at him.

"You were all thinking it."

Beck glared at him. "Claud and Charley don't need to hear that shit out loud, though."

"What's with the costumes anyway?" Denver asked, grinning at us. "Other than to provide us all with masturbatory fantasies."

I grimaced. "Thanks for that. And the costumes are for a *costume* party."

"Party?" Beck asked Claudia before taking a drink of beer and sitting back down at the table.

"We were invited to a party on Simpson Loan behind the university so we can only stay for a little bit. I'll text you the address so you guys can catch up after your set if you want."

"Sure." Lowe nodded and then caught my eye. "I get the feeling I'm only going to get to see this once in my entire lifetime, so I'm making the most of it."

"Me too," Beck agreed, smiling wide at us. He flicked his eyes casually to Jake and Melissa. "You guys coming with?"

Melissa looked to Jake for the answer and he nodded. "Sure." Sensing my gaze, Jake looked up at me. I had to admit, I was a little disappointed he didn't treat me to the almost X-ray perusal Lowe and Beck had. Instead his mouth twitched. "Supergirl? Finally embracing it, huh?"

I rolled my eyes at his boyish grin. "Claudia wanted to be Wonder Woman and she thought that this was funny. She's very difficult to ignore when she wants something."

"She must be very persuasive." I could tell he was dying to laugh at me.

"Why?" Melissa asked quietly, a little furrow between her brows.

Jake didn't take his eyes off me as he replied, "Because Charley's had the nickname Supergirl since she was fourteen and doesn't like it so much, and then there's the fact that she never wears skirts. Claudia has performed a miracle."

Although Jake didn't see it, I saw the uneasiness in Melissa's face and understood what it meant. She didn't like the reminder that Jake knew me well. I didn't like it, either, but for a completely different reason.

"Why are you nicknamed Supergirl?" Lowe asked curiously.

"Because—"

"Jacob Caplin, you tell that story and I will kill you," I growled.

Just like when we were younger, Jake found the growl cute instead of menacing and he ignored my warning. "She threw her older sister out of the way of an SUV when she was fourteen, took the impact instead. Broke her leg and ribs. The town started calling her Supergirl."

"Why do ye no want people tae know that story?" Rowena looked as mystified as the rest of the group. "That's a great story."

"Because people make such a big deal out of it and anyone would've done the same."

"No, they wouldnae," Rowena argued.

Instead of glaring at her, I threw my dark look at Jake, who just laughed. Annoyed at him, I decided to cool off at the bar. I took everyone's drink order and ignored the comments from other customers—whether sleazy or teasing.

I'd only been standing in line to be served for a minute when I felt a warm body press close. When I tilted my head around, I was surprised to find Melissa looking down at me. I couldn't read her expression at all.

"You're not making this easy," she told me softly, matter-of-factly.

I swallowed hard, feeling suddenly much too hot in my costume. Throat parched, I croaked, "What?"

She sighed and ducked her eyes away. "You're his first love and you knock people out of the way of moving cars, and you want to be a cop, and you're smart, and you're confident, and you have the guys eating out of the palm of your hand every time you open your mouth ... and now you've gone from pretty to every guy's fantasy in a superhero costume. I want to hate you." Her eyes lifted back to mine now. "I really want to hate you, but I can't because Jake's the one who wronged you. And maybe that's part of the problem too."

Seeing the real pain and concern in Melissa's expression, I felt a need to reassure her somehow. As much as it hurt me to admit it to her, I found myself saying, "There's nothing romantic between us anymore. According to Beck, you helped Jake get over what happened. He wouldn't let me do that for him. I think that speaks volumes. You're the one he loves." Every word of it felt like a piece of me was being ripped out, but I pasted on a fake, breezy smile. "As for me, I have an appointment with a hot senior with a cool accent, so we're all good."

Melissa studied me, so I kept my smile light until she finally gave me her own shaky smile in return. She stayed with me as I ordered the drinks and helped me back to the table with them. The whole time we walked across the bar together, I felt Jake's eyes burning into us. Not once did I meet them with my own. I was afraid if I let him look into me, he'd see I was just a little nudge from falling apart.

That's why, as I settled down beside Claudia with our drinks, I leaned over and murmured into her ear that I wanted to leave early for the party.

"You okay?" she whispered back, scanning my face for the answer.

I gave her a subtle shake of my head. "I don't want to be here."

Claudia squeezed my hand under the table, instantly understanding. "We'll finish these and go."

The guys seemed a little confused that we weren't staying to hear their set, but we promised we'd make it up to them another time. Claudia gave them the address of the party and they told us they'd see us there later. I didn't look at Jake. Not once.

The sight of Aaron's appreciative gaze when we walked into their party was a soothing balm to the burn in my chest from the heart-to-heart with Melissa. In a bid to get rid of the feeling completely, I got drunk. Claudia followed me right down the liquid path.

We were having a great time, laughing and dancing, the four of us in our own little bubble among the crowded party. The apartment was super swank with an open-plan living space and kitchen, floor-to-ceiling glass windows, and sliding doors that led out onto a balcony big enough to hold a good portion of the partygoers. All that plus free food and booze? No wonder the place was filled with people, most in costume. This made Claud and I feel a little less out of place. Aaron and Zach were in dark suits, hats, and sunglasses—the Blues Brothers. I thought that was cool.

Being drunk, I thought everything was cool.

It was a good few hours later and Claudia had disappeared with Zach, leaving me on the corner of their massive L-shaped couch with Aaron. When he started kissing me, I let him. I was drunk and fuzzy and hurt and confused and his kisses, his touch, let me forget all that. The kiss deepened and I cupped Aaron's face, holding him to me, silently asking him to keep going. He was a great kisser and the way he caressed my upper arm with the tips of his fingers was nice.

When he finally let me up for air, he murmured, "Wow," against my lips. I grinned, a little embarrassed that we'd been making out in public. I turned my head to make sure no one was paying attention and felt my muscles lock as I spotted Jake across the room with Melissa. My vision cleared and I suddenly felt very sober. He was staring straight at me, his face perfectly blank. My stomach flipped as he quickly looked away and frowned at something Melissa said to him.

"Hey, Charley," Beck's voice called from above. I twisted around to see him standing behind the couch. "We just got here. Do you know where Claudia is?"

I shook my head, frowning. "I haven't seen her in a while. She's not around?"

He shook his head.

"Let's look for her."

A hand gripped my leg and I looked back at Aaron. "She'll be fine."

"I'll be back," I promised and stood up, taking Beck's hand as he helped me around the couch.

"You both had a lot to drink?" he asked, scowling down at me.

"We're just having a good time."

"With a bunch of guys you don't know."

"We didn't know you," I pointed out.

He sliced me an unamused look from the corner of his eyes but didn't say anything. We searched the balcony and the bathroom, but no Claudia. I was beginning to get a little worried. Claudia wasn't the kind of girl to lock herself in a bedroom with a guy she barely knew, so I moved down the hall toward the bedrooms with renewed determination to find her.

Just as we were drawing to a stop at the first door, the second bedroom door opened. Claudia strolled out giggling at someone behind her, readjusting her bustier and hair. "I didn't think I was going to get that back on," she laughed, still unaware of us.

"I'm a master with women's apparel," Zach smirked as he emerged from the room. His chin lifted when he caught sight of us and seeing his expression, Claudia spun around and jerked in surprise.

I raised an eyebrow at her, completely shocked that she'd gone far enough with Zach to lose clothes. It was unlike her, and it hit me that I'd been so busy with my own problems, I'd completely missed the fact that Claudia was going through something too. The tension magically disappeared out of her body and she threw Beck a flirty smile and said, "What? *You* were the one who said I was a good girl. Not me." She brushed past us, a confused Zach following in her wake.

I needed to have a serious talk with my girl.

Feeling his tension beside me, I glanced up at Beck. His jaw was taut and his hand clenched his beer bottle so tight, it was a wonder the thing didn't shatter.

"Beck ..." I didn't know what to say because I honestly didn't know what was going on between them.

However, I might as well have been a ghost.

"Fuck it," Beck muttered. He turned and strode back into the party without a word to me.

As soon as I shook myself out of the confusing scene, I wandered back into the party to find Beck had a girl pressed against the wall, flirting his ass off. That boy moved faster than a cheetah.

"Charley!"

Strong arms wrapped around me and my feet left the ground as Matt gave me a bear hug. When he settled me back on the ground, I found myself standing beside Jake and Melissa.

Great.

And Jake wouldn't look at me.

Double great.

"Having fun, Supergirl?" Matt winked, raking his eyes over me again.

"I will be once you get me a beer."

Finally, Jake honored me with his attention. "Don't you think you've had enough?"

What is your problem? I'm not your girlfriend! Your girlfriend is standing right next to you. I'm the girl you dumped, remember?

"No, Dad, I don't," I answered, my drunken, loose lips about to get insulting when arms came around my waist and pulled me back into a strong chest. Aaron.

"I need to steal Supergirl away for a bit," he told the group, laughter in his voice. "She needs to rescue me from a dire, dire situation ..."

I laughed and let him drag me away, hoping it annoyed the fuck out of Jake. Uneasiness settled over me almost immediately, though, when Aaron led me down the hall to bedroom number one.

I tugged on his hand and he looked over his shoulder. "What?"

"I'm not going in there with you." I shook my head and tried to pull my hand out of his, but Aaron held tight.

"Come on, Charley. Loosen up a little with me."

Annoyed at his persistence and annoyed at myself for giving him the wrong impression, I yanked my hand back. "I'm not sleeping with you."

Aaron's handsome face darkened. "Are you kidding me? I've wasted all night on you. I thought it was clear that this was just going to be a fuck."

My ears were ringing with his brutal honesty, so I didn't reply.

He sighed heavily and brushed past me, leaving me standing there feeling stupid and worthless. In the morning I'd be pissed that I let him make me feel that way, but right then, I was too drunk to push my gloomy feelings away.

Back in the main room Beck was making out with some random girl and Denver, Rowena, Jake, and Melissa weren't anywhere to be seen.

Lowe and Matt were chatting and drinking at the kitchen island.

Lowe gave me his sexy, flirty grin as I approached. "Babe, you're killing me in that outfit. You should wear skirts more often. You've got great legs."

I drunkenly cuddled into his side, leaning my head on his shoulder. "Thanks," I murmured.

His arm came around me, hugging me. "You okay?"

Hearing the concern in his voice, I pressed even tighter against him, trying to bury myself into the comfort he was giving me by just being him. "Fine. Where did everyone go?"

It was Matt who answered, appearing a little awkward. "After you left with that a-hole English guy, Jake got a little moody. Mel noticed. They got into an argument and left. Den and Row got bored, so they left too."

I was put more than a little off-balance by Matt's not-so-subtle insinuation that I'd caused some kind of rift between Melissa and Jake. However, it wasn't just the insinuation. It was the thought that

Jake was pissed at me for being with another guy. What the hell did that mean? What was he trying to do to me?

Lowe's arm tightened around me. "Don't worry about it, babe." He sighed. "This party is terrible and I'm exhausted. You want us to walk you home?"

I nodded. Yes. I wanted out of there so I could pass out on my bed and forget everything about tonight. "Let me get Claud first."

Finding my friend on the balcony with Zach and a couple of his friends, I pulled Claudia aside and told her that I wanted to leave.

"Okay, we'll go," she assured me.

I glowered at her. "Don't think we won't be talking about what happened with you."

"Not now." She brushed me off and called a goodnight to Zach.

Seeing us preparing to leave with Lowe and Matt, Beck abandoned the girl he was with and followed us out of the apartment. Hitting the street, I was glad I had alcohol in my blood to keep me warm in the freezing cold.

"You might not feel cold, but you are," Lowe said, pulling me into his side. He was only wearing a thin shirt. "So am I," he grumbled and rubbed a hand over my arm.

Ahead of us Claudia walked between Beck and Matt, Matt chatting away, oblivious to the obvious tension between his companions.

"What happened with the guy?" Lowe suddenly asked.

I curled my lip at the thought of Aaron. "As soon as I made it clear he wasn't getting any, he dropped me like a bad habit."

"What a charmer."

"Mmm."

He squeezed my waist. "Will you sleep with me?"

I smiled at his teasing question. "Not tonight."

His laughter rocked against my side. "That wasn't a no."

"I'm leaving my options open."

Lowe chuckled. "A guy wants a girl, he has to hope to God she wants him back. A girl wants a guy, all she's got to do is say the word and bam! He's naked. You got all the power."

"I am Supergirl."

He laughed again and kissed my hair. "That you are."

"And you know … I think it's more to do with the fact that girls need to be attracted to more than just a penis to want sex. I get the impression straight men are just attracted to the vagina."

This only made Lowe laugh harder. "You'd be surprised." He sighed and after a minute quietly muttered, "Jake's a fucking moron."

I decided it was best I didn't ask him to confirm what he meant by that.

Chapter Ten

Indiana, Thanksgiving 2008

There was so much food inside my stomach, I was impressed I'd managed to fold myself into my mom's car and drive myself to Jake's. I'd just spent Thanksgiving dinner with my parents, and my mom had gone overboard, illogically compensating for the fact that my sister wasn't with us. Well, she was kind of with us. We'd sat my laptop at the end of the table and Andie had Skyped with us from Dublin while we ate. I'd have felt sorry for her watching us scarf down Mom's delicious turkey dinner and incredible pumpkin pie, but Andie had made her own little Thanksgiving dinner for her and a couple of her fellow Americans. Since she'd inherited Mom's cooking gene, I could imagine it had been pretty good.

When I told my parents I was going over to see Jake, my mom was the one who protested. "Isn't it enough that one of my daughters isn't here for Thanksgiving?" she bemoaned. Surprisingly, it was Dad who came to my rescue.

"Let her go. They haven't seen each other in twenty-four hours. It must be killing them," he said, flashing me a teasing smile before returning his eyes to the game. The Eagles were playing the Cardinals, neither of which were my dad's team, yet still he watched.

Somehow in the last few weeks, Jake had weaseled his way into my dad's good graces. Whether it was because I was happy or because Jake could charm the pants off anyone, I don't know. All I did know was that last Sunday, I'd gone into the kitchen to get Jake a soda and when I returned, he and Dad were watching the game and I might as well have been invisible. They made disparaging comments about the Rams and reassured each other that their team (the Chicago Bears) would pull it together. In the end, the Bears whipped the Rams 27-3 and that victory seemed to cement some kind of bond between Dad and Jake. I didn't care that it took football to do it. I was just glad it was done.

It was freezing outside, so despite the fact that my cheeks were blazing and my whole body was warm with Delia Redford's cooking, I bundled into my winter coat and scarf and got into Mom's car. Thankfully, it hadn't snowed yet this month so I had clear roads to Jake's. He lived on the other side of town in a newer development built in front of the creek, so he had beautiful views from the rooms at the back of his house. Including his bedroom. I'd been in his bedroom a couple of times, but his mom made us keep the door open while we studied. He still managed to sneak in quick make-out sessions, but the heavy make-out sessions were reserved for the inside of Hendrix. We couldn't use the truck bed because of the weather, but I'd already begun fantasizing about next summer and the possibilities to be had.

"Charley, so good to see you, sweetie," Mrs. Caplin greeted me at the door. "Happy Thanksgiving."

I hugged her tight. "Happy Thanksgiving, Mrs. C."

She led me into their large sitting room and I met Jake's eyes as soon as I entered. He smiled at me and lazily got up off the couch, sauntering over to me for a hug.

"Don't squeeze me too tight. I'm full," I mumbled against his chest, clutching onto his back.

Jake chuckled and turned me in his arms so he wasn't blocking me from everyone. I said hi to Lukas and Mr. Caplin, and waited for Jake to introduce me to the older woman who I knew was his nana—he'd told me she was visiting. She was sitting on the arm of Mr. C.'s chair, her long, gray hair pulled back on each side with glittery slides. She wore a long gypsy skirt and a warm, knitted pink sweater.

"Charley, this is Nana. Nana, this is Charley."

She raised her eyebrows at him. "How many girls you got, boy?"

I tensed against his side and Jake squeezed my arm. "Cut it, Nana."

"No," I pulled out from under his arm, crossing mine over my chest. "How many girls you got, Jake?" I tilted my head in question, half teasing, half concerned.

Mrs. C. rubbed my shoulder. "Jake's nana is just teasing. Amanda Reyes dropped by this morning with a pumpkin pie and was a bit obvious about her crush on Jake. It was sweet. She blushed a lot. Poor thing. She must be the only one in town who doesn't know my boy is head over heels for you."

Although her comment made me melt into goo inside, I knew Jake's mischievous nana was waiting for a reaction. She instantly reminded me of Lukas. Now I knew where he got his cheeky devilishness from. Projecting nonchalance, I nodded and turned back to the room. "Her pie any good?"

Jake's nana chuckled, her eyes bright on me. "Good answer."

"If you're done causing trouble, Charley and I are going to hang out upstairs."

"You're not watching the game?" I didn't want to interrupt him when it was obvious that's what he'd been doing before my arrival.

"Not my team." He shook his head, gently pushing me out of the sitting room.

"Keep your door open!" Mrs. C. shouted after us.

I climbed their wide staircase, feeling my remaining energy begin to dissipate under the weight of my food intake. "Are you saying if it had been your team, you wouldn't have left to have alone time with me?"

"That's not what I'm saying. There is such a thing as a record button, you know."

"You're not like other boys," I mumbled and then face-planted on his bed. "I ate too much," I said, my mouth pressed against his pillow. It sounded more like, "M mm mm mmuh."

I heard his deep chuckle behind me and then the bed depressed as he sat on it. "Let's get your coat off before you pass out."

Reluctantly, I sat up and let Jake unwind my scarf and slip off my coat. The whole time I stared at his mouth, my eyes lidded and heavy with food exhaustion. He brushed his mouth over mine and settled us back on the bed so I was lying on my side, my back to his chest, his legs intertwined with mine. Snuggling me closer, Jake wrapped his arm around my waist and clutched my hand. "I missed you today," he whispered against my shoulder.

I smiled sleepily. "I love you."

I was out before I even realized I'd said it out loud.

My eyes opened to the dark. Where was I? What had happened? I shot up into a sitting position, willing my eyes to adjust to the light, and then swallowed a shriek at the feel of a warm hand on my lower back.

"Baby, it's me," Jake whispered. "You fell asleep."

It came to me that I was in Jake's bedroom. I relaxed back against the pillow as his face formed in the dark from the crack of light streaming in from the window above his bed. He put his arm around me and drew me into him.

"What happened?" I whispered against his mouth.

"Mom called your mom to let your parents know you fell asleep here."

"And they just let you stay with me?" I asked incredulously, keeping my voice low.

Jake laughed softly. "Yeah, right. I'm supposed to be on the couch. I came back up after everyone went to bed."

I dropped my head, nuzzling my face against his throat. A few weeks ago, I'd gone on a shopping trip with Mom to Chicago and on impulse bought Jake cologne that made my mouth water. He'd worn it every day since and every day since, I found an excuse to bury my head against his neck and inhale him.

Jake held me tighter and I felt him grow hard against my upper thigh. My breath caught and I moved my leg over his hip. He rocked gently against me, shooting delicious tingles through me. I lifted my head and met his eyes two seconds before I kissed him. The kiss turned deep and hot fast, and Jake rolled me beneath him, my inner thighs clutching his hips as he tortured me by rubbing his denim-clad erection against the denim seam between my legs.

Breathing shallow, Jake broke the kiss and cradled my head in his hands as if I was a piece of something incredibly fragile. The light moved over his face and I caught my breath at the way he was looking at me. "What my mom said earlier … about me being head over heels for you …"

"Yes?"

"I love you too, Charley. I've been in love with you since our first date, and every day since I've fallen deeper and deeper for you."

For a moment I was so busy floating on a cloud of pure euphoria that it took me a minute to realize he'd said "I love you *too*." I gasped, remembering my mumble before I fell asleep. "I said it out loud, didn't I?"

He nodded. "It would be nice if you said it again, though."

Even though I was lying down, I felt a little dizzy with adrenaline as I gazed up into Jake's soft, warm eyes. His confession that he loved me like I loved him made me feel right in a way I didn't know how to describe. I was only sixteen, so I hadn't been looking for it, but now that I had it, I realized it was something I guessed we all looked for our whole lives. We all are looking for a place in life, somewhere we fit. It's not a place that changes who we are or what we do—perhaps it *shapes* us, makes us better, makes us *more*—but mostly it shelters us with a sense of peace, a sense that whatever we do, whoever we are, we're not alone in it.

I was lucky enough to find that place when I was sixteen years old. It was carved deep in Jake. And that scared the hell out of me.

"I'm scared, Jake," I whispered honestly. "We're so young. There are a lot of years ahead of us to lose this."

"Don't think like that," he replied, his tone hard and implacable. "We're never going to lose this, Charley. I promise. Now tell me you love me."

I sucked in a deep breath. "I love you, Jacob Caplin."

He grinned and kissed me hard, his hand coasting down to the waistband of my jeans. "Can you be quiet?" he murmured against my lips.

I smiled at his cockiness. "I'm sure you'll find a way to muffle my cries of ecstasy, Sex God."

He laughed into my mouth and it felt beautiful. When he lifted his head, Jake looked happier than I'd ever seen him. "Don't ever stop being a smart-ass. It's one of my favorite things about you."

"I'm not a smart-ass." It was my immediate response to such claims. "But if I were, I'm glad you like that about me."

"I love everything about you."

"Even my freakishly long big toe?"

Jake shook against me, dropping his head to my shoulder. "Even that," he whispered, laughter in his voice. "I'm trying to get lucky here."

Since we hadn't had sex yet, I found myself wondering if he meant going all the way, and as much as I was ready to go all the way with Jake, I didn't want to go all the way with his parents in the next bedroom. "*Lucky* lucky? Or lucky-to-a-certain-point lucky?"

I felt his teeth on my earlobe and shivered. "Not sex. Just all the good stuff we've done before."

At the mere suggestion, I felt my body grow ready for him. I felt another smart-ass comment take the stairs down from my brain toward my mouth, but I tripped it up before it could ruin the moment. Instead I turned my head to find Jake's mouth. "I won't ever stop loving you," I promised him.

"Good," Jake replied, and upon hearing how hoarse his voice was with emotion, I felt tears prick my eyes. "I won't ever stop loving you. No matter what."

Chapter Eleven

Edinburgh, November 2012

Between the two of us, Claudia and I were racking up an insane amount of angst over boys. Boys! I wanted to be fifteen again when I didn't give a crap about them.

The day after Halloween, I nursed a hangover and split my time among wallowing in confusion and self-pity, writing my paper, and attempting to get the truth out of Claudia.

After downing an aspirin and shoveling back the falafel wrap Claudia had gone bravely in search of, I broached the subject I should've broached pre-Halloween booty call.

"What is going on with you?" I asked, concerned, pulling my knees up to my chest and curling into one of the waiting room chairs in the kitchen. We were alone and the night before was fresh, albeit hazy, in my mind. It was as good a time as any to hash this out with her. "Something is bugging you."

Claudia was lying on the hard linoleum floor, her dark hair spread out around her head, her hands flat on her stomach. Her golden complexion looked a little pale—I wasn't the only one who had seriously overimbibed last night. She closed her eyes at my question. "It's obvious there's something between me and Beck, right?"

I snorted. "Um, yes."

"It's obvious to everyone." One eye opened as she peeked at me. "The sexual tension is killing me." She closed it again. "But he wants the best of both worlds. He wants the closeness of a girlfriend without committing to it. And to get his rocks off, he sleeps with other girls he's made no such promises to."

Seeing the strain in her features, I asked softly, "Is he hurting you?"

"Is Jake hurting you?"

I took that as a yes. "Should we stop hanging out with them?" It occurred to me that I didn't know what I wanted her answer to be.

"I wish I could say yes … but I don't want to stop spending time with Beck." Claudia sighed and pushed up into a sitting position, tugging her fingers through her hair. "Last night was stupid. I was attracted to Zach, I'm not saying I wasn't, but it was stupid. I'm pissed off about Beck and I just went for it. You know what, though?" Her expression was a little sheepish as she confessed, "Beck walking in on it made it worthwhile. It made my point. He doesn't want me, fine. But other guys do."

"He definitely seemed annoyed."

"And then he started making out with some random."

I winced. "You saw that, huh?"

Claudia rolled her eyes. "He's such a coward. And trying to get reactions out of each other, hurting each other? That's not good. Definitely not good. I thought last night might have pushed us in a final direction, but he texted me this morning as if everything is fine."

"Probably because he doesn't want to stop hanging out with you, just like you don't want to stop hanging out with him."

"We're a mess."

"So ..." I shrugged like it was no big deal. "Sleeping with strangers?"

She cut me a sullen look, as if I'd judged her. "I just wanted to try it."

"Don't get defensive. I'm not judging. I swear. It's just not like you."

"I know."

"Well? What was it like?" I was genuinely curious.

Claud wrinkled her nose. "It was good, but not great. Kind of like eating vanilla ice cream when you really only ever eat chocolate."

I wanted to say I understood that analogy but I didn't.

"What about Jake? Anything of note happen last night?"

I grunted and proceeded to tell her about him leaving the party in a mood over my escapades.

Now it was Claudia's turn to look concerned. "Spending time with each other is obviously confusing you. Maybe you should stay away from one another for a while. And don't say I should take my own advice." She groaned again and flopped back on the floor. "We suck at this right now."

"I don't think it'll be a problem for me to stay away from Jake. Unlike you, I didn't get a text this morning and I doubt I will. Ever." It was hard keeping my tone light, casual, when the very thought of not speaking to Jake again felt like an impossible and painful prospect.

Just as it had felt almost four years ago.

After saying such to Claudia, I was taken aback to find Jake waiting at the gates to our courtyard a few days later. I was heading out for the gym on our usual day and Jake always met me there. But I hadn't expected to see him after the Halloween party.

Trying to calm my heart, I slowed to a stop in front of him. He was leaning against the wall, his hands inside the pockets of the black, double-breasted wool coat he wore over his black jeans. A soft blue scarf was tied around his neck, bracing him against the Scottish Fall. Could it have killed him to not look good … just once?

I was wrapped up warm in my own coat and scarf but I was wearing my gym clothes underneath. Jake was here … but by his attire, I could assume he wasn't coming to the gym with me. So why was he here?

Jake lifted his gaze from the ground and once again, my body reacted to the impact of his dark eyes. I shivered and crossed my arms over my chest in a protective gesture.

"I'm sorry about the other night," he apologized softly.

"It's okay." I knew we were both wondering if I meant it.

The silence between us became too thick to bear and I made a little huffing noise before telling him dryly, "I didn't sleep with him. And he wasn't happy about it." Why was I explaining myself? Was I really that afraid of him being mad at me? After what'd he'd done? It occurred to me I might need therapy.

As I pondered over whether it was a bad idea to get free therapy from Andie, since she was hardly impartial over the subject, a dangerous alertness leapt into Jake's expression. "How not happy? Did he do something to you?" he pushed off the wall, bristling with aggression.

I hurried to assure him. "No, no. He was just a jerk. But an honest one."

"Lowe didn't say. He just said he walked you home."

"Yeah."

The silence returned.

Two girls walked past, their eyes glued to Jake. As they walked up hill away from us, they started giggling and casting smiles at him over their shoulders.

Some things never changed.

"It took me off guard," Jake suddenly said.

I turned back to him, frowning in confusion. "What?"

"Seeing you … with him. It took me off guard. I reacted badly. I'm sorry."

Even more confused than I'd already been, I dragged a hand over my head and down through my ponytail, trying to think what the best answer was. Something not confusing. Something that reminded us where we were now. I didn't do it gently. "It's been a while, Jake. You must know that there have been other guys." *Guy* singular, but he didn't need to know that. I'd already explained myself when I didn't need to, confusing the situation even more.

If I were anyone else, I would've missed that little flare of anger in the back of his eyes. He hid it well and he hid it quickly. "Of course. I'm just trying to wrap my head around all of this. Sometimes it feels like only yesterday we were lying in the back of my truck, you know."

"Well, it wasn't."

Jake studied me a moment and I tried my best not to squirm. Finally, he nodded. "You're right. I'm sorry. I just came here to see if I hadn't fucked everything up again."

I wanted to scream at him—demand to know why he'd fucked everything up in the first place, and then stuck the knife in deeper by bringing another girl to the place we'd planned to come together. Instead, I nodded tightly. "We're good."

He appeared to relax a little and he gave me a small smile. "We'll go to the gym together next time, yeah?"

My answering smile was equally small. "Sure."

"So your mom says Jacob Caplin's there and that you're spending time with him."

Silently, I cursed my mother. I should've known she wouldn't be able to keep this from Dad. Thankfully, Dad and I were talking on the phone and not on Skype so he couldn't see my murderous expression. "Mmm-hmm."

"Don't 'mmm-hmm' me. Were you ever going to tell me?"

"There's not much to tell, Dad."

"That boy broke your heart. I don't want him near enough to do it again."

"That's not going to happen."

"I'm not convinced."

"Dad, I don't want to talk about this with you."

Dad sighed, causing the line to crackle. "You were just a kid, Charlotte, and he changed you. One minute you were happier than I'd ever seen you, and the next you were closed off. I didn't like having to watch that."

I bowed my head, feeling at once loved and sorry that I'd done that to my family. "I'm not anymore," I promised him softly.

"You sure about that, sweetheart? Because I don't see any other boy hanging around. Let's not even get started on Alex."

"I don't want to talk about Alex, either, Dad. There's nothing to talk about."

"Maybe you should come home."

I laughed and then immediately sighed. "I'm okay. I won't do anything stupid. Lesson learned."

"You know you can still trust people, Charley, without it turning into another lesson. I think Jake is just this reminder that you can't depend on people, and I don't want my daughter feeling that way."

"I don't feel that way about people ... I feel that way about Jake. There's a difference."

"Then why are you hanging around the boy?"

"Because he's friends with my friends," I lied.

Before my dad could say anything else, I heard Mom calling him to get his breakfast. It was Saturday, early there, and Dad had called before he had to head to work. It would've been nice to talk to him about something other than Jake.

"Got to go, sweetheart. You take care, all right? We'll speak soon. Love you."

"Me too. Bye, Dad."

I hung up and growled at my cell. I was going to kill my mother.

Hearing masculine laughter from the kitchen, I wondered if it was Beck and decided to go in and keep him and Claud company. The two of them were very busy pretending everything was cool between them. However, Claudia confided it helped when they weren't alone.

And yet they still spent time alone together. That completely made sense. Not.

Strolling into the kitchen, I discovered it wasn't just Beck and Claud in there. Lowe, Jake, Gemma, and Matt were sitting around chatting.

"Hey," I greeted as I came to a stop near Jake. We'd been to the gym together since our little chat outside at the gates. We'd also grabbed coffee and taken a stroll through Regent Gardens and into Leith, wandering around the cold city and talking about everything. Everything except us. We'd distracted ourselves from that by joking around in tourist shops trying on tartan hats with ginger hair glued inside them, and drinking Starbucks while we nibbled on sugary Scottish tablet that made our teeth ache. I'd also attempted to take a photograph of Jake standing next to a bagpiper dressed in full tartan regalia. The piper— not the same guy every time— stood on the corner of Princes Street and Waverly Station. He wasn't there every day but he was there a lot, and I got used to his pipes playing the soundtrack to my life in Scotland. Some people didn't like the pipes, but for me they were like this sentient being that totally got me. As soon as I neared New Town it was like those pipes sensed me and whatever mood I was in its tune would change, as if it was saying, 'Me too'. Some days it was lively, its high pitched song in harmony with me as it said, 'I'm feeling good today too. The air is crisp, I'm in a land full of mystery, and I feel up for an adventure'. Other days, more often of late since Jake came so thoroughly back into my life, the pipe's song swung from reflective to almost mournful. Sometimes I'd stand on the opposite side of the street, the pedestrians and traffic quieting to a hum beneath the pipe's story. Like Scotland itself, the melancholy tune was quiet, dignified, braving life and keeping the secret of its pain buried. Its haunting wail never failed to cause the hair on the back of my neck to rise. Twice now Jake had come upon me just standing there listening to it. Twice now he'd just looked at me as if he knew exactly what I was thinking but was afraid to bring it up—an action (or inaction rather) that was becoming common between us.

After the guys greeted me, Jake suddenly reached up, grabbed my hand, and jerked me down onto the arm of his chair in an unconsciously familiar move. When I looked at him, he just gave me a small smile and turned back to listen to what Beck was saying.

I, on the other hand, searched the room to see if anyone's expression resembled mine. My eyes immediately locked on Lowe, his eyebrow raised in my direction.

Shrugging at his silent question, I watched on bemused as he smiled and took a sip of his soda. While I stewed over Jake's behavior, Lowe returned his focus to Beck and Claudia.

Glancing down at Jake, I tried to ignore the squeeze in my belly as I watched him smile at whatever Beck was saying. He had enviously thick eyelashes and a beautiful mouth. A perfect mouth.

I'd spent hours when we were together nibbling on his lower lip, which was classically fuller than his top.

Sensing my study, Jake looked up at me and I covered my longing with feigned casualness. "Where are Melissa, Den, and Row?"

"Mel's with some friends and Den and Row are still sleeping."

I nodded, relaxing more now that I realized Melissa wasn't going to be appearing out of the bathroom and asking me why on earth I was perched on the arm of her boyfriend's chair. "What have you all been talking about?"

Claudia whirled around, her long hair whipping Beck in the chest. He barely flinched, silently telling us he was used to it. I knew I was. She once almost took out my eye with her hair whip.

"We're talking about Thanksgiving. Since none of us are going home for it, I thought we could bring it to us. I've offered to do the cooking."

I didn't argue with that. Although Claudia only cooked when she could be bothered, she was actually pretty good at it. "Sounds great."

"Why am I turned on at the thought of Claud and Char cooking for us?" Matt asked, seeming genuinely bemused by his predicament.

"Because you're a horny dick and you need to get laid," Lowe grunted at him.

"You can remove Charley from that fantasy," Jake added, laughter in his words. "She can't cook for shit."

His behavior minutes ago, plus the conversation I'd just had with my dad, made me suddenly irritated by Jake's overfamiliarity. "Maybe I can cook now," I scowled down at him.

He raised both eyebrows. "Can you?"

"No," I huffed, "but it's been almost four years, Jake."

He was scowling back at me now. "Point being?"

"Stop acting like you know me."

The muscle in his jaw ticked. "A little hard to do ... because I *do* know you."

Thus commenced a death stare match.

We glared into one another's eyes, neither refusing to give in, and then suddenly, memories of arguments ending in kisses flared behind my eyes.

I knew the moment Jake remembered too because the air between us wasn't angry anymore ... it was sexual.

My skin flushed and I flexed my hands, trying to ignore the pulsing throb in my neck and the blood whooshing in my ears. It was hard to do when I recognized all too well the look in Jake's eyes.

"I can cook it on my own," Claudia announced loudly, shattering the moment. I jerked my head around to see her giving me a look that screamed, "What the hell are you doing?" before turning back to Beck. "It's cool. We'll get a bird and everything. I can handle it."

At least one of us could handle something.

For once the kitchen didn't seem so cold with eight of us crammed around the table. True to her word, Claudia had cooked Thanksgiving dinner and to our surprise, Lowe had helped. Maggie, Gemma, and Laura had left us to our traditions, as had Rowena. That meant Jake, Claudia, Beck, Lowe, Melissa, Matt, Denver, and I were cozied together at the table.

We were tucking in, lots of "mmms" and "Claud, I love you" being thrown around the table. It was easy to forget everything else, to forget the very real awkwardness between Melissa and me for instance, when we were all just happy to have something to remind us of home.

Edinburgh was great, but I think we were all missing the States just a little bit.

"This is so much better than home," Claudia announced, taking a sip of her wine as she proved me wrong.

"It is?" Melissa frowned.

Claudia nodded, her eyes wide as she replied, "God, yes. Well, it was." She threw me a grin. "I spend it with Charley's crazy family now, but pre-Charley … right about now, I'd be curled up on the couch by myself in a house that's way too big for three people while my parents either fuck other people in Cabo or each other in Switzerland. No phone calls home to wish me Happy Thanksgiving, nothing, nada. They pay their cook Consuela to make and serve me Thanksgiving dinner every year, and every year I give her a couple of days off without telling them. That would kill them," Claudia smirked. "My parents hate paying for anything when they don't have to. I'm saving it up for the right moment. Who knows … it might piss my mother off so much, she may actually manage to make an expression through the Botox."

Beck, Lowe, and I laughed, which relaxed everyone else who, by the uncomfortable expressions on their faces, clearly felt weird by Claudia's oversharing.

Lowe shrugged. "I don't mind Thanksgiving. Mom passed a while ago, so it's just me, my older brother, and my dad. My dad is a litigator and always working. So Josh and I just get takeout and sit back, have a beer, and watch the game."

I hadn't known that about Lowe. Although he'd spoken casually about his mom, there was a definite tightness in his tone. Since he was sitting beside me, I felt the tension in his body. So no one would notice, I put down my cutlery, lifted my wine glass with one hand, and gently squeezed Lowe's knee under the table with the other.

Two seconds later I felt his warm hand cover mine and he gave me a squeeze back. I looked at him out of the corner of my eye and saw he was giving me a small, grateful smile. His muscles relaxed and I let go of him as Beck started sharing.

"My mom and stepdad always go on vacation at Thanksgiving because Mom hates the cold. That leaves me either stuck in the house by myself, much like Claud, or if my dad's coherent, I'll drop by his place with some food."

I wondered what the comment about his dad meant and as I looked around the room, I knew only two other people understood exactly what it meant—Jake and Claudia had hard looks in their eyes, the kind of look a person gets when someone they care about is mistreated.

Shit. Beck didn't have it great at home. It didn't surprise me that Jake knew ... but Claudia? I was beginning to think she and Beck were a lot closer than any of us realized.

"Well," Matt smiled, breaking the tension, "Thanksgiving at home is awesome for me. I live with my aunt and uncle because my parents died when I was little, which isn't awesome obviously, but my aunt and uncle are cool and my aunt can cook the shit out of anything. Seriously, our table is, like, immense. We've got three different types of bird, three different types of potato, gravy that I think I'd kill for, chocolate pie, and pumpkin pie. Neighbors try to get an invite every year, it's that good. There's always so much food, my aunt invites a different couple of people every year. I swear it's like they've won the lottery when she chooses one of them. And she's got to be careful she doesn't show someone too much favor because that drama lasts a whole fucking year."

We smiled at him, imagining a table piled with food and neighbors clamoring to get to it.

"Thanksgiving is good for me too," Melissa smiled contemplatively, leaning closer into Jake. He smiled at her and put his arm around her chair. The turkey in my mouth turned to ash. "It's usually just me and my dad, my stepmom, and two stepsisters. My stepmom isn't the greatest cook, but she always insists on doing it. I go behind her, fixing her mistakes, and she doesn't have a clue," Melissa laughed. "She's sweet. So are my sisters." She shrugged. "We just laugh a lot."

"It sounds nice," Claudia smiled. "It sounds really nice."

"Well, you're more than welcome to come to Thanksgiving at my house next year," Melissa offered kindly. I wanted to stick my fork in her eye. She had my ex-boyfriend. She was not getting my best friend.

Claud looked ready to burst into laughter, as if she knew exactly what I was thinking. "Thanks, Mel, but I've forced myself onto Charley's family and I'd feel rude if I stopped doing that."

Chuckling, I shook my head. "She has not forced her way in. I swear to God, my parents like her more than they like me."

"Do you have a nice Thanksgiving, Charley?" Lowe asked quietly.

I nodded at him. "Me, my mom, my dad, my big sister Andie. My grandmother sometimes too, and now Claud. I'm the only female in my family who can't cook, so I get to sit and watch the game while they all cluck in the kitchen."

"Cluck?" Claudia asked, clearly offended.

"Like a hen." I nodded. "*Who's mashing the potatoes?* They all answer at once—cluck, cluck, cluck. *Who checked the bird last?* Cluck, cluck, cluck. *We've all brought our best pie dish, which one should we use?* Cluck, cluck, cluck, cluck."

The guys laughed and Claudia twisted her mouth into a moue. "That is a gross misinterpretation of the situation. I don't own a pie dish."

"Oh, really?"

Claudia exhaled. "Okay, I do. And maybe we cluck a little, but the hen noises are worth it once the food is on the table. No one makes pumpkin pie like Delia Redford."

"Amen, sister."

"What about you, Jake?" Claudia turned her attention rapidly to him. "How's Thanksgiving at your house?"

I lowered my eyes, knowing the answer to that one. I'd dreaded his turn since we'd started sharing. It reminded me all too well of the best Thanksgiving I ever had.

"It's always good. The immediate family—me, Mom, Dad, my little brother Lukas, and my dad's mom. Some of my best memories are from Thanksgiving."

I tensed at this confession, wondering if he meant what I thought he meant. Quickly, so no one would notice, I glanced up at him from under my lashes to see if he was looking at me. Instead, Jake was studying his plate, apparently intent on not making eye contact with anyone.

"Thanksgiving at my house is crazy," Denver informed us loudly. "I mean, we got my whole family, which is me and my three brothers and my parents, plus we got cousins, uncles, aunts, grandparents, nieces, nephews. The house is packed with people and food. I swear to God, I need a vacation just to get over the holiday."

"I bet you wouldn't trade it for the world," Claudia said.

He shrugged, a guy equivalent of agreement.

Lowe leaned forward, shoving his now-empty plate aside. "Where do you think you'll be on Thanksgiving five years from now? *Who* do you think you'll be?"

"You go first," Beck grinned at him before taking a sip of beer.

"Okay." Lowe relaxed against his chair, his arm casually draped around the back of mine. "I'm in a hotel room in London with some random hook-up while I get ready for a show at the O2 Arena with my band, The Stolen."

The guys grinned. Matt relaxed back in his chair. "Well, I guess that's my future plan."

"Yeah, you're our fucking roadie because you've been replaced by Dave Grohl," Denver grunted.

Beck chuckled and threw a potato at Denver. "You're a shit."

"Where will *you* be, then, smart-ass?" Matt asked Denver.

"Getting sucked off by—ow!" He glared at Claudia as he rubbed his head where her hand had cracked across it. "What the fuck?"

She glowered back at him, unmoving. "It's Thanksgiving. Thanksgiving doesn't involve that kind of language, thank you very much. Apologize."

"Jesus, okay, I'm sorry." He winced, feeling his head for blood.

The rest of us all looked at one another, trying—and failing—to hold in the laughter. We collapsed into hysterics as Denver attempted to annihilate us with his eyes. Claudia sat prim and unmoving.

Beck grabbed her by the back of the neck and pulled her close so he could kiss her forehead affectionately. She relaxed and rolled her eyes, settling back into her seat.

"Where will you be?" Lowe asked me as soon as the laughter died down.

I felt my cheeks warm as they turned their focus on me. "Uh … either having Thanksgiving with my family or patrolling the streets of Chicago as a rookie with a really crap work schedule."

He smiled at me. "And nothing else. No guy? Or girl?" he winked at me.

"You can squash that fantasy, Lowe. I'm not into girls." I shoved him playfully and then stared at my plate, avoiding Jake's gaze. "It would be nice to think there will be a guy. Who knows?"

Lowe snorted. "There will be a guy, Charley," he said, sounding absolutely convinced on the matter.

I raised an eyebrow. "Are you clairvoyant?"

"Nah. I'm just not blind. It's a miracle you're single at the moment."

The compliment hit me in all my good-for-nothing places and I shook my head, trying to laugh it off with everyone else. It wasn't easy when I could feel Jake's eyes burning into me.

"Claud, where do you see yourself in five years?" Matt asked her. "With me, right?"

I laughed as Claudia rolled her eyes for the second time that night. "If I'm going to be with anyone in five years, it will be Will McPherson."

"Who the hell is Will McPherson?" Beck grumbled.

I answered for her. "The hot TA Claud has been lusting after for two years and has been too chicken to approach."

"Why would you be too chicken to approach?" Matt guffawed. "Have you seen you?"

"Are you trying to kill me with compliments, Matt?"

"Seduce, Claud, not kill."

"I don't think it's working," Beck said, smirking at him.

"Well," Melissa spoke up, her tone overly cheery, "in five years' time, I'm hopefully going to be working on my postgrad, and spending Thanksgiving on vacation with my whole family and Jake."

My fingers clenched around my wine glass. When I dared to look over at her, she was giving me a firm but pointed look. I managed to keep my flinch inward and calmly took another drink of wine.

Nice Melissa was gone then. Determined-to-keep-her-boyfriend Melissa was in town.

"Jake?" she turned to him, "what about you?"

He didn't look at her, just sat staring at the beer bottle in his hand as he picked at the label. "What about me?" he answered a little flatly.

"Where do you see yourself in five years' time?"

He shrugged and then shot the table a strained grin. "A roadie for The Stolen." The guys laughed, helping him out. Lowe quickly turned the conversation elsewhere.

As I collapsed into my bed later that night, I wondered not for the first time that evening whether Jake spent the entire dinner remembering our first Thanksgiving together … and our promise that we would never stop loving each other.

Chapter Twelve

Indiana, December 2008

For the first time since rescuing my sister from the SUV, I wished to God I were Supergirl. I'd never read the old comics but surely Supergirl wouldn't have been this nervous about going all the way with her boyfriend? Or maybe she would have, I didn't know. Maybe like me, Supergirl put up this front that she was confident about everything, when in reality she was just as scared as the next girl.

I didn't know why I was so nervous about my plans to lose my virginity to Jake. Throughout the last four months, I'd been the one making the moves, pushing for our first kiss, pushing for fooling around. We'd done a lot of "stuff" together, and although I'd felt a little flurry of jitters when we'd first started out, I hadn't felt nervous or anxious the way I was now feeling nervous and anxious.

The truth was I didn't want to disappoint Jake in any way. I'd gotten it out of him that he'd lost his virginity when he was only fourteen. He wouldn't tell me how many girls he'd been with, which worried me more than a little, but he promised it was nowhere near as scary a number as I probably had in my head. Still, Jake was experienced for his age. I guessed part of that was due to the fact that he didn't look sixteen.

Take Stacy Sullivan, the waitress at Hub's, for instance. I knew the rumors that Jake had slept with her were true. I knew this because since dating Jake, I'd hardly been inside Hub's and the reason was because Jake didn't appear to like it all that much. That was ridiculous—Hub's had great food—so I suspected it had more to do with the fact that he'd nailed Stacy.

So Jake was experienced. And I wasn't.

I knew it was ridiculous to have those concerns. Jake loved me and he wanted to be with me no matter what. That didn't mean I didn't want to be the best he ever had.

"Ugh," I groaned and dropped my head against the bathroom mirror, trying to take calming breaths. I jerked my head back, jumping out of my skin at the sound of my cell binging.

It was a text from Jake.

Coast is clear. I'm outside x

I sent him an affirmative text back, drew in a deep breath, and hurried out of the bathroom. Mom and Dad were at work, so at least I didn't have to hide what I was up to.

It was a Saturday and Jake's parents and Lukas had gone Christmas shopping in Chicago. Chicago was actually an hour closer to Lanton than Indianapolis, plus Lukas was meeting up with some old friends. Jake had begged off the family day trip with the excuse that he wasn't feeling great.

In reality, we just wanted his house to ourselves.

Two weeks ago when Jake had mentioned the shopping trip, I'd instantly thought about having an uninterrupted day with Jake in the vicinity of a bed. We spent most of our time fooling around in Hendrix in Brenton Fields and a couple of those times, things had gotten seriously frustrating for the both of us. It was bad. It had gotten to a point where I was zoning out in class because all I could think about was Jake's hands on my body.

That's why I casually suggested that he didn't go with his family.

Assured that I meant it and that I was ready for us to have sex, Jake had eagerly jumped on board with the idea.

Bundled up in my winter gear, I hurried out to Jake's truck, jumping in out of the cold and rubbing my hands together. I gave him a small smile. "Hey."

He stared at me a moment, his eyes searching. "You okay?" he asked softly.

I nodded quickly. "Yeah, let's go."

Instead of going, Jake put Hendrix in neutral and pulled up the handbrake. He twisted around, sliding his arm behind my seat so his body was turned into mine. "Baby, we don't have to do this. If you've changed your mind, it's okay."

As his reassurances and kind expression sank in, I thought that I was amazingly lucky to have found Jake Caplin. I'd said it before and I'd say it again: he was not like other boys. However, I'd obviously done something to deserve him, so I was content to accept his adoration and devotion for the rest of my life. I smiled at him now, some of the nerves dissipating. "I haven't changed my mind. I ... just want this to be good for you."

He frowned. "You're worrying about that?"

"Well, yeah, aren't you?"

"Yeah," he nodded, "but because I'm the experienced one and I want to make it as perfect as it can be. You don't need to worry about that."

"Jake, I do," I insisted. "I'm just as concerned about making this perfect for you. You've been with girls who know what they're doing—"

"I'll stop you right there," he cut me off, tugging on my hand so I had no choice but to fall forward against him. Jake cupped my cheek, his thumb stroking my skin as he pulled me into his dark gaze. "Everything we've done up to now is the best I've ever had. It's the best because it's with you and we're great together. This will be no different."

"Seriously, did you grow up on another planet or something where immature adolescent males are forbidden?"

He laughed and shook his head. "I don't want to fuck this up by being an immature dick. And believe me, I have plenty of experience in that department too."

"Okay," I rolled my eyes, gently pulling back from him. "Let's get out of here before you say something to change my mind."

Jake's house was silent, thick with it, in fact, as if it was breathless with anticipation right along with me. We hadn't said a word in the truck as we drove to his place, both of us preoccupied with what lay ahead, nerves and sexual tension making the atmosphere potent enough to kill conversation.

Jake locked the front door behind us and helped me take off my coat and scarf. I watched silently as he removed his own. Taking my hand, he felt it tremble and gave me a sharp look. I squeezed his hand and reassured him once more with my eyes.

I followed him up the stairs, my breath coming harder and faster now. As soon as we entered his bedroom, Jake reached over for a piece of paper on his desk and then handed it to me.

Eyebrows drawn together, I unfolded it and blinked rapidly when I realized what it was. "You got tested?" I whispered.

He nodded solemnly. "I wanted you to know that I'm clean. You deserve not to have to worry about that."

Swallowing hard, I folded the paper back over. "How many girls *have* you been with?"

"Enough to know 'the one' when I find her." Jake pulled me against him, his arms strong around my waist. "My friends back in Chicago think I'm crazy when I talk about you. They keep telling me that I'm too young to feel this way. I'm not too young, Charley.

I know with more certainty than I've ever had about anything in my life that you're my future. I know that when we're ready, after college or whatever, we're going to get married and that you're going to be the mother of my kids. I know that deep in my gut."

Overwhelmed by his heartfelt confession, by his surety in me, and honestly by the restless sexual chemistry between us, I found myself close to tears. I hit his chest gently. "You're going to make me cry. You know I don't like that."

He chuckled and cuddled me closer, his chin resting on my hair. "It's the good kind of tears, though, right?"

I nodded, nuzzling my face into his throat. "I love you so much. I don't care if people think we're crazy."

"I love you too," he murmured, stroking my back.

Pretty quickly his soothing caress became something else and I pressed my lips to his throat. Jake groaned, tilting his head back a little as I kissed my way up to his jaw. I didn't get a chance to reach for his mouth because Jake was already reaching for mine.

His kiss was soft, coaxing, his tongue gently teasing mine. As I melted into it, I slipped my hand under his shirt, forcing the fabric up as I explored his abs. Taking my hint, Jake broke the kiss to pull off his shirt and I did the same with my sweater. Goosebumps awoke all over me.

It was going to happen for us.

Yes.

I grinned at him and he smiled back, his warm hands coasting lightly around my waist as he pulled me back to him. We started kissing again, this time our lips pressing harder, our tongues sliding deeper, and the goosebumps disappeared in a flush of fire. Deftly, Jake took off my bra and still kissing, we fumbled with one another's pants.

Laughing and stroking and kissing, we eventually ended up on his bed naked, his body braced above mine. When he slid a hand between my legs, the laughter disappeared and our breathing grew stilted. I lifted my hips, widening my legs, welcoming his touch and groaning with sheer pleasure when he slipped two fingers inside me.

He'd done this before, playing me to the point of explosion.

This time he pressed deeper and I flinched at the uncomfortable pressure.

Jake pulled back, his muscles straining. "It'll hurt the first time, but I'll try to make it as good as I can for you."

"I know." I wound my arms around his shoulders. "I trust you."

He kissed me, lowering his hips against me so I could feel his hot erection pulsing at my core. I thought for a minute we were going straight into it and I tensed, bracing myself, but Jake left my mouth to follow an invisible trail down my body with his lips. He kissed every inch of me, sucking on my nipples until they were distended and tender, kissing between my legs, his tongue laving at my clit until I came. And then he started all over again—his thumb on my swollen clit, his fingers pushing inside of me.

"Jake," I moaned, my nails biting into his back. "I can't ..." I felt shattered, like I was only held together by the tiniest cracks of light and if Jake pushed me one more time, I was going to break into a million pieces. My body wanted that but I didn't know if I could take any more.

"I can't wait any longer," he breathed harshly and I nodded, silently asking him to do it, to move inside me and end the torture he'd started. He leaned over the bed and opened the drawer of his bedside table. He removed the small foil condom package and ripped it open with his teeth. With a proficiency I pretended not to notice, Jake rolled the condom on.

I felt his hands depress the mattress on either side of my head, his chest lifting up off my body. He nudged my knee with his and I opened my legs wider at his silent request.

I looked up into his eyes.

He stared back at me, his cheeks flushed, his eyes dark with a mixture of tenderness and love. "You ready?"

My chest gave way to the strange sensation of fluttering beats. I gripped him harder, needing to anchor onto him to fight the nerves. "Yes," I managed. "No. Wait."

He swallowed hard, his arms shaking a little. "Okay."

"Do it fast."

"Baby, no. I've got to be gentle. I could hurt you."

"It might hurt more. Think of it ..." I struggled to draw a full breath. "Think of it like a Band-Aid."

He didn't look certain at all. "I don't think—"

"Please."

I knew he could never deny me. He nodded slowly and I nodded back reassuringly.

"Do you know how beautiful you are?" Jake muttered, his gaze still hot but adoring. "So beautiful. I used to think there was nothing prettier than looking up at the stars. That feeling I got, like I was part of something bigger than anything I could ever imagine. It's one of my favorite feelings ... and I get it every time I look at you."

I felt my eyes grow wet as the connection between us tightened. "I know," I said. I did know because I felt that way every time I looked at him.

Our kiss was just a lip brush at first but I pulled him back for more, something deeper, and as I sucked on his tongue, I must've snapped what little self-control Jake had left. I felt him press between my legs, and then he shifted his weight ...

I cried out as Jake thrust inside me hard, pushing deep. A flare of pain rippled up from my lower back to sprinkle shivers across my shoulders and I tensed as Jake hovered above me, not moving.

"Baby, you okay?"

As the pain dissipated, I was left with this uncomfortable fullness, a strange sensation I wasn't sure I liked. But when I looked up at Jake's face and saw the bead of sweat on his forehead, saw the untempered heat and desire in his eyes, I knew Jake liked whatever *he* was feeling. "I'm okay," I said softly.

At my assurance, Jake moved, pulling back until he was almost gone and then pushing back in. I ached, still unsure, but held on as he repeated it. As he withdrew again, I felt his thumb circle my clit and the ache disappeared under the stir of pleasure. The next time Jake withdrew, I muffled a cry of surprise at the delicious sensation that moved through me and I arched my hips trying to pull him back.

"God, Charley," Jake growled and I felt his thrusts pick up speed.

Soon I'd forgotten where we were, and all I cared about was our bodies and what his was doing to mine. I slid my hands down his back and clutched at his buttocks, pulling him into me.

"Baby," came Jake's guttural response. "I'm going to lose control."

"I want you to," I replied, my words choppy and breathy.

"I'm trying to go slow," he reminded me through gritted teeth.

"No." I pressed him deeper.

He gasped and his hips slammed against mine, his dick moving so deep in me, it was almost painful. By that point I didn't care. He thrust into me a couple of more times and then stilled, his neck muscles straining as his hips jerked against mine in hard climax.

Finished, he tried to catch his breath and melted on top of me, his hands moving down my waist as he rested his forehead on the pillow next to my ear.

I stroked his back, running my hands soothingly over his damp skin. I smiled as his hand squeezed my waist. He was still inside me, his body heavy on mine. Wonderful contentment settled over me.

I'd just given my virginity to Jake Caplin and he'd just given everything to me too. This was it. This was our lives now. Laughter and kindness and affection and friendship and great sex.

Lucky didn't even begin to describe how I felt.

"I tried to wait," he muttered, lifting his head to stare into my eyes. "Sorry."

"Don't be sorry," I stroked his cheek, my smile probably a little goofy. "It was amazing."

"You'll come next time," he promised, brushing his lips over mine before he lifted himself up onto his hands again. I flinched a little as he pulled out and realized that I was actually pretty sore. He saw my flinch. "You okay?"

I smiled, this time flirtatiously. "A little sore but I'm definitely okay."

Without saying another word, Jake got up and disappeared out of the room. A minute later he returned condomless and carrying a cloth. He crawled back into bed and pressed the wet cloth between my legs.

"What are you doing?"

He smiled, his love for me so glaring, I wanted to dive all over him again. "Taking care of my girl."

"You know I don't need you to," I teased, "but I like that you want to." I arched an eyebrow at him playfully. "Do you promise to take care of me for the rest of forever, Jacob Caplin?"

His eyes were grave as he replied, "I promise. For the rest of forever."

Chapter Thirteen

Edinburgh, December 2012

It was nothing short of a miracle that I'd managed to secure a table in the main campus library. I had my laptop all hooked up and was going through my notes for class. Exams started in a week. Fun.

It would be even more fun if I could concentrate. I pushed my laptop aside and opened one of the books I'd had to buy for class. By the second page I gave up and pushed that aside too. Not a thing was penetrating my thick skull—my thick skull that was painted with images of Jake from last night.

For the third time since Thanksgiving, Jake stopped by the apartment to hang out. I deliberately steered us clear of my room so we hung out in the kitchen. Sometimes the girls dropped by, but for the most part we were alone. Like we'd been last night.

Last night reminded me too much of the old Jake. Although we were good with banter, we'd kept things fairly light conversationally since our foray back into a friendship. Until last night ...

"Something's up with you."

At the pronouncement, I glanced over at him, sitting in the corner at the window, his long legs stretched out and resting on another chair. I was tucked in a corner opposite him, his feet only inches from me. Jake had his head tilted to the side, his face searching, concerned.

"What makes you say that?"

"When you're really with someone, you give them your entire focus. When something's on your mind, you give rote answers. And you're way less of a smart-ass."

"I'm not a smart-ass," I responded automatically, my lips curling up at the corner.

Jake smiled back at me but nudged my knee with his foot. "Come on. What's up?"

"Nothing is up." *Everything is up. My mom and dad still won't talk to me about being a cop. They're annoyed I'm hanging out with you. My best friend is in some weird semi-non-relationship. And then there's you.*

"It's the law school thing, isn't it?"

My brow wrinkled in consternation. "What makes you say that?" It bugged the hell out of me that Jake would be the one to notice my preoccupation with my career issue.

He shrugged. "You've been talking more and more about being a cop. It's as if you're trying to plant it so deep inside you that when it comes to telling your parents you don't want to be a lawyer, you'll be in too deep for them to try again to talk you out of being a cop."

"I hate that you know me so well," I replied quietly, sadly, without even thinking.

Jake gave a short, sharp huff of laughter, hurt flickering across his countenance. "I guess I deserve that."

I instantly felt guilty. "Jake, I didn't mean—"

"I think you did." He gave me an unhappy, rueful look. "But whether you like it or not, it's true—I know you. So ... talk to me."

Still sliding down the guilt spiral, I sighed and gave in as recompense for wounding him. "Law school is expensive."

"That's it?"

"No. I have the money but it just seems stupid to spend it on law school, especially when my mom needs money for the store."

Jake gave me a small smile. "You don't want to go to law school because your mom needs the money more than you do? Charley, you haven't changed a bit."

I grunted. "So you keep saying."

"It's not a bad thing. But that's not all, is it?"

"Would you stop doing that? Get out of my head. It's messy enough in there without you cluttering it up."

I watched him determinedly keep a straight face. A wise decision. Exhaling, I leaned back against the wall and looked out the window. "The more I try to talk about being a cop with Mom and Dad, the more they push the lawyer thing. I've never done anything to let them down before, and if I don't go to law school, I'd be letting them down hugely. I know I make jokes about it and I tease Rick to mentor me, but in reality, I don't know if I can let my parents down."

"If you do what they want, you'd be letting yourself down." Jake sat up, shifting his chair closer to me and tugging on my hand, demanding my attention. I had nowhere to look but into his sincere eyes. "Baby, since as long as I've known you, you've wanted to be a cop and Delia and Jim know that. Yeah, it can be a dangerous job. Yeah, they'll worry about you. *I'll* worry about you. But it's what you want to do. Who knows … you could go to the academy and do a year or two of being a rookie and absolutely hate it. But at least you'll know. At least you'll never regret not going for it."

Unconsciously, I rubbed my thumb across his hand, an affectionate gesture of thanks. "I should talk to them. Make them listen."

"Yes. You should definitely do that." He eased back from me, letting go of my hand. I looked away from him again.

"Do *you* have any regrets?" Why oh why did I ask that?

Clearly I was a masochist.

Jake was silent so long, I didn't think he was going to answer. Finally, he replied, his voice thick with … everything, "Yeah, I've got a few of those."

Hearing the emotion in his voice, I couldn't help but turn back to him. I *needed* to. When I did, I sucked in my breath at the blaze of anguish in his eyes. There was no mistaking that the anguish was all for me. I felt my cheeks burn, my blood quickening with fire in an instant. Dry-mouthed, pulse throbbing, I was frightened to move, sure that if one of us did, something would happen. Something we couldn't take back.

The door to the kitchen blasted open and Claudia burst in, books tumbling out of her arms as she leapt toward the kitchen table. Once her load was deposited on the table, she turned to us and pulled off her wooly knit cap. "I hate studying." She pouted, looking adorable with her cheeks rosy red from the cold.

We just stared at her, both of us still trapped in our moment.

Claud made a face. "You two okay?"

I searched my brain for something, anything, to say. "They call studying 'revising' here, did you know that?"

Jake laughed shakily and stood up. "I did not know that. Does that make sense? Isn't revising editing?"

Claudia looked from Jake to me and her eyebrows dipped with suspicion.

"I think you're right."

"Hmm." He nodded and then clapped his hands together. "Well, I'm going to go." He lifted his chin to me and smiled at Claud as he strolled out of the room.

As soon as we heard the front door shut, Claudia turned to me, her hands braced on her hips. "What the hell was that?"

I opened my mouth to lie and then thought better of it. Instead I groaned and let my head fall between my knees, my hair brushing the ground as I replied, "I think that was Jake telling me he regretted dumping me."

"WHAT?" My head was suddenly shoved back up, Claudia's fingers curled in my hair as she stared wide-eyed into my face. "Say again?"

I grabbed her hands, wincing as I uncurled her grip on my hair. "It wasn't said in so many words."

"Explain."

So I did, leaving Claudia convinced that Jake and I were playing with fire. I wasn't sure she wasn't wrong. However, I didn't want to stop hanging out with him. I was afraid I was addicted to him again, and since Melissa obviously didn't seem to be too bothered by us hanging out, I wasn't going to feel guilty about it. It wasn't like I had any intention of making a move on him. Jake might have inadvertently admitted that he regretted leaving me, but that didn't mean he loved Melissa any less. In fact, I was sure of it.

Sitting in the library I doodled over my lecture notes, willing myself to concentrate.

I didn't get far, but that wasn't my fault.

The chair across from me screeched across the floor, the noise jolting me in my seat. Jake slid into it. Seriously, I needed to stop thinking about him. It made him magically appear everywhere!

He beamed at me, dumping his books on the desk. "You found a table? What, did you get here at six o' clock this morning?"

I blinked. "Where did you come from?"

"Evanston, Illinois."

I made a face. "Smart-ass."

"Hey, that's my line."

I searched his amused expression for any trace of awkwardness concerning the night before, but nope. Nothing. It was like it had never happened.

Ignoring a prick of anger I settled back in my chair, my demeanor prim. "I hope you haven't stopped by to bother me. I'm studying."

Jake pretended to look offended. "Moi? Bother you? As if I would."

"You've been bothering me since the eleventh grade," I grumbled.

He seemed far too pleased by this, so I thought it necessary to kick him in the shin under the table. "Oww!" he jerked back in shock.

"Ssshh!" the girl sitting at the desk in front of us admonished, glaring.

"Apologies," Jake raised a hand in placation. "I'm just a victim of violence."

She glowered harder and then finally looked back down at her books.

"Your charm failed you that time, Caplin."

"You should know I bruise like a peach," he sighed, tutting under his breath. "Marring my perfect body with your Uggs ... terrible."

I fought laughter, not wanting to get us kicked out. "Jake, they're Uggs. How much damage can they do?"

He leaned down to rub his shin. "A fuck of a lot, clearly. That shit hurt."

"You're such a baby."

"What was that?" he cupped his ear toward me playfully. "I'm such a babe?" he winked. "Already know that, sweetcheeks."

I laughed. "What is with you today? You're very chipper."

"You mean for a guy who just got nailed in the shin by a hundred-pound girl?"

"Oh, we are in the mood to charm today." *A hundred pounds, my ass.*

"I'm in a good mood." Jake shrugged, his boyish smile causing heat to spark in me. I wish it wouldn't. He was acting an awful lot like the old Jake and I had to admit, I'd missed him. "I'm not allowed to be in a good mood?"

I pushed my books to the side, knowing I definitely wasn't going to get any studying done with him sitting across from me. "Of course you are. I'm just wondering what it's all about. You're extra Jake-like today."

"Extra Jake-like?" He smiled and shrugged. "What is extra Jake-like?"

"I don't know." I fiddled with my pen as I tried to pinpoint what it was exactly that was making him extra Jake-like. "Lighter," I said suddenly. "You're lighter. Like you used to be. Ever since ... and even now, you seem ..."

"Seem what?" His amusement had left him and he was leaning across the table, his eyebrows drawn together.

I didn't know if it was wise to finish my sentence, but since we'd been teetering on a lot of cliff edges lately, I didn't think one more would make a difference. "More serious. Which is only natural with everything ... and you being older ..." I trailed off.

He huffed and sat back in his chair. "Only natural," he agreed.

Silence fell between us and I wished to God I hadn't said anything. I'd ruined his good mood.

"I do feel lighter lately, though."

I couldn't look at him. If I looked at him, I'd only find ways to make it seem like that meant something, something to do with us. Honestly, I just really needed to start remembering there was no longer an "us."

"Good," I muttered, pulling a book back to me. "I'm glad."

When I didn't say anything else, Jake shifted in his chair. When I still didn't say anything, he shifted again. Finally he threw a pen at me.

"What, are we twelve?" I threw his pen back.

"I wanted your attention." He was back to boyish Jake. Pity I found him irresistible.

Crossing my arms over my chest, I relaxed back in my chair. "Okay, well, you have it."

"So," Jake leaned forward, hands clasped in front of him, as if we were sitting down to discuss something of great import. "Have you noticed what's been going on with Beck and Claudia?"

I choked on a giggle. "You want to gossip with me?"

He lowered his voice, "It's better than studying."

"Okay, I'll give you that." I pushed my books out of the way once more. "They're definitely into one another but Beck seems reluctant to start a relationship."

"That's because Beck doesn't *do* relationships."

Jake gestured me closer and when he spoke, it was a whisper. "Shit family life. I'm the closest he's got to family. It's messed up his whole thinking but I leave him to it. Still, I've noticed he's been agitated lately. In particular these last few days …"

I nodded knowingly. "Claudia started dating this Scottish guy."

Jake sighed. "I wish Beck would pull his head out of his ass."

"Should we help him?"

"Pull his head out of his ass?"

"Yeah. I know Claudia cares about him and it's obvious he cares about her. Maybe there's some way we could give them a little shove?"

"Would you like someone to give you a little shove in your relationship?" Jake looked less than convinced.

I shuddered at the thought of someone interfering with mine and Jake's fragile friendship. "Okay, good point."

"I just wanted to know if you knew if Claud felt the same way, that's all."

"Why?"

"Something might still come of it. For Beck's sake, I hope it does. He needs someone like Claudia in his life. She's a great girl."

I smiled affectionately. "She is. She's the best."

"You didn't have a friend like *her* in high school."

I thought of Lacey and Rose and our somewhat shallow friendship. "No, I did not."

"But for now, I guess we just sit back and watch the show."

I thought of the relationship that had built between Claudia and Beck over the last few months. They seemed very close but because there was this animal attraction there, the whole friendship seemed ready to implode. As I stared at Jake, it occurred to me that our friendship might be mirroring our friends'.

Since I was choosing to believe we had more control over our relationship, I pushed that scary, ticking-bomb thought to the back of my head.

"What are you thinking?" He cocked his head to the side, his lids lowered in thought.

Before I had to scramble for a lie, a shadow fell over our desk. Melissa stood staring at us, books pressed tight to her chest. Everything about her was tense and I knew right away when her gaze fell on me that it was because of my presence. More to the point, it was because I was in Jake's presence. Alone.

Huh. I thought she was over it.

"What are you doing here?" she asked Jake quietly. There was a definite note of accusation in her voice.

"Studying," he answered calmly, but I could hear the edge in his answer.

Melissa pointedly looked at our unopened books. "I'm going back to my dorm to study. Come with?" It wasn't really a question. Her cheeks were flushed and her mien was brittle. She was roaring for a fight.

Resolved to his impending doom, Jake gave her a tight nod and stood, collecting his books. For the millionth time I ignored the ache in my chest at the sight of them together, both dark and tall and beautiful. They were perfect for one another.

I felt the sting in my nose and quickly ducked my head, yanking a book toward me.

"See you, Charley," Jake said softly.

I nodded, not looking at them. "See you tomorrow at the gym."

"Gym?" The question was asked sharply and by Melissa.

I lifted my chin, surprised by her almost caustic response. She glowered at Jake and he blanched. Annoyance tore through me and I locked my jaw to stifle the curse words I wanted to throw at him. This whole time I thought Melissa knew we were spending time together, but of course, she didn't. What girlfriend in her right mind would be okay with a guy spending that much quality time with an ex? I was such a willful idiot.

I slunk farther down in my chair, listening to them walk away and wishing like hell I'd kicked Jake's shin hard enough to cause a dent. He had hurt Melissa by not being honest with her, and he'd pulled me into it, making me feel guilty when I hadn't done anything wrong.

Right?

Claudia had been on three dates with the Scottish student she'd met at the library. He was cute and funny and she really seemed to like him. He wasn't Beck, but she was in denial and frankly I was right there with her, so I wasn't going to be a hypocrite and attempt to yank her out of it.

Claudia was out on a date with the Scottish guy, and The Stolen were busy with other plans. Since I hadn't made much headway with my roommates, I found myself huddled in my room alone, my hands wrapped around a warm mug of cocoa as I stared at the photos pinned to my wall, pictures of our group here in Edinburgh—some great shots of Beck and Claudia who looked stunning together, of Rowena and Denver, of Matt, Lowe, and Beck, of Jake and Beck, of Lowe and me. Even one of just Jake and me. I wanted to say we didn't look right together. But we did. Not perfect in the way that Jake and Melissa looked. No. But we looked *right*.

I clunked my mug down on my bedside table and reached up to pull the picture off the wall. Within seconds it was scattered across my bedspread in pieces.

"Sometimes I wished I hated you, Jake Caplin," I whispered hoarsely.

And as if he'd heard me, my cell rang. It was him.

Cautiously, I answered it.

"Charley," Jake breathed, as if relieved I'd picked up. "You okay?"

"I'm fine," I replied flatly. "Melissa didn't seem so fine."

"Yeah. She just ... she feels a little threatened by our history."

"Is that why you didn't tell her we hang out all the time? Because I was under the impression she knew."

"Mel's an understanding girl, but I didn't know if she'd understand this. You are my ex."

I didn't say anything.

Jake exhaled heavily. "Look, I called because Mel told me something tonight. Something you said and I want to know if it's true."

"What would that be?"

"Did you really tell Mel that I loved her because I let her help me and because I didn't let you help me I obviously didn't love you?"

My chest tightened at his question. As I switched the phone to my other ear, it shook in my trembling hand. "I said that you wouldn't let me help you, but you let Melissa help you and to me, that speaks volumes."

"Bullshit," Jake responded, taking me aback with his vehemence. "You've got to know that's bullshit, Charley. I pushed you away but it wasn't because I didn't love you. I was crazy about you. You know that. It had all just happened, though. I was a fucking mess. No one could get through to me. I met Melissa a long time after it. Enough time to not be in that dark place anymore."

Feeling sick, I shook my head, even though he couldn't see. "I don't want to talk about this, Jake."

"I know. It just … it would kill me if you thought I fell out of love with you. Or worse … that I was never in love with you."

"Jake, what are you doing?" I asked, panicking now. "There's no point to any of this. You're with Melissa."

"And I love her." I closed my eyes at his declaration, fighting tears, desperate not to give into them. "But I didn't even know her when I applied to study here for the year."

Fighting the tears meant choking on them. I had to take a minute before I responded. "You knew I'd be here."

"I *hoped* you'd be here, yes."

I covered the phone while I tried to catch a painful breath. After I counted to ten, I exhaled and put the phone back to my ear. "And then you met her."

His breath crackled on the line. "Yeah."

I was going to break. "Jake, I have to go."

"Charley—"

"Claudia's at my door."

"Oh. Okay. I'll see you tomorrow?" he sounded unsure.

"Yeah. Bye." I hung up and threw my phone on my bed just in time to catch the sob in my throat. It choked me as I fought it, my hands clenched into fists as I pushed back the tears. He wasn't getting any more from me. He'd had plenty in the past.

I wished I could hate him. It would make it all so much easier if he'd just dumped me, if all that shit hadn't happened to him and his family. I needed him to be the bad guy, all black and white, no shades of gray. It was the only way I could move on.

But unfortunately, that wasn't reality, and Jake wasn't the bad guy. Not completely. I turned on my side, curled into a ball. I was still making excuses for him when he had to have known how much it hurt me for him to say he loved someone else.

It was decided then. I needed to stop spending time with him.

The thought of not talking to him, laughing with him, clawed at my gut but I had to do something before I turned into one of those whiny girls I wanted to thrust a spine into.

Chapter Fourteen

Indiana, January 2009

The smell of Hub's burgers, fried onions, and coffee was welcome and familiar. As was the same playlist of country music installed in the old-fashioned jukebox in the corner. No one cared that they'd had to listen to the same music for ten years—Hub's was always so busy, conversation drowned out the crooners. I think the people of Lanton would've put up with cat's nails dragged across blackboards just to get a taste of one of Hub's burgers.

As for me, I'd put up with the fact that one of the waitresses had slept with my boyfriend. That's how good Hub's freaking burgers were.

I sat across from Jake in a small booth near the front entrance, chewing on a fry and watching him munch on his burger. He suddenly made a face and put it down, swallowing his food to complain, "I got pickle."

"Give me," I waved my fingers at him. "The taste of it will undoubtedly help me get over my disbelief that you don't like it."

Jake took the pickle off the burger and held it out to me. I smiled and leaned across the table and closed my lips around his fingers. His pupils dilated as I pulled back, chewing on the pickle. "Seriously? In public?"

I laughed and shrugged, picking up my own burger. "It's not my fault you can't control yourself."

His expression pretty much said "you'll pay for that later," but I continued to eat happily, not too concerned about it. Jake's payback was always yummy. "We definitely have an audience now," he mumbled before taking a sip of his Coke.

I didn't need to ask what he was referring to. Sitting behind us, closer to the bottom end of the diner, were some of our classmates and my so-called friends. Taking up two booths in the back was Alex, Brett, Damien, and a couple of their friends, as well as Lacey and Rose. Since Jake and I had walked into Hub's, they'd been watching us. I heard their pointed laughter when I took a seat that wasn't in Stacy's section, and I felt their burning gaze on my neck the whole time we ordered food.

The fact that Lacey and Rose were with Brett and his idiots should've bothered me but honestly, I was done. The girls and I had grown distant since I started dating Jake. Yes, I spent time with him but even when I did spend time with the girls, all they did was bitch about the fact that I also spent time with Jake. Since I couldn't cut myself in half, I didn't really know what they wanted me to do about it.

And then Lacey started dating Brett.

Brett and his father hadn't stopped their campaign of hate against the Caplins, so as soon as Lacey became his girl, he made it clear that I was to be treated as the enemy. She hadn't spoken to me in three weeks.

I knew Jake was angry and also feeling inexplicably guilty. That pissed me off and as I chewed on my delicious burger, I grew annoyed that my senses were too distracted to enjoy it to the fullest. The muscle ticking in Jake's jaw told me he was pissed.

"Whatever they're doing behind my back, ignore them."

"They're just staring, trying to intimidate me."

I frowned. "Not Alex, though, right?"

Jake shook his head. "As always, that douchebag looks uncomfortable."

"He's not a douchebag."

"He's best friends with a douchebag and as such is a douchebag by association."

"Jake—"

"Don't even," he warned. "You know I don't like that crowd. They're bullies, baby."

I agreed that Brett and some of the others were bullies, but Alex and his senior friends weren't. Still, I didn't want to argue about it with an audience.

His voice was hushed as he continued. "Now they've got your two best friends turning against you and why? Because of me."

"Babe, as much as they want it to be, this is not the O.K. Corral. Ignore them."

"And Lacey and Rose?"

"Ignore them too. From the moment Lacey turned fourteen, she's been desperate to be popular. When Alex and I broke up, she was plotting to fix me up with every jock who walked by just so she could be a part of this high school fantasy she created in her head. She met you and thought you were it, Mr. Popular, and since you weren't interested in her, she wanted you to meet me. She talked about it all summer when I called home. Unfortunately, you and I failed in that endeavor, so she's hooking herself to another star. Do you really think I'm that upset over someone so disloyal?"

"What about Rose? I thought she was a nice girl," Jake said, his eyes dim with disappointment. "I hate that me being with you has caused this."

"It's high school drama, Jake. Rose has always done whatever Lacey tells her to do. Even if she feels bad about it, she still does it. If it hadn't been you shaking things up, it would've been something else. Lucky for me it was you, and just so you know, I'd choose you over them in a heartbeat every single time."

The right side of his mouth quirked up in a little smile and he nodded, chewing on his fries.

I grinned. "You know, since you got here you've looked everywhere but at Stacy. Your aversion to Hub's and your behavior right now is proof that you slept with her."

Seeming stunned that I'd had the balls to bring it up, and so abruptly at that, Jake said, "You want to talk about this here? Now?"

"No. I just think you should know that I actually prefer knowing who you've slept with so I don't feel like a total chump when I'm in the room with them."

"And that's it? You're not ... jealous?" He eyed me warily.

I shrugged. "I'll always be jealous of any girl who's had that part of you, but I'm not worried about it. If you wanted her, you'd be with her. But you're not. You're with me. A sound choice, I might add." I smirked suggestively.

Jake threw his head back in laughter. "God, my girl is cocky."

"Pot, meet Kettle."

"Good thing we're both attracted to cocky, then, huh?"

"Good thing."

We smiled intimately at one another before turning our attention back to our food. Over the last few weeks, our relationship had grown pretty intense. It was already intense before so that was saying something. People were right when they said sex changes things. For Jake and me, it had brought us closer but had also added this edge of possessiveness that I wasn't expecting. On both sides. If I saw him laughing with another girl, I'd feel a pang in my chest I didn't like and I had to remind myself that Jake loved *me*. It became pretty clear, however, that Jake was as susceptible to those emotions as I was. Case in point, his attitude toward Alex. I still talked to Alex at school and two weeks ago when Jake came upon us laughing at my locker, he'd made it clear on the ride home that he hadn't liked it. We argued. There was shouting and yelling and even some growling. My intention had been to jump out of Hendrix angry and without saying goodbye, but Jake hadn't liked that, either—proving so by yanking me across the cab and practically into his lap so he could kiss the anger right out of me.

I talked to my mom about our arguments but she said she'd been the same with Dad when they were just starting out. They butted heads quite a bit and their "discussions" could get heated, but it was all in passion, not volatility. They were just trying to figure each other out.

They still butted heads and were still crazy about each other, so I wasn't going to worry about petty clashes between Jake and me.

It was far better putting my thoughts toward the next time and place we could use to be *alone*. Sneaking around to have sex was not easy when both sets of parents took preventing that very seriously. However, it wasn't quite impossible. Since our first time six weeks ago, we'd had sex seven times. Yes, I was counting. We managed to find alone time at least once a week, but since the sex just kept getting better and (oh my God) better, it was difficult to focus on anything other than sex with Jake.

Andie had come home from Dublin for Christmas break, taken one look at Jake and me together, and *knew*. I'd gotten the safe-sex talk from her and now she was urging me to go on the pill, something I knew Jake wanted me to do too. It wasn't that I didn't want to—it was just that in a small town like Lanton, these things had a way of getting back to parents.

The thought of having to discuss my sex life with my parents?

They may call me Supergirl, but I wasn't *that* brave.

I'd have to do it sometime soon, though. I knew that.

Fun.

"Did you tell your mom and dad about Edinburgh?" Jake asked, wiping his mouth with his napkin. I knew that satisfied look on his face. He was such a liar when he said he didn't like Hub's food.

"Yeah? Did you?" Just before Christmas I'd told Jake that I wanted to spend my third year of college abroad. Andie was having such an amazing time in Dublin and she promised me that it was an experience that would change me and help me grow up a little. I'd always wanted to travel, so a year abroad sounded awesome. My aunt Cecilia had visited Scotland years ago and when she came back, she showed us all her fantastic photographs. The ones of Edinburgh and its awe-inspiring castle resonated with me and I'd never let go of the idea of visiting someday. Why not for a study abroad? The University of Edinburgh had a fantastic reputation as an international school and Cecilia's money was sitting in the trust fund waiting for me to spend it.

As soon as I'd mentioned it to Jake, he was all for the idea. After a ten-second conversation, it was decided he was coming with me. This was similar to the discussion we had regarding the schools we were applying to back home. We'd decided to apply to Northwestern, Purdue, and the University of Chicago. It depended on who got in where but we were planning to either attend the same college or go to the colleges that were closest to one another. At least with those three, we were talking a few hours at the most.

"Yeah," Jake answered, "they think it's a great idea. They like the influence you have over me." He winked at me, and I so wished his winking wasn't as hot as it was.

"My parents are resigned to the idea as long as I apply for pre-law."

"They're still on about that huh?"

Delia and Jim Redford just couldn't get to grips with the idea of their daughter becoming a cop. I think they were now just beginning to realize that this wasn't a phase I was going through. Now they were pushing hard for law school. My mom had even downloaded brochures.

"I think they'd be okay with it if my intention was to be a deputy here."

Jake smiled affectionately. "But of course, you want to join the illustrious ranks of the Chicago PD."

"I do. I want the chance to advance, you know. Specialize."

This caused a little furrow between Jake's eyebrows. Although I'd talked at length with him about being a cop and he'd spoken at length about getting into engineering, we both just listened in that I'm-there-for-you-and-I-care-that-you-do-what-makes-you-happy-but-I-have-no-idea-really-what-you're-talking-about kind of way.

"You've never mentioned that."

I shrugged. "It's just something I've been thinking about more and more lately."

"Well, specializing to what?"

"I don't know. Homicide, maybe."

Jake tensed and then moved back in his seat. "What?" I noted the concern in his voice and hoped to God I wouldn't have him to contend with as well as my parents when it was time to apply to the academy. "Do your parents know this?"

I nodded, sighing. "I told them a few nights ago. Please don't tell me you now agree with them?"

Jake rubbed his eyebrow in thought and then shook his head. "You should do whatever will make you happy, but Charley ... a homicide detective in a place like Chicago? You'll see things you can't erase. Ever. Why would you want to see that shit every day?"

The reason was something that had been in the back of my mind since it happened. It wasn't something I'd shared yet with Jake because it was pretty sad, but I wanted him to understand me like no one else did. "I've always wanted to be a cop, ever since I knew what one was. I just …" I smiled ruefully, "I wanted to do something that mattered, that makes people feel safe. Working in homicide? Well … three years ago my big cousin Ethan was shot and killed in his Miami apartment for his laptop and some cash. The police never caught the guy. My aunt and uncle don't have any closure. It was a mindless crime and there's no one to perpetrate justice on. You can still see that in their eyes." My throat constricted and I felt that same rawness inside of me that I'd felt last summer when I spent a month in Miami with them. They got through each day for my cousins Emily and Seth, but it was like something was weighing them down, something eating at any chance of contentment they might have. "I guess if I can't give them closure, I'd like to try and do that for other people. And I know that I'll see some really horrific stuff, Jake, but I also know I want to at least try to see if I can handle it."

Jake regarded me with an intensity that held me still. "I bet you can." He slid his arm along the table until his hand found mine. He squeezed it, rubbing his thumb over my knuckles. "I'm sorry about Ethan."

"What's this? Young love?" a rough voice mocked as a shadow fell over us.

Jake and I looked up at the intruder and I tensed. Jake's grip on my hand tightened and suddenly, it was me squeezing his reassuringly.

"Mr. Thomas," I murmured unhappily, eyeing the weathered, obnoxious face of Trenton Thomas—Brett's dad.

He shot his son's table a smirk before turning back to look down on me. "I see all your friends have dumped you since you started dating the enemy. Maybe you should think on that, Charlotte." He grinned, as if he'd cracked the world's funniest joke.

I sneered. "Grow up."

Just as abrupt as a blackout, Trenton's face darkened. "You watch who you're talking to, young lady. Around here, we treat our elders with respect."

So I was supposed to respect this forty-year-old bully just because he had twenty-four years on me? I didn't think so. "You want respect? *Earn* it."

Trenton was practically bearing his teeth at me. "Pfft, just like your momma. Delia was a stuck-up bitch too."

Flinching at the insult to my beautiful mother, I had to take a couple of breaths, concentrating on Jake's hand in mine. Before I could respond calmly, however, a familiar voice said, "Delia just didn't like you, Trenton. That's why she said no when you asked her to prom, and that doesn't make her a stuck-up bitch. That makes her smart." Hub, the owner of the diner and a six-foot-four bear of a man with a scruffy beard and usually kind eyes, was standing beside Trenton, wiping his hands on a dish towel. His kind eyes were sharp and filled with warning. "If you're smart, I won't hear you speaking about Delia or any good woman like that again, and I won't hear you trying to intimidate kids in my establishment or elsewhere ... or you and I got problems. Understood?"

It took everything I had not to grin triumphantly at the strained look on Trenton Thomas's face. Tall at six foot and strongly built, it wasn't as if Brett's dad couldn't handle himself, so it was galling when he came up against someone who wasn't afraid of him. Especially someone as well liked and integral to the town as Hub.

We watched as Trenton gave Hub a short, sharp nod and then turned tail and stormed out of the diner.

Hub sighed and then looked at our empty plates. "Enjoy that, did you?"

I laughed. "The food or the show?"

Hub chuckled and shot Jake a sly smile. "Hope you can handle this one. She's as sharp as her mom."

As soon as he'd disappeared behind the counter, conversation started up in the diner again and Jake pulled on my hand to get my attention. "I can handle you. I want to handle you right now."

I shivered at the look in his eyes. "Are your parents home?"

"You want to check?"

"What do you think?" I chuckled and slid out of the both.

Jake paid for the food and I didn't bother arguing with him. We'd already had a massive blowout about this. I told him I was a modern girl and I wanted to pay my own way, or at least take turns paying, and Jake told me he was raised in a world where the man paid. This seemed awfully old-fashioned for a sixteen-year-old boy, but he would not be budged. Today I was too interested in fooling around to get pissy about it.

Pulling up to Jake's house, I felt the mood in the truck plummet. His dad's car was in the drive. Jake sighed. "What now?"

Groaning in annoyance, I shook my head. "My parents are home too."

"Our parents need to get lives."

I laughed and followed him out of Hendrix and up to the house.

As soon as we walked inside, we knew something was wrong.

Logan Caplin was pacing the living room floor, and he was seething. Jake's mom, Beth, stood to the side, a grim expression on her face.

"What's going on?" Jake asked quietly.

"What's going on?" Logan growled. "What's going on is that I'm going to teach that son of a bitch a fucking lesson!"

"Logan," Beth snapped. "Charley is here."

"It's okay," I assured her, frowning with concern. "Mr. C., what's going on?"

He stopped, shaking his head as he tried to control his anger. "I stopped by my office early this morning to pick up some papers I needed over the weekend. My office was trashed. Papers shredded, my computer smashed to bits, and there was pig excrement smeared everywhere."

I gasped and Jake choked out, "What the fuck?"

"Jacob!" Beth admonished. "Just because your father is angry does not give you an excuse to use that word."

"Sorry, Mom," he said before focusing back on his dad. "Please tell me it wasn't Trenton Thomas."

"Who else?" Logan threw up his hands, an angry vein throbbing in his neck. "Sheriff Muir and his deputies have lifted some fingerprints and have taken the tape from the cameras outside so we'll know soon enough. I don't need the evidence, though. I know it's that fucking moron."

Beth blanched at the continued cursing and I blanched for an entirely different reason. Both Jake and Logan looked ready to blow, and I didn't want them retaliating. Trenton and Brett Thomas weren't worth it. They were school bullies and always would be. Jake and his dad were better than that.

Beth walked cautiously over to Logan. She placed gentle hands on his chest and murmured to him to calm down. When that didn't seem to work, she took his hand and led him into the kitchen.

The kitchen door had only closed milliseconds when Jake whirled around and started toward the front door.

"Whoa, there, mister," I ran after him and grabbed his arm, jerking him to a stop. "Where do you think you're going?"

Jake's handsome face was taut with fury. "My dad's a good guy. He doesn't deserve this shit and we don't deserve the snide comments and alienation we're getting at school. I'm sorting this out between me and Brett."

"No," I pulled him harder when he tried to dislodge me. "No, you're going to calm down and come upstairs with me and forget about it. We're going to make out and fool around until we hear one of your parents coming up the stairs. It's Brett ... or me." I narrowed my eyes. "And I'd consider your answer very carefully or you'll have bigger problems on your hands than the Thomases."

Jake glared at me for a couple of seconds until I felt the tension slowly melt out of him. "You're a pain in my ass, Redford."

My lips curled up at the corner in triumph and I turned and started walking up the stairs. "And you're a pain in mine, Caplin, but I'm stuck with you."

"I'm sorry for the hardship," he teased. I smiled harder at his changed tone, knowing I'd won.

At the top of the stairs I turned and began walking backward into his room, unzipping my jacket as I went. "Don't be. I'll survive ... as long as you lose some clothes."

Jake smiled and quietly shut his bedroom door. He strode toward me with purpose, "Anything you say, baby."

I pulled off my jacket, grinning as he came to a stop inches from me. He reached for me but I pressed a hand against his chest and shook my head with a secretive smile. When I pulled the small envelope out of my jacket pocket, Jake frowned.

"Happy seventeenth birthday, Jake."

His eyes instantly brightened and he gently took the envelope from me. "It's not until Monday."

I gave a little shrug. "I know, but you won't get to thank me properly in front of everyone at school if I give it to you then."

He was still smiling as he opened the envelope. His smile grew huge and gorgeous when he saw what was inside. "Two tickets to Blind Side? Are you kidding me?"

I laughed, happy he was happy. Blind Side was a really cool indie band from Seattle who Jake had come across on the Internet. We'd spent the last few months listening to them. "I've been stalking them and found out they're doing a small concert in Chicago in June."

Jake kissed me, still smiling. When he pulled back, he gestured to me with the tickets. "This is a great fucking present." He frowned as he reached over to put them on his dresser. "I've just got to find someone to take with me."

"Funny."

He laughed and caught me by the waist, swinging me off my feet and crashing me down on the bed. I held onto him, giggling like crazy, as he followed me down. "I'm going to show my appreciation now."

I relaxed and gave him my best seductive smile. "Bring it."

As he kissed me deep, I wrapped myself around him, content in the knowledge that not only had I gotten him a great birthday present but I'd completely distracted him from Brett "effing" Thomas.

Chapter Fifteen

Edinburgh, December 2012

Frankenstein was a cool pub/club on George IV Bridge that Claudia and I had discovered at the beginning of the semester. On the ground floor was the bar and dance floor where people could get their pictures taken at the Frankenstein statue and watch costumed bar staff dance on the bar top to music from the *Rocky Horror Picture Show*. If you were looking for something a little more low-key, their basement sports bar was a lot more chill. That's where my Edinburgh gang and I found ourselves on a cold Thursday night in December, playing a pub quiz.

All of us except Jake—who was talking to his parents and had promised to catch up later—were seated around a mammoth booth. Lowe was sitting in between Claudia and Beck and Claud kept leaning around Lowe to argue with Beck about the answers to the emcee's questions. Rowena and Denver sat across from them trying to be helpful, but sometimes they had to resort to stealing the answer sheet from Beck. Matt had fallen asleep next to an exasperated-looking Lowe, who appeared to want to be anywhere but where he was—stuck in between the most frustrating non-couple ever.

To my surprise when we'd slid into the booth, Melissa had slid in beside me. She'd been giving me friendly smiles since we'd all met up out on the Cowgate. I had no idea what to do with that since the last time I saw her, I was pretty sure she wanted to kill either me or Jake.

"What is the largest omnivore in Britain?" the guy on the mic asked. "I'll repeat, what is the largest omnivore in Britain?"

"What kind of question is that?" Beck asked.

"Does Britain have omnivores?" Claudia's expression pretty much mirrored Beck's.

"I'm going tae pretend ye didnae ask that." Rowena shook her head and pulled the paper toward her. "It's a badger, people. A badger."

Melissa put a gentle hand on my shoulder, drawing me out of the conversation and into a little bubble with her at the back of the booth. I raised an eyebrow in question. "You okay?"

She looked determined but also a little nervous, a strain visible in her pretty blue eyes. "I wanted to apologize for my behavior at the library. I know things are complicated and I'm trying. Really."

"Melissa, you don't have to—"

"No," she held up a hand to cut me off, "I really need to explain, because right now I'm just this girl with a name who is dating your first love. You don't know me and I only know you from what Jake's told me. So I need to explain." Melissa leaned into me, her voice just loud enough for me to hear. "When I met Jake, he was just coming out of what I'd later discover were a few messy years. Drinking, partying, sleeping around, and refusing to make a connection with anyone who wasn't Beck. Luckily, he was starting to get pretty bored with that life and was pulling himself together, so when we started talking, he didn't want a relationship but was open to a friendship. I liked him so much, I took what I could get. As soon as it dawned on me that I woke up each day excited about seeing him, I knew I'd fallen for him. We grew close enough that he trusted me with what happened—with you, with … everything. So I know," she nodded, her regard kind and understanding and so not easy to hate. "I know what you meant to him, I know how special he thinks you are, and I know that he hurt you and that things between you are unresolved." Melissa took a shaky sip of her beer before turning back to me. "But I'm not just some girl he met, Charley. I'm one of his best friends.

"I've never judged him, and I like to think I helped him finally realize that what happened wasn't his fault—that he's not a bad person. Every day since meeting me, Jake has smiled a little more. He laughs at my stupid jokes because he cares enough to. I know that he can't start the day without black coffee, that he texts his brother every day about random stuff as an excuse to check in with him, I know he treats listening to Pearl Jam like a religious experience, and I know that when he sleeps on his back, he snores. I know him. We share the same views on practically everything, we never fight—well, until you—and I know that that means a lot to him. I love him and he loves me and I give him peace.

"Thing is, I know that he cares about you too and that he wants to be your friend. That isn't easy for me and I imagine that my existence isn't easy for you. But we both care about Jake, so I want to give friendship a shot. I think if we try to be friends with each other as well as Jake that it might help." She smiled. "I can be pretty cool when you get to know me."

I swallowed hard, feeling everything she'd said like a burning log in my throat. "I can see that," I replied a little roughly. "And thanks. For being honest."

"Jake says you appreciate people being upfront and straightforward."

I nodded, not sure what to say, how to respond, and thanking God when our group got loud as they greeted someone. Jake. He grinned at us, his warm eyes coming to a rest on Melissa and me. Noting our expressions, his own grew thoughtful.

"Here, man, I'll let you in." Beck began sliding along the booth.

"Let me out first," I called, trying to keep the panic out of my voice. "I need a drink. Anyone else?"

Everyone but Claudia was set, so they let me out and as I stood, Jake moved in. Looking up into his face was a big mistake. It made what Melissa had said hurt that much more.

He looked into my eyes and flinched, concern immediately puckering his brow at whatever he saw in me. His lips parted and I knew a question regarding my welfare was coming, so I hurried toward the bar and hoped he'd slide in next to his girl and forget all about me.

I leaned against the bar, trying to catch my breath and stem the shaking in my hands.

Every time I thought it couldn't get any worse, I got smacked in the face. Everything she said was enough to cut through me and finally put me in my place. She gave him peace. They didn't fight or argue over stupid shit. They were good. They were perfect together. She gave him peace.

She was his one.

And I just had to hope to God that Jake wasn't *my* one.

A warm body nudged into my side and I glanced up from the broken place I'd just been in to stare into Lowe's gorgeous face. He winced, a reaction fairly similar to what Jake's had been when he looked at me a minute ago. Lowe put an arm around my waist and tugged me into his side. "He's my friend and he's a great guy, but right now I could kill him."

I reared back a little, my gaze speculative. "What?"

"Charley, your poker face is slipping and he knows it. He saw it, the pain in your eyes after whatever the fuck Melissa said, and if that isn't enough to get him to stop being a selfish bastard and back off so you can move on, then I might have to hurt him. He wants you both. He can't have you both and needs to wake the fuck up and see that."

I tried to pull away from him, not wanting to discuss this with him, of all people. "I can handle it."

Lowe gripped me tighter, refusing to let me retreat into myself. "Sure. You're a tough badass."

"You know it," I muttered.

Lowe laughed softly and gave me a squeeze. "We go back to that table and you sit with me so I don't have to sit in between Sid and Nancy over there."

I chuckled, attempting to pull myself out of the tugging weight of heartache. "I don't need you to rescue me, Lowe."

"No, but I need you to rescue me from Claud and Beck."

"Fair enough."

I paid for the drinks and walked back to the table at Lowe's side. We slid into the booth and I leaned into him as he casually put his arm around me, turning to say something to Beck.

Glancing up quickly at Jake, I found him staring at me with that little pucker between his brows again. Bolstering myself, I gave him a carefree smile and shot it Melissa's way too. She looked relieved and snuggled into Jake's side.

Ignoring them, I laughed at Beck as he tried to steal a sip of Claudia's drink and got slapped for it. He smiled at her mischievously. "It's the closest you're going to get to my tongue, babe, so I'd let me have a drink."

Claudia made an affronted "ugh" sound at the back of her throat. "If I wanted your tongue, I could have your tongue. Put my drink down, you Neanderthal."

"A little overconfident in your charms, gorgeous."

My best friend threw her hands up in the air and turned to me. "Why am I letting him wind me up?"

I gestured helplessly, laughing. "I don't know. Why are you?"

She narrowed her eyes on Beck. "Maybe because he's been a broody asshole for the last two weeks but tonight he's himself again and I don't want to ruin that but if he doesn't put down my drink my stiletto is going through his foot."

Beck gave her an appeasing smile and slowly lowered her beer. "Let's not get crazy now."

Rolling my eyes I glanced up at Lowe and we shared a knowing look. Beck was in a good mood because Claudia had stopped dating the Scottish guy from the library. It was a good thing because she'd been fake enthusiastic about the whole thing for the past week, and the reason why was sitting next to her.

Beck and Claud needed to sort themselves out already.

I relaxed back into Lowe and asked him when the guys were playing next, happy to let an attractive, great-smelling guy do what he could to take my mind off Jake and his one and only.

Chapter Sixteen

Indiana, March 2009

Despite Brett's efforts to make both Jake and me persona non grata, Alex was too cool a guy to listen to petty slander. That's why when Alex invited Jake and me to his seventeenth birthday party, I told him we'd be there. Jake hadn't been certain we should go, but I was sick of the drama and didn't want my senior year to be as loaded with it as my junior year had been. Don't get me wrong—I would go through it all again to be with Jake, but that didn't mean dodging certain classmates and having to think up clever retorts when I couldn't dodge them wasn't a pain in the ass.

Things between Jake and Brett had only grown more strained when Doug Clare, one of Trenton's oldest friends and well-known Trenton follower, was arrested and charged not only for breaking and entering Logan Caplin's office but for vandalism and destruction of private property. Sheriff Muir knew that Trenton put Doug up to it, but without any evidence and Doug being idiot enough to take the fall for his friend, there was nothing Muir could do about Brett's father's involvement. This meant that Jake was always just seconds away from punching a smug, taunting Brett Thomas in the face. During the last few weeks, I'd used *a lot* of distraction techniques to make sure Jake kept his cool.

Alex promised me he'd had a quiet word with Brett and that he felt he'd finally gotten through to him. My ex wanted to make amends for the crap Jake and I had put up with; I just wanted Jake and his family to start feeling like Lanton was their home. So I dragged Jake to the party.

"I'm telling you," Jake sighed, taking my hand, "this is not a good idea."

I smiled at a classmate as we strode up the wide white timber-frame porch of Alex's home. His parents lived in a large house at the edge of Jake's neighborhood. A long drive led up to the five-bedroom house, and right now that drive was packed with cars. Alex's birthday had actually been a week ago but Mayor and Mr. Roster were vacationing in Cape Cod for their twentieth anniversary, so Alex had pounced on the opportunity to throw a kegger behind their backs. It was a bad idea, and I told him so. He grinned at me with boyish excitement, a look I knew, and a look there was no point arguing with.

"Jake, it'll be fine. We need this." I squeezed his hand as we walked into the packed house together. Hip-hop pounded throughout the ground floor, kids were dancing and drinking in the large living area, talking and drinking in the dining room and hallway, and bodies littered all the way up to the second floor.

"Hey, Jake!" Amanda Reyes stumbled to a stop in front of us, her cheeks flushed but her eyes focused. I noted the can of Red Bull in her hands. She wasn't drinking, which wasn't a surprise. Neither was her enthusiastic greeting toward Jake. Her crush had not waned one iota. I was surprised that she was at the party, however. Amanda wasn't really part of the social scene outside of school. It looked like she was trying to change that. Her eyes flicked to me and although they dimmed a little, she still gave me a smile. "Hey, Charley."

"Hey, Amanda," I answered.

"Amanda," Jake gave her a friendly nod and then walked around her, his hand still in mine. He did this every time she approached him. He was friendly but not too friendly, and when I was with him, he emphasized it by keeping me close. I got the impression her obvious crush made him a little uncomfortable.

I gave Amanda an awkward wave and her face fell as she watched Jake drag me away.

As soon as we were out of earshot, I pulled on Jake's arm. "Dude, we need to find her a guy."

Jake's eyes widened in agreement. "You think."

I laughed. "You should be flattered."

He tugged me closer to his side as we waited to get past a group of kids standing in the kitchen doorway. "I am. But every time she gives me those sad puppy eyes, I want to run a mile. Sad puppy eyes from a girl I know is bad enough, but from a girl I don't …" He shrugged as if to say "I don't know what to do with that."

"Charley, Jake, you came," Alex smiled as we entered the packed kitchen. He squeezed through to greet us at the door. "I wasn't sure you would."

I glanced over at his shoulder to see a very drunk Brett give us the stink-eye before he wrapped an arm around Lacey's neck and stumbled outside with her. Turning my attention back to Alex, I teased him. "And miss your birthday-slash-excuse to wreck your parents' house? How could we?"

He laughed. "Whatever. It'll all be good. They don't get back for another four days, so I've got plenty of time to clean up. I also roped a couple of sophomores into helping out with cleanup tomorrow."

Jake snorted. "How'd you manage that?"

Alex leaned into us. "I'm paying them fifty bucks each," he admitted, as if it were some genius secret.

"They're cleaning up a royal mess for a measly fifty bucks?" I said.

"Hey, these are desperate times," Alex laughed and then pointed to the counter to our right. "Lots of drink over there. Help yourselves. I am going to hunt down a certain senior who slipped her phone number in my ass pocket at school."

"Good luck with that."

He winked at me and brushed past us.

Once Jake and I had grabbed a couple of beers, he pulled me back out of the kitchen and out of the house to the porch where it was a little quieter. "So you and Alex seem good," he said, but I could see the question in his eyes.

Hoping this wasn't leading into a familiar fight, I leaned back against a pillar and replied casually, "We are. You know we are. It was weird at first for him, but he's over me."

Jake nodded into his beer. "I know I haven't always been a big fan of his because of Brett, but I think you might be right. The guy goes out of his way to be cool to me at school. I'm letting this shit with Thomas skew that."

"How about," I leaned into him, my fingers tangled in his shirt, "for tonight, we don't think about any of that?"

His eyes glittered and he nodded, bending down to brush his mouth over mine. I smiled happily into his face and settled back against the pillar.

"We met at a party like this."

"Six months ago."

I studied him in the low light, wondering how it was possible I'd only known him for six months. "That doesn't seem right somehow, does it? I can't remember what it feels like not to be with you."

"Ditto, baby." He took a pull of his beer, his affection focused on me. "This is it from now on. You and me. Sure you can handle that?"

"Well, it'll be a hardship, but what doesn't kill you only makes you stronger," I teased.

"Hardship, my ass." He wrapped an arm around my waist and pulled me into his body, grinning wickedly down at me.

"Oh, people I know!"

We turned as Lois McKinley zeroed in on us from across the porch, her beer spilling as she dragged her best friend Deke over to us. Lois was the editor of the school paper (and sick of hearing Lois Lane jokes) and Deke was her computer-geek sidekick.

"Hey, guys," I eyed Deke. "Not working at Hub's tonight?"

He shook his head,. "I swapped shifts. It's not every day you get invited to a party at Alex Roster's house."

Settling back against Jake, I nodded. "It does seem like the boy went all out inviting everyone."

"Alex is cool," Lois shrugged. "He's not like Brett and the others, you know, picking and choosing who's worthy enough to talk to." This was said with a slight hint of bitterness and resentment, something I understood since Brett and his idiot friends ragged on Lois on a weekly basis. She was short and somewhat voluptuous and showcased her curves in vintage fifties clothing. Her dark hair was always styled like a pinup girl's and she was never without bright red lipstick. I thought she was awesome, but some people just didn't get that Lois had a style and didn't care if you approved of it.

I grunted. "Alex's mom is going to freak if she comes home to find out about this party."

We stood chatting for a while, me with my back against Jake's chest, his chin in my hair as we drank and relaxed with Deke and

Lois. Deke was quiet but he was also smart and quick-witted and really fun to hang out with.

It was only about an hour later when Lois's phone rang. After watching Lois groan and whine for about five minutes in the corner, she finally got off the phone and grumbled that her mom had been called into work at the hospital and she needed Lois to return home to watch her younger brother. Deke was Lois's ride, so to our disappointment, the two of them left.

"They're cool." I turned around to face Jake once they were gone. "We should hang out with them more."

"Then we will." He gave my waist a squeeze. "Want another beer?"

"Sure."

Jake kissed my nose before taking my empty and disappearing back into the house. He wasn't gone but a few minutes when a drunk Lacey wandered out onto the porch, clearly looking for me. I braced myself.

"Charley," she weaved a little as she approached. "I've been looking for you."

"Oh?"

"I'm so, so sorry, Charley." She tripped a little and I had to steady her. "I've been such a bitch."

I didn't disagree.

"I want to make it up to you. Will you let me?" She leaned in too close and I could smell the apple sours on her breath.

"Lacey, how much have you had to drink?"

She put her finger and thumb together and scrunched up her face. "Just a little."

"I'm thinking you've had more than just a little. Come on, let's get you water."

Her tight grip on my wrist stunned me. "No," she said vehemently, her smile wobbly. "Just stay and chat."

I narrowed my eyes on her as I peeled her fingers off me. "I think water would be better."

"No!" she cried, trying to pull on me again. "Stay."

Suddenly, the blood was rushing in my ears as my heart started to race. "What ... are you stalling me?"

At her wide, blinking eyes and guilty expression, a sense of disquiet drifted over me.

Jake.

"Fuck," I breathed and pushed past her, shoving my way through bodies as I hurried toward the kitchen. The pounding in my chest only grew harder and faster when I saw a commotion around the French doors at the back of the kitchen. People were gawking outside, questioning what the hell was going on.

I bulldozed them, ignoring the yelps and complaints as I forced my way through and outside. The porch wrapped around the entire house and I had to push past the people standing on it, drinking and staring excitedly down on the backyard. As soon as I got past them, I could see why. The Rosters' backyard was split into three parts. At the bottom was a fountain and pond, reached by a pebbled pathway in the middle of landscaping. At the top, the porch steps led onto a wooden patio with a large family patio dining set on the right and a monster grill on the left. Standing near the grill, Jake had his back to me and swaying in front of him was Brett. Damien, Jackson, and a couple of their teammates stood behind Brett, and Alex was nowhere to be found. I could feel the hostility building between Brett and Jake from up on the steps.

My gut churned with unease as I hurried down toward Jake. Brett's eyes flicked to me, his lip curled in a sneer, and Jake looked over his shoulder, his eyes narrowing. "Charley, stay back," he warned, holding a hand up to me.

Something in his voice caught me and I stopped. Returning my gaze to Brett, I saw the light from the house glint off the object in his hand. "Brett, what are you doing?" I whispered, horrified.

He had a large kitchen knife.

"He's not going to do anything, Charley, he's just talking with your boy," Damien assured me with an arrogant smirk.

Brett laughed and stumbled with the movement.

I edged a little closer to Jake whose whole body was tense, ready to move if Brett got it into his dumb head to actually use his weapon. "I think he's a little too drunk to be handling a blade," I snapped at Damien. "Take it off him."

"Don't," Brett waved the knife in my direction and Jake moved, blocking me from his view. "Don't talk like I'm not fuckin' here. Shurrup. This is between me and your boy."

"What the hell is going on?" Alex pounded down the porch steps behind me, two of the seniors at his back. He stopped abruptly at my side when he saw Brett was waving a knife, his cheeks paling. "Brett, what are you doing? You're shitfaced. Give me the knife and stop being an idiot."

Brett's already rosy cheeks darkened. "I'm the idjit?" He took a step toward Jake, concentrating so that he didn't sway this time. "I'm not the one who let thish fucker take my girl. He ... he and his family'sh not welcome. Need to know it." He swung his arm at Jake and I lunged forward only to be hauled back by Alex.

My heart was in my throat as Jake jerked to the left, narrowly missing the knife edge. He backed up a few paces, his hands help up in placation. "Come on, Brett, you're wasted, man. You don't want to do this. Put the knife down." His words were calm, coaxing, but I could see the anger burning in his gaze.

"Pfft." Brett faltered again, his left arm spreading out for balance as his right one still pointed the kitchen knife at Jake. "You dessherve a cuttin'. Fucked nearly all the girlsh at thish party. Now you're fuckin' a prime piece like Charley. Not right. She ain't yoursh. This town ain't yoursh. Don't want fuckin' Caplinshes in our town. We'll get you out." He grinned, an uncontrolled leer. "Then I'll get your girl on her back and show her how real men fuck."

Alex's fingers bit into my arms at Brett's crude taunt. The anger I felt brewing from him was unfortunately already at the boiling point for Jake. I shook my head, not wanting to distract him by speaking, but willing him to remain calm, to not let Brett rile him.

Even in his drunken stupor, Brett caught the rage in Jake's face. He laughed. "Yeah, that cut deep, knowing ash shoon ash you're gone, I'm puttin' my dick in that—"

"Brett, shut the fuck up!" Alex shouted, pushing me behind him as he took a furious step toward his friend.

"—and she'll love every minute." Brett ignored Alex and finished off by springing at Jake again, his right arm swinging upward as he tried to slash him from stomach to chest.

I whimpered, every part of me desperate to stop him but knowing anything I did might make it worse.

Jake slid back on the balls of his feet, dodging the cut, and then he moved too fast for a drunk Brett to compute. He tripped to the side away from Jake, shaking his head, and I watched the muscles bunch in his shoulders with anger as he stupidly and devoid of coordination swung around and ran at Jake. Jake sidestepped him again, making sure he was moving away from Damien and Brett's other idiots.

Brett couldn't slow his momentum.

He fell over his own feet, crashing awkwardly onto the patio floor, face planting against it.

Everyone was silent as we waited tensely for his next move.

But he didn't move. Instead he elicited this strange, muffled whine.

I knew the moment we all realized something was wrong. I felt the shift in the air, the breathless waiting.

"Brett," Damien said, laughing hollowly, "come on, man, get up." He strode over to him and bent down, gently pushing Brett over.

People cried out behind me and I heard the guys cursing. Brett stared up at Damien, fear in his eyes, and then he dropped his gaze to the knife lodged in his ribs. "Get it out, man," he cried hoarsely, tears in his voice, his trembling hands reaching for the blade.

"No!" I shouted, rushing toward him. "Don't let him pull it ou—"

But it was too late.

Brett yanked out the blade and blood soaked his shirt.

I fell to my knees beside him, ripping off my light jacket and bundling it into a ball I pressed against his wound. He gave a pained grunt but I held it there, keeping pressure on it. Shaking, I shot a command at a pale, trembling Damien. "Call 911!"

He didn't move, frozen with shock.

I glanced back over my shoulder at Alex who stared down at his friend in horrified disbelief. My eyes flicked to Jake whose hands were in his hair, desolation written all over him. "Jake, call 911!"

He looked like he wanted to puke but he pulled himself together enough to take out his cell.

"Char ..."

I turned back to look down at Brett, his terrified eyes on mine, tears sliding down his cheeks. Swallowing hard, I forced my voice to stay calm. "You're going to be okay. You're going to be fine."

Warmth touched my fingertips and my attention fell on my jacket. The blood was soaking through it, the bitter tang of copper making me breathless. His body began to shudder hard beneath my touch and he coughed, little flecks of blood spraying out from between his lips.

"No," I whispered, panicked adrenaline tightening my chest. Not only was he going into shock but I had the dire suspicion that he'd punctured a lung. "Guys, he's going into shock." Looking up at his friends I told them fiercely, "We can't let him. We need to keep him warm. We need blankets. Give me your jackets now."

His friends fumbled with their clothes as Jake murmured that the ambulance was on its way.

I heard Alex tell me he'd find blankets. I heard crying and gasps and questions and fear and horror settle in behind me. I ignored it, bowing my head toward Brett, feeling helpless as he shuddered and choked, his eyes begging for help.

The guys tucked their jackets around Brett and Jackson pulled off his T-shirt and handed it to me. I balled it up and quickly replaced my soaked jacket.

Although it tore me up inside to meet Brett's gaze, I had to. He pleaded with me. *Pleaded.*

"We'll get you taken care of Brett. Okay, we'll get you fixed up." On my peripheral I saw Damien tuck his jacket around Brett's sides. "Yeah," I whispered numbly. "Keep him warm."

Suddenly Brett's choked sounds drew quieter to a wheeze. Then to a stutter.

"No," I shook my head, applying more pressure, "Brett, stay with me. The ambulance is almost here, buddy."

His eyes were wide as they stared into mine and I knew that no matter what I said, he just couldn't hold on. The shuddering faltered ...

His body relaxed.

His breath ... stopped.

The panic was gone from his eyes.

In its place was nothing.

"I've got the blankets!" Alex shouted, his footsteps smacking against the wood as he hurried toward us.

I fell back on my heels, my blood-soaked hands unsteady. I felt like I was in a nightmare. The darkness pressed down on me as I turned to look up at Alex.

His mouth fell open at my expression, his eyes darting to his friend, before coming back to me, questioning me through a shimmer of tears.

I shook my head, the tears blurring my vision. "He's gone."

"Will you tell him I'm asking for him?"

Mrs. C. nodded at me, her expression sympathetic. "I will, Charley."

Feeling as though I was wading through water thick with mud, I walked back to my car. For a moment I stared up at the Caplin house, hoping that the front door would open and Jake would come out before I pulled away.

The engine of the car purred to life.

No Jake.

My reverse lights came on.

Still no Jake.

The car backed up onto the street.

Not even a twitch of a curtain.

Feeling sick, I pulled away, noting the police car sitting just around the corner. Was that for the Caplins? Worry bit at me the entire drive home, and when I eventually pulled my mom's car into the drive, I couldn't remember how I got there.

Two nights ago, on an ordinary Friday night, at an ordinary high school party, Brett Thomas lost his life. My classmate. A sixteen-year-old kid. He bled out under my hands from a self-inflicted knife wound that punctured his lung. He might have survived long enough for the ambulance to make it if his body hadn't gone into shock.

I wanted to blame someone. I wanted to blame Brett for being a complete moron, or his dad for raising a complete moron and then encouraging him to be the king of morons. But there was too much blame already flying around, and since my boyfriend was a target of that blame, I was kind of sick of the whole verb.

The wee hours of Saturday morning were a blur. We all existed in a fog of unreality as those of us who witnessed the attack were taken to the police station. To my surprise, Amanda Reyes had been there to witness it all. I hadn't even noticed her. Thank God she was, though. She was one of only a handful of extremely credible witnesses since there were only a handful of sober kids at that party. Good thing too she was on Jake's side.

Damien and Jackson heaped all fault on Jake, maintaining that Jake hit Brett and he went down on the knife. Alex, Amanda, the seniors, and I told the truth, and when Sheriff Muir asked Damien and Jackson to repeat their witness accounts, they admitted that in the end, Brett tripped over his feet. Still, they irrationally maintained that Jake was responsible.

Jake was detained longer than any of us, but from our witness accounts and those of the students on the porch, along with the results of Brett's blood alcohol level, word reached me on Sunday that Sheriff Muir wasn't pressing charges, and that the case was more than likely going to be closed as an accidental death.

Trenton Thomas had been loaded ever since Saturday, telling anyone who would listen that it was all the Caplins' fault. It didn't help that Trenton's own brother-in-law advised the likelihood of prosecution was minimal because of the lack of evidence against Jake. Now that Muir was near to closing the case and no one had been arrested (i.e., Jake), I knew the sheriff and his deputies were on alert for Trenton's reaction. That's why they had a car outside Jake's home.

I looked down at my hands on the steering wheel and an image of them bloody flashed before me. Clenching them around the wheel, I drew in a deep breath and slowly exhaled.

My dad was waiting for me as soon as I walked inside. "How is he?" he asked, his face pinched with concern.

I shook my head. "He won't see me."

In the aftermath, Jake had frozen me out. He wouldn't talk at the station, which I put down to shock, but that Saturday afternoon my calls and texts went unanswered. I'd tried calling his house but his dad said Jake was sleeping. Finally, going out of my mind with worry for him, I decided to pay him visit.

Mrs. C. wouldn't let me in the door. Jake wasn't up to a visitor.

A visitor? I wasn't a freaking visitor!

But nope. He didn't want to see me.

Patience. I just needed to be patient. What had happened to Jake, the position he'd been put in, was absolutely awful, and I knew Jake. I knew that right now, he was in his room blaming himself for what happened. That thought caused a splinter in my chest, and all I wanted was to go to him and make sure he knew that no one else believed that.

Of course, with the exception of Trenton Thomas, but that guy was an asshole.

An asshole who'd lost his son.

I slumped, shaking my head. No one, not even an asshole like Thomas, deserved to go through that kind of pain.

Whatever my dad saw in my eyes, it had him hurrying across the room to pull me into a tight hug. I held onto him, shaking but forcing myself not to break down. My mom stood in the kitchen doorway, her sad, glittering eyes telling me she loved me and that it would all be okay.

Pulling back from Dad, I sighed. "I should maybe go to bed."

"Your sister has been waiting on Skype for you. You want to talk to her?" Dad asked.

I nodded, feeling a little crack appear in my armor. It sucked that Andie wasn't here. It had been a long time since I really needed a hug from my big sister.

The laptop was waiting for me in the dining room and I slid into the chair at the head of the table. After sending her an invite, her face popped up on screen.

"Hey, Supergirl," she greeted me sadly, "how are you?"

I shrugged, holding it together.

"Oh, sweetie," Andie leaned closer, "do you need me to come home?"

"No," I shook my head. "Don't ruin your trip. I'm fine. I'm just worried about Jake."

Andie grimaced. "Poor kid. He's going through a lot."

"He won't answer my calls, Andie. I haven't spoken to him since Friday night. I don't know what to do."

"Give him time. I imagine he's in a pretty dark place right now. And don't feel bad that he's not letting you in. Sometimes people just need alone time. No matter how much you love someone, you can't always be what they need in that moment."

Grasping onto that, I whispered, "You think?"

"Yes, sweetie, I do." Her brows puckered together as she searched my face. "Now what about you? How are you handling it? Mom told me you were there. That you tried to help Brett."

His eyes were imprinted on my brain.

My lips trembled, this feeling building up from my chest, this pressure, a need to let it blow out like a massive gust of wind. "I felt so helpless," my voice cracked on the last word, my eyes dropping. "He was so scared and he was just looking at me, silently pleading with me to do something." The sobs burst forth, my shoulders shaking, my ribs rattling. "I can't get it out of my head."

"Ssshh, sweetie, it's okay."

I shook my head, unable to see her through the tears. "It's not. It's not. I tried to help and then he was gone and … and," I took a shuddering breath, "I kept thinking 'I'm so glad it wasn't Jake.'"

I jolted a little at the feel of my dad's strong arm encircling my shoulders, pulling me back against him. His lips brushed my forehead and I sagged against him, crying harder than I ever remember crying.

Staring at the tributes placed at the foot of Brett's locker, I barely heard the bell ring. Shell-shocked students pushed past as they hurried to get to class while I remained frozen on the spot.

Brett's funeral was to be held on Thursday.

I shook myself, looking around as the halls started to empty. Since stepping foot on school grounds that morning, I'd felt alone. I saw that Lacey's eyes were red from crying, but not once did they settle on me. She was ashamed. Probably feeling guilty for her part in it. If we'd been friends, I would've told her to learn from it, to not let it eat at her, to let it help her grow the heck up. But we weren't friends. Her boyfriend was dead. All it would've taken was a small twist of chance and it might've been Jake everyone was grieving for.

I couldn't bear the thought of it.

Jake wasn't in school; neither was Lukas. They were probably waiting for the flames to die down.

When I walked into school, to my surprise it was a quiet Alex who kept me company. From him I'd discovered that Trenton

Thomas had been arrested for disturbing the peace outside of Jake's house last night. Luckily that cruiser had been sitting there and they took him in before he could do much damage. As soon as Alex told me, I sent a text to Jake asking if he was okay.

It was past lunchtime now and still I'd heard nothing back.

Alex and I had sat in the cafeteria by ourselves, not talking but keeping each other company nonetheless. There was no Alex now. He wasn't in my next class or the one after.

Screw this, I thought.

My feet took me out of the school, out the gates, through town, and forty-five minutes later, I was at Jake's.

The sight of Mrs. C. on her knees, yellow rubber gloves on, scrubbing at the porch, made me slow to a halt, annoyance and frustration ripping through me. My eyes washed over the porch, catching sight of dried yoke and eggshells.

Mrs. C. glanced up at me, her eyes tired. "Why aren't you in school, Charley?"

I shrugged and then gestured to their house. "You okay?"

"It's the second time it's happened since we moved here." She sat back on her heels, her mouth tight.

"There are a couple of idiots in this town, Mrs. C. You just have to ignore them." I knew that was easy for me to say. My house hadn't just gotten egged. "Can I help?"

She shook her head. "Not with this."

"With Jake, then?"

Mrs. C. ripped off her rubber glove and ran a shaky hand through her dark hair. "He says he doesn't want to see anyone, but frankly, I'm just so past the point of worried right now … I think you should go up. See if you can get him to talk."

I nodded. "I'll try."

The music throbbing from his room meant that he probably didn't hear me climb the stairs or cross the hallway. When I pushed his door open, my gaze zeroed in on him lying on his bed, his hands behind his head as he stared at the ceiling, listening to some screaming band he'd never shared with me.

Thank God, because they sucked.

He lowered his gaze and the breath was knocked out of me at the emptiness in his eyes. "I don't want to talk to anyone," he told me flatly, returning his focus to the ceiling.

I'd never encountered this Jake. If we were mad at each other, we were loud about it. This emotionless robot scared the crap out of me.

But for him, I'd be brave.

As I shrugged out of my jacket, I kicked off my shoes. Quietly I crossed the room and lay down beside him, careful not to touch him. My own eyes met the ceiling.

"You don't have to talk," I promised him. And he didn't. All I wanted was to remind him that he wasn't alone. That he had me if he needed me.

My hope was that eventually he might say something, but I met my match in Jacob Caplin because he kept his mouth zipped for two and a half hours, replaying the screaming band until my ears almost started bleeding. Finally my mom called and I had to admit defeat for the day and go home.

"I have to go." I leaned over and pressed a soft kiss to the corner of his mouth, but he didn't move, didn't even flinch. I held my sigh in and got up. "When you're ready, I'm here. I love you, Jake."

For the first time ... he didn't say it back.

Chapter Seventeen

Chicago, December 2012

O'Hare was filled with that high-level hum of conversation, just a mishmash of chatter that if you let it in it could make your head throb. Melissa was the last to grab her suitcase but finally it circled around on the baggage carousel and I could feel the guys breathe a deep sigh of relief with me. We'd just flown from Edinburgh to London, London to Chicago, and all together our traveling time (including waiting around at Heathrow for our flight) was around twelve hours. Jake, Melissa, Beck, Lowe, Matt, and I were exhausted and there was nothing more irritating than a baggage carousel when you were exhausted.

Now we were moving through the airport toward the pickup point where I knew my dad was waiting for me. He was supposed to be waiting for both me and Claudia, but a week before our flight home for Christmas vacation, she got a phone call from her mom, Rafaela, to tell her they were hosting a huge Christmas party this year and she'd need Claudia to stay out of the way of preparations when she got home. It had never occurred to Rafaela Jenkins that her daughter didn't actually spend lonely Christmases at home, so when she discovered Claud wasn't going to be there, she got pissed and started speaking in rapid-fire Portuguese (which Claudia didn't understand since her mother had never taken the time to teach her).

In the end, she demanded—in English—that Claudia be there.

Claudia was mad that she wasn't going to be spending her Christmas vacation with the Redfords and I have to say, I was disappointed too. The two of us were so used to being in each other's space all the time, it was kind of like missing an arm when she wasn't there. However, underneath it all, I think my best friend was secretly pleased that her mother was adamant she be home. It meant she was actually taking notice of her.

"I had to hit a whole other continent for her to notice me, but whatever," Claudia said, smirking.

Although I'd miss Claud for the next three and a half weeks, I *was* looking forward to some distance from the Jake-and-Melissa show. Because of them, my head was in a weird, messy place and I knew my family would recognize it right away. This pretty much blew since I didn't want anything marring our reunion.

The six of us strolled outside bundled up in jackets and scarves. I smiled as the cold wind hit my face. It was pretty mild, actually, for December in Chicago. No snow yet. It was warmer here than what we'd left behind in Scotland. The guys were talking about meeting up to do a gig the day before Christmas Eve, but I was too busy bobbing my head, trying to see past people to find my dad. I had no clue what they were saying beyond that.

And then I saw him and my face split into a huge grin.

Leaning against the hood of his SUV, my dad watched the crowds with focus. My dad was in his mid-forties and as my mom often noted in a dreamy voice that cracked me up, he was the kind of man who only grew more handsome with age. He had little sprinklings of gray in the sides of his dark brown hair, hair I often bemoaned that I didn't inherit. Andie got his hair and his eyes. I got his eyes, but Mom's hair. I didn't know why the genetics god couldn't have gone all out and given me my mom's gorgeous pale blue eyes as well.

Damn you, genetics god, damn you.

Seeing Jim Redford waiting for me filled my chest with warmth. He never went to college, and neither did Mom, but they worked it out and did well for themselves in our small town. I was proud of my parents. I was proud to walk through a crowd of people at an airport knowing that the handsome middle-aged man leaning against the hood of his SUV was my dad and that he loved me.

It hadn't taken Thanksgiving with my new friends, listening to them talk about their mixed backgrounds, for me to realize how lucky I was to have been raised by Jim and Delia Redford. No. All it had taken was a glimpse into Claudia's world, growing up in Coronado with parents who lived on inherited wealth and spent their lives dashing around the world and ignoring their only child, for me to realize what I had at home.

Pretty freaking great parents.

My dad's eyes came to a rest on me and he beamed huge when he saw me, standing up off his car. I waved as he started toward me.

"That's me, guys. I'll see you back in Edinburgh."

Lowe pulled me into a hug, and I ended up getting my ribs squeezed by him, Beck, and Matt. Jake and Melissa received an awkward wave instead of a hug.

When I turned around, Dad was right there. "Dad," I said. I threw my arms around him, something I hadn't done in a long while. He lifted me off the ground in a bear hug.

"Hey, Supergirl," he murmured softly as he gently set me down.

Thickness suddenly developed in my throat and I swallowed it, surprised by the emotion. I don't know why I bothered. It was a perfectly acceptable reaction considering I'd been gone for three months, the longest time I'd ever been separated from my parents.

My dad glanced over my shoulder and I turned to see he was looking curiously at Lowe. "Dad, these are my friends. They go to Northwestern. This is Lowe."

"Hey, Mr. Redford," Lowe greeted congenially and held out a hand.

My dad smiled and gave him a firm handshake. "Nice to meet you."

I introduced Beck and Matt who shook my dad's hand with respectful hellos.

The friendly, warm atmosphere plummeted to below freezing when Dad turned to greet the next person in line. His whole body tensed with recognition.

"Uh, you remember Jake, Dad. And this is his girlfriend, Melissa."

Dad actually flinched at the introduction, his eyes narrowed on Jake, moving from him to Melissa before slicing back to me with a look so incredulous, he didn't even have to say "are you nuts?"

"Mr. Redford." Jake stepped forward and held out a hand. A peace offering. An olive branch.

The look my dad bestowed upon him could've shriveled even the biggest badass's smile. With a grunt of disgust he spun around, grabbed my suitcase, and started to walk away. "Let's go, Charley."

Awkward.

I didn't know where to look.

"Dude," Matt laughed quietly, "I thought he was going to smack you."

"I was kind of hoping he would," Lowe muttered. Shooting Lowe a look that clearly told him to put a sock in it, I was merely rewarded with a smile. "Your dad rocks."

However, my choked laughter quickly vanished when my eyes met Jake's. He looked ashamed, and, worse, lost. There wasn't anything funny about that. Dad's attitude had told Jake one thing I hadn't told him—just how badly his leaving had affected me. So badly that Jim Redford, a man who had eventually welcomed Jake into his home and treated him like a son, could barely stand the sight of him.

"Charlotte!"

Exhaling through the sudden tightness in my chest, I gave my friends a wave. "Bye, guys. Have a great Christmas."

"You too, babe," Lowe stepped forward and pressed a soft kiss to my forehead. When I lifted my eyes to smile at him, he winked, making me feel not so lost. Grateful, I squeezed his hand and then spun around quickly, darting through the crowd toward my dad and away from Jake.

There was no snow to drive through and Dad said he'd made the trip in just under two hours. Two hours in the car with a dad you hadn't seen in three months should've been a breeze. We had lots to catch up on, but after the Jake encounter, Dad was quiet. Tense and quiet.

"How's Mom?" I finally asked, fed up with the silence. I was tired enough I could close my eyes and go to sleep, but I'd just gotten home. I wanted to chat with my dad.

Dad's hands clenched around the steering wheel. "I can't believe he had the audacity to offer me his hand."

I sighed. Really, this shouldn't surprise me. Dad was a stewer—he stewed until he was ready to vent. It had taken him twenty minutes of stewing to get to the venting part. Damn. I really should've closed my eyes. "Dad—"

"I didn't agree with him being back in your life but your mom told me to leave it, that you were a grown-up and could make your own decisions ... but to see him standing there, and with his arms around another girl right in front of you."

"Dad—"

"No, Charley." He shook his head, his brow wrinkled with deep furrows. "I'm a realist, okay. Most sixteen-year-olds aren't going to end up with the person they're dating in high school. That's reality. Most of it is puppy love or temporary love or just plain old lust. But I watched you two together and I thought, well, they're just like me and Delia."

He'd never admitted that to me before.

Pain cut through me and I looked out the passenger window, trying to control the emotion.

"I was like Jake in high school. Ask your mom. I had a bit of a rep for fooling around with a lot of girls and yeah, I know you don't want to hear that, but it's the truth. Then I came home after one summer at my grandma's in Virginia and I walked into class and there was Delia. Sitting on her desk, feet on her chair, laughing her ass off at something her girlfriend was saying. As I approached she turned her head to smile at me, and I swear to God, that smile ... it knocked me on my ass. I don't know why I never noticed her before, but there she was and I couldn't take my eyes off her. I was a goner." He sighed. "First time I saw Jake smile at you, I thought, hell, here we go again. And because of that I saw myself in him and I began to trust him with you. And I'm not stupid. I know he took *everything* from you—"

"Oh, God, Dad ..." I groaned, mortified.

"—but I thought to myself, these kids are forever. I let myself care about that son of a bitch. I was cut up for him over what happened to Brett. Then he broke my little girl. Stomped all over what she gave him. Now he's back offering me his hand as he willfully messes with your head. Flaunting another girl in front of you. I ought to swing this car around and kill him."

Somehow I managed to keep calm as I looked back at him. "Dad, I have to move past it."

"Move past it ..." He glanced at me, still furious. "He wasn't there. He didn't watch his little girl—the strongest, bravest kid I've ever met—cry for days when he left and then just go numb. I remember it was months before I heard you laugh again. And even then, we never got you back the way you were. With what happened to Brett and then Jake taking away so much, you grew this look, this cynical little look in your eye no kid your age should have."

I shuddered, wrapping my arms around my stomach. "Dad, don't."

"I'm saying this now and then we're done talking about it." He shot me a hard look. "Letting this boy back in your life is a mistake. Fix it before he breaks you again."

Every year a six-foot Christmas tree took pride of place in front of the sitting room window. Pale white lights glittered over every branch. Metallic strings of red and silver wove from branch to branch like scalloped lace. You could tell which gifts Mom had wrapped because they matched the tree. And even though we were twenty and twenty-four years old, stockings hung from the mantel for Andie and me. To my delight, this year a third stocking hung in the middle with Rick's name on it.

I had to admit it I almost peed my pants laughing upon discovering my mom had sewn his name on and hung a stocking for a thirty-four-year-old police detective.

Apparently Rick had graciously thanked her, his mouth twitching with laughter. Andie had had to leave the room so she wouldn't embarrass Mom by collapsing into a fit of giggles.

I wasn't nearly as considerate.

Mom didn't even flinch. She just couldn't see what was wrong with mothering a man who was only ten years her junior.

"So did you try haggis?" Rick asked, sipping at his hot cocoa. Mom had made cocoa for all us of and we were snuggled up warm in the sitting room. It was Christmas Eve, the fire roaring, the light darkening in the early afternoon sky. The five of us were relaxing and just enjoying being together. Rick was raised by his single mother—he'd never met his father—but she passed five years ago. He'd gotten a Christmas vacation this year and was spending the whole time with Andie and us. We wouldn't have it any other way.

I was lying with my back pressed against the bottom of Dad's armchair, my legs stretched out alongside the fire. I sipped my cocoa and nodded. "Yeah, it wasn't as bad as you'd think, but it's hard to fully enjoy something when you know it's encased inside sheep stomach."

Andie made a gagging noise. "I can't believe you tried it." She frowned. "No, wait, scratch that. It's you. Of course you tried it."

"I also tried a deep-fried Mars bar. I'm ashamed to admit I tried it a couple of times."

"That's revolting," Mom huffed. "You told me you were eating well."

"At least I'm eating."

That garnered a grunt.

"I hope you aren't drinking too much with you being legal over there?" Dad asked, pulling gently on my ponytail.

I craned my neck to grin up at him. "Would I overimbibe just because of a legality?"

"Yes."

Laughing, I turned back around, my expression mischievous as I shared a look with Andie. "I've hardly touched a drop, Dad."

"Don't lie to your father, Charlotte, it's beneath you," Mom teased.

"Then don't ask questions you're not going to like the answer to."

"She's got you there, folks," Rick murmured, smiling into his mug.

Mom used Rick's input to turn the conversation to grandbabies (Mom could somehow manage to turn any conversation to grandbabies) and my phone buzzed, distracting me.

A text from Jake.

Supergirl is on the television. Made me think of you. Hope you're having a nice time at home.

There was something placating in his text. Usually he teased me or cracked a joke, starting a battle of wits. I wondered if he was still stinging from Dad's cut, and then I wondered why I felt bad about that. Feeling too hot all of a sudden, I got up and wandered into the kitchen. Leaning against the cool countertops I stared at my phone, trying to decide whether to answer him.

"Was that Jake?"

I jerked my head over my shoulder in surprise, unaware that Andie had followed me. "Yeah."

My big sister's lips pinched together. "You look miserable. I mean, you're putting on a good front but we all see it."

Honestly, I was sick of everyone telling me what it was I was feeling. I was sick of everyone reminding me of what Jake had done and how I'd reacted. It was hard enough attempting to wade through my own emotions without having to bear the weight of my family's feelings regarding Jake too. "Maybe I'd be okay if everyone would stop going on about my relationship with Jake like it was this epic thing."

"It was. It is." Andie took a determined step forward. "You know it was. That's why you're hurting so much. Please don't rewrite history in order to accommodate him in your life again. Look, it's obvious Jake cares about you still or he wouldn't be so adamant about remaining in your life. But he has to know how selfish it is of him to put you through this. So ask yourself if that's a friend worth keeping."

What she said was scarily similar to what Lowe had said and I immediately felt a headache coming on. "I'm going for a walk." I strode toward the kitchen door, shoving my feet in my boots. "Will you let Mom and Dad know? I've got my cell."

Andie nodded. "Yeah, sweetie. Take all the time you need."

I left the house, taking in deep breaths of crisp air. My feet really did the thinking and before I knew it, I was standing in the empty parking lot of the high school.

All around me was silence but in my head, I could hear the hum of chatter, the shouts, the laughter. In front of me was just a parking space but in my head was a crowd standing around a figure curled up on the ground ...

Chapter Eighteen

Indiana, March 2009

It was Wednesday, the day before Brett's funeral.

Still no word from Jake.

Although Lukas had returned to school, Jake was still not in attendance. I'd gotten a sympathetic nod from Lukas at the main entrance yesterday morning but he'd disappeared when I'd approached to ask after Jake.

I felt like a leper and the only one brave enough to be around me was Alex.

Today, however, there was a tension among all the students. The pall that had cloaked the school on Monday was back as Brett's funeral approached, and honestly I just couldn't be around it. All it did was give me flashbacks to pleading eyes and bloody hands.

Not exactly feeling like an exemplary student these days, I'd decided to head out of school grounds for lunch and drop by my mom's store. I needed a friendly face. So Mom it was.

As soon as I stepped out the front entrance to the school, I heard the commotion. My eyes darted across the parking lot, following the sounds. I saw a small crowd had gathered around something. I was going to ignore it, but then I saw Damien's hardened face appear in the center as he stared down at something or someone on the ground. When I saw that Jackson was with him, instinct told me what was going on.

Fury fuelled me as I dropped my backpack and tore down the stairs and across the lot, shoving people hard out of my way, my eyes dipping to the ground to see Lukas in a fetal position on the ground, bleeding.

"You asshole!" I screamed, shoving Damien back with all my might.

It sent him stumbling into Jackson. I stepped around Lukas, putting myself in front of him.

"Get out of the way, Charley," Damien hissed. "This has nothing to do with you."

"You want him, you go through me." I beat a hand against my chest.

He narrowed his eyes.

"Come on, Damien!" I cried disdainfully. "You can beat up a freshman, two juniors against one freshman kid, but you won't lift a hand against a girl? That's a fucked-up set of principles."

"I won't warn you again. Move, Charley."

"You want Lukas? You're going to have to hit me to get to him."

"Charley, don't," Lukas grunted, and I felt movement behind me as he tried to sit up.

"Move out of the way, Charlotte," Damien took a step toward me, "or I will make you move."

"Dude," Jackson didn't seem so sure, putting a hand out to stop him.

Damien shook him off. "She's on their side. Brett's dead, her boyfriend saw to that, and this kid is smart-mouthing us about it and she's trying to protect them both. She's a traitor to this town. She deserves what she gets." He moved toward Lukas as Lukas stood but I pushed Jake's brother behind me, jutting my chin out in determination.

"I mean it, Damien," I warned him. "You'll have to fight me first before I let you touch Luke. And I fight dirty."

"Bring it."

I braced myself, ready to take a beating so Lukas wouldn't have to.

In the end I didn't have to either because suddenly Alex was there, fury on his face as he shoved Damien away from me. "Are you crazy!" he shouted, pushing him harder.

Damien stumbled, shock and betrayal in his eyes. "They killed Brett, man."

"Fuck you, Damien. I was there. So were you. Brett fell on his own knife. It's not Jake's fault and it's definitely not Lukas's and," he dropped his head, getting in Damien's face, "it's definitely not Charley's. She tried to save his life, remember? I swear to God, if I ever see you come at her again, I will kill you."

The two friends started to argue in quiet voices so I turned to Lukas, cradling his left side. His nose was bleeding and his right eye was swollen shut.

The anger caught in my throat again and I glanced up across the parking lot to the security cameras. Those bastards were going down. Without saying a word, I grabbed Lukas's bag and held his arm, gently asking him to follow me. He did, his head bowed in humiliation.

"You have nothing to feel embarrassed about, Luke. They're bigger and older than you and it was two against one. They're the pathetic ones."

"Where are we going?" he sucked in his breath as he tripped on the curb. I winced in sympathy.

"To see Sheriff Muir."

"Uh, why?" he stopped.

"Because if we report it to the school, the likelihood is that Coach will try and talk the principal into letting Damien and Jackson get away with it. I tell Sheriff Muir and also give him the heads-up that the school security cameras caught the whole thing, he'll make sure Principal Watts does something about it."

"It's fine, Charley."

"It's not fine, Lukas," I snapped. "Jake gets dragged through the mud and he's completely innocent while those assholes are the biggest bullies I've ever seen and they get away with it. Even now … Brett is the one who pulled the knife. It's tragic what happened but he did it to himself. Not Jake. And I won't have Damien and Trenton Thomas try to say any different, or bullying people into believing different. Not in my town."

Luke cocked his head to the side, giving me a small, weary smile. "You're hot when you're mad, Charley Redford."

Affection and tenderness and anger for what had been done to him warred within me. "I'm sorry that they did this to you, Luke."

He winced and hobbled beside me. "Don't. You've got nothing to be sorry for. You're, like, one of the best people I know."

And that just made me want to go back and smash Damien's face into the ground.

Instead I settled for getting Lukas to the station. Sheriff Muir took our statements and called Mr. C. out. I insisted on going with them to the nearest hospital a half hour outside Lanton. The doctor had just finished telling us that Luke had probably fractured a rib or two when I felt him enter the room.

I turned, my breath catching as Jake strode in with his mom, his hard eyes on Luke. They flickered to me for a second before moving quickly back to his little brother.

As he took in the mess of Luke, Jake's fists curled around the foot of the hospital bed.

Mr. C. saw. He shook his head at his eldest. "Don't even think about doing anything stupid. Charley saw to it that those boys will pay for attacking your brother. Don't make your situation worse by demanding your own retribution."

"They can't get away with this, Dad. They should leave us alone."

"They won't get away with this. I told you Charley saw to it."

"She was awesome," Luke grinned up at Jake, his eye now completely swollen shut. "She jumped in front of me and told them that if they wanted me, they had to go through her. If it hadn't been so emasculating, it would've been hot."

I smirked at him. "It wasn't emasculating."

"Dude."

I took that to mean he disagreed.

Jake's head whipped to me and I flinched at the blaze in his eyes. "You were going to take a beating?"

"I knew they wouldn't hit me."

"Uh, I don't know. I think Damien definitely would've swung for you if Alex hadn't stopped him," Luke grimaced.

The muscle ticked in Jake's jaw, a sure sign he was ready to lose it.

Jake kept silent as the doctor finished up with Lukas. It wasn't until we were out in the hospital parking lot that Jake finally spoke. "Can you guys wait in the car? I need to talk to Charley."

His family nodded hesitantly and slowly walked away, shooting us concerned looks over their shoulders.

Feeling ill, I glanced up at Jake. He gestured for me to follow him. We moved far away from the entrance, giving us a modicum of privacy.

"I know you're mad at me," I started, "but—"

"Just be quiet, Charley." He sighed, his expression blank again.

I tried to swallow my annoyance over his tone, over his attitude, but I couldn't. "Jake, I know you're going through a lot but I would really appreciate it if you'd stop speaking to me like that. And stop shutting me out," I hissed.

"Our front window got smashed in yesterday," he answered flatly. "Our phone keeps ringing and then the callers hang up. Trenton and his goons are getting restless," he muttered.

I closed my eyes, resenting Trenton. The man was going through a lot, but he did it mostly to himself. "Jake, I'm sorry. But it's just Trenton. Everyone else knows you didn't attack Brett. They know it was an accident."

"I should've walked away, called his bluff." He shook his head, his eyes hollow. "He died because I wasn't smart enough to walk away from a drunk. I didn't put the knife in him but I've still got blood on my hands."

"Jake, he swung at you. If you'd walked away, turned your back, he was drunk enough ... he might have hurt you ..." I reached for his hand and squeezed it but he gave me nothing back. "We'll get through this."

He stared silently at me in answer and I felt that horrific weight settle in my stomach again.

"Jake?"

"I have to get through this on my own."

"What?"

"I can't do it with you around me."

I shook my head, panic pressing down on my chest. "Are you ... breaking up with me?"

He looked away, unable to meet me eyes as he replied, "Yeah. I'm breaking up with you."

I couldn't catch my breath. "And everything between us ... everything you promised ... that's just gone?"

He tensed and then shook his head. "I'm not sticking around to listen to this."

"Don't walk away from me!" I cried, anger thankfully breaking the panic into pieces. "You owe me!"

And suddenly the fury was back in his face when he stopped and whirled to face me. "I owe you? I owe you? I played a part in a kid's death. Do you know how fucked up that is? How fucked up I feel right now? Can you think of someone other than yourself for just a second?"

"I am!" I argued. "I've been thinking about you constantly for days. I've been worrying nonstop. All I want is to help you. I don't understand why this is my fault?"

"I told you we shouldn't have gone to that party." He was back to unbridled anger again. "We should never have been there and none of this should ever have happened."

I felt like he'd punched me. "So you blame me?"

"No," he grew quiet, "I'm just done." Jake turned to leave me again and I ran after him, yanking on his arm.

"Don't," I growled up into his face, feeling a pain and ire I'd never felt in my life. "Don't you walk away from me like I don't deserve better than 'I'm just done.' You promised me!" I pushed him and he took it, stumbling back. "I gave you everything." I shuddered, trying to control myself. "Every piece of me. So if you're breaking up with me ... I deserve an explanation."

"The explanation is that I need to be alone. Don't make it hard for me. I'm exhausted. I don't need this ..." He gestured helplessly to me.

I swallowed hard and dragged a hand through my hair, trying to think of something to change his mind, to stop this. In the time it took me to do that, Jake had started walking away again.

"I'm sorry he did this to you, Jake. I'm sorry his dad is still doing this to you." He hesitated so I continued, "But I'm standing by you, ready to help you work it all out. Doesn't that count for something?"

The look he gave me ripped me apart. "No. I can't be here, in this town with these fucking people. And you're one of them. When I look at you, that's all I see."

Desolation crashed over me. Nausea rose through me, my eyes burning with tears I was determined to keep in check around him. But the realization that he'd ended it, that we'd never talk again, that I'd never feel his warm hand in mine, that no one would ever look at me or make me feel the way he made me feel ever again shattered me. The tears started to fall and Jake looked sharply away.

Swiping at the traitorous teardrops, I curled my lip in disgust. "You're just as big an asshole as they are—" my voice broke as the emotion became too much. "I can't believe I gave you everything," I whispered.

"Yeah, well, we all do stupid shit sometimes." He shrugged callously, turned and walked quickly out of my life.

Five days later word reached me that the Caplins had gone back to Chicago. Two days later a for-sale sign went up in the front yard of their home. Someone, I imagine Trenton, re-broke the window that had been fixed.

Jake's departure re-broke me.

Chapter Nineteen

Indiana, December 2012

"It feels like a lifetime ago. How is that possible?"

I spun around at the intrusion, a soft smile playing on my lips as I drank in the welcome sight of Alex Roster. "Hey, you."

He grinned and took two steps toward me on the lot so he could haul me into a bear hug. "Your sister thought you might be here."

"It's official," I sighed, easing back to stare into his handsome face. "My sister is creepy spooky."

Alex took hold of my hand as I stepped back. "Missed you this semester."

After Jake had left, I'd felt lost for the first time, not really sure where I fit in the town I'd loved my whole life. Alex had been feeling the same way after Brett's death and we'd clung to each other, finishing out high school as best friends and heading off to Purdue together. From there things had gotten complicated until I'd uncomplicated them. "I missed you too. How's Sharon?"

"She's great. She's home in Tampa with her family. We're still not quite at the spending Christmas with one another's family stage."

Sharon was a sophomore Alex had met almost a year ago. She was tiny, cute as a button, loud, girly, the complete opposite to a now-reserved Alex. I thought they were great together. She loosened him up. "It's been almost a year. Holidays-with-the-family time is approaching."

He rubbed a hand over his close-shaven head and nodded. "She's talking about coming here in spring, so I think you're right." His gaze flickered behind me to the parking lot before they returned to me, his study careful and perhaps a little worried. "So I'm guessing from everything you told me that you're here because of Jake."

Other than Claudia and Andie, Alex was my closest confidant. Despite the convoluted history between us, I told him everything because at the end of the day, he was one of my best friends. This meant I'd kept in close contact with him while I was in Edinburgh and he knew how messed up I was feeling over Jake being back in my life. Although he'd always been neutral in our conversations as he quietly advised me to follow my gut, I was braced to hear him tell me what everyone else was recommending: to get Jake out of my life.

"It's gotten really hard to be around him and Melissa," I confessed quietly. "He changes me, Alex. I become this neurotic, whiny girl, and I don't want to be that person."

"One: you could never be a neurotic, whiny girl. Two: just because he makes you feel weak doesn't mean you are. Three: this whole time you haven't been honest with him. I know you were close, and I know he thinks he knows you, but has it crossed your mind that he actually has no clue you still care about him? Char, he said some unforgiveable things to you. He took every bad feeling he had out on you. If I were him, I would presume a girl like you would've moved on from a guy who treated her like that."

I shook my head. "He knows, Alex."

"Maybe he does. Maybe he doesn't. The thing is, you do. It's your decision."

I glanced back over my shoulder at the school, angry butterflies stirring inside me. I shoved them aside, determined to get myself back on track. When I looked back at Alex, I nodded. "I know what I have to do."

Reading the decision in my wounded eyes, Alex yanked me toward him and curled me into his side. "Come on. Your mom was taking a pecan pie out of the oven when I stopped by, and I am not leaving town until I have myself some of that goodness."

"It's great to see you," I snuggled into his side.

"You too."

"How are your mom and dad?"

Alex snorted. "Annoyed I dropped politics."

"You told them?" Damn, now I was the only coward between us. The Rosters had pushed politics on Alex since the moment he got into Purdue. He'd taken it as a double major with law to appease them but never had any intention of going into politics. I couldn't believe he'd gathered the courage to tell them when I still hadn't talked to Mom and Dad about applying to the police academy.

My friend scowled down at me. "Please don't tell me you're still considering the whole police thing?"

Unfortunately, Alex being Alex, overbearing but caring, like my parents he'd never wanted me to pursue a career as a cop. It was one of the many reasons I'd uncomplicated things between us.

"Don't tell them," I told him sharply. "I'm still working toward that."

He shook his head. "Sweetheart, your head must be a whole bunch of mess right now."

I made a pathetic face and nodded.

Alex huffed in sympathy, hugging me closer to his side as we made our way back to my parents' house.

Pots, pans, trays, cutlery, foil, and scraps littered the kitchen. Smack bang in the middle of it was Rick and I. Since Mom and Andie had cooked Christmas dinner, Rick and I were stuck with cleanup duty. My parents and Andie were lying almost passed out in the sitting room watching a comedy while I was elbow-deep in dishwater and Rick was attempting to keep up with the drying so we didn't have a pileup situation on our hands. Looking at the dishes, I couldn't believe five people could eat so much.

"Are you surviving another Christmas with the Redfords, then?" I teased Rick.

His lip curled at the corner. "You know it."

"My sister loved her gift." And wasn't that an understatement.

The two of them had been house hunting for months. Andie found a house in Beverly that she loved, but it was a little over their budget. Rick did okay as a detective but he wasn't exactly a high flier, and Andie may one day make good money as a psychiatrist but they weren't there yet. She'd been really disappointed when Rick refused to stretch the budget because she was a goner for the house and the area.

This morning she'd opened an envelope with documents showing he'd put a down payment on the house.

My reserved sister elbowed me in the face launching herself at him.

He smiled, his blue eyes warm with tenderness. "I got that."

"Do you like the house too?"

"It's a great house to raise a family in. Good neighborhood. I wouldn't have put a down payment on it if I didn't like it."

"Still, it's like a half-hour drive into the city."

"Longer during rush hour."

"Aren't you going to miss it? You've lived in the city for years."

He shrugged, still smiling. "Beverly is still the city—it's just got more of a suburban feel to it. And I've got to grow up sometime. We make sacrifices, we compromise. That's the way it works. You know that better than anyone, Miss Pre-law."

Grimacing, I hunched my shoulders at the reminder. "Don't."

"Charley, you need to talk to them again. Aren't you supposed to be applying to law school soon?"

"I'm supposed to register to take the LSATs in June after I get home from Edinburgh. If I do well, I start the application process in the fall."

"So what are you going to do?"

My expression was a little sheepish, my voice low as I replied, "What do you think, Rick? I've made a nice attempt at pretending to compromise with them because I love them and I don't want to upset them, but this is me. I never do anything I don't want to do. That is exactly why I keep putting off telling my parents that when I graduate, I'll be applying to the Chicago Police Academy."

My sister's fiancé's grin was contagious and I felt a warm glow in my chest at the pleased glimmer in his eyes. "Good for you, sweetheart."

I nodded, and even though I was nervous about telling my folks, I felt a sense of peace rest around me at having finally admitted it out loud to a member of my family.

"So, something I've never asked you before because I was trying to keep my nose clean of the issue so I didn't upset Jim and Delia ... but, why a cop?"

"Why are you a cop?"

Rick didn't hesitate. "Because I was too wild. I barely got through a bachelor's degree. I was partying too hard, and mostly just wasting my time. I was angry and I needed some discipline. It was this or the army, but being a cop kept me closer to home so I could watch over my mom."

"I don't even think I have an exact answer for why I want to be a cop. I know people will say it's a thankless job and that it involves long hours and the pay isn't what it should be ... and who knows, maybe I'll get into it and that's all *I'll* see. But I don't think so. I've just always wanted to do this." Rick grunted and I narrowed my eyes. "What?"

"Charley, you want to be a police officer because you have a hero complex. Why do you think the nickname Supergirl stuck?"

I wrinkled my nose. "I don't have a hero complex."

"Third grade you masterminded a plan to contain some kid in his locker at recess because he kept stealing the weaker kids' lunch and lunch money."

"Henry Ames," I nodded in disgust. "His family moved to Lanton in third grade and left in fourth. He was such a little prick." I frowned. "Did my sister tell you that?"

He laughed softly. "Yeah. She also told me in sixth grade you led a town search for your friend's missing tortoise."

"Lacey's tortoise, Micky D. He disappeared out of her pond. She was devastated. Turns out Jackson Emery 'borrowed' him and freaked out when I organized the search party. He waited three hours before confessing and his parents ended up buying the entire search party ice cream and lemonade. It cost them a small fortune. Jackson was grounded for a month." I smirked.

Rick continued to grin. "Freshman year, you knocked your sister out of the way of a moving vehicle." His smile disappeared. "Junior year, you tried to save a boy's life, and then almost took a beating trying to protect another."

Glowering now, I turned fully to him. "Is my sister doing a paper on me? Because I will mess her up so bad ..."

He shook his head, chuckling softly. "Sweetheart, she just talks about you. She's proud of you. She admires you. She thinks you'd make one hell of a cop."

I felt a surge of happiness from my sister's belief in me. "And what do you think?"

He shrugged. "I think you'll have obstacles to overcome. Sad but true, but looking the way you do, you'll not have an easy time of it from some of the male officers. You'll have to work harder to prove yourself, especially if you're chasing a promotion. It's nowhere near as bad as it used to be but it's still there." Before my shoulders could slump in deflation, he continued, "But I think if anyone can do it, it's you, and I'm looking forward to witnessing it."

I smiled at him gratefully. "Thank you."

"No problem." He eyed me carefully. "I've got something else to say and then I'll take my advice elsewhere."

"*Okay.*"

"This kid, this guy who's messing with your head ..."

I sighed wearily. "Please, don't, Rick—"

He held up a hand. "Hear me out."

Ready to be lectured on what an idiot I was for even thinking about letting Jake back into my life, what my sister's fiancé actually told me came as a surprise. And one that confused me even more. "Your sister told me everything about Jake. And I already know how your dad feels about him, believe me. And I get it. Had I been in Jim's shoes and watched my kid's heart get broken, I'd probably want to swing for the guy too. But ..." His eyes filled with sympathy and understanding as he said, "I remember being a confused seventeen-year-old guy, Charley. Never mind confused. I remember being seventeen. We seem to expect and yet at the same time, hate, how fast kids grow up today, but no matter how fast we think they're growing up, emotionally they're still just kids. Jake was, what, barely seventeen? He'd been hassled for months, targeted unfairly, and then a kid died during a fight with him. That's not an easy thing to get through, and if you're the kind of person who would feel to blame for that ... well, that kind of blame when you're just a kid ... could he have handled it better? Hell yes. But just because he didn't doesn't make him a bad guy, Charley. It made him a fallible kid who's probably walking around with a whole lot of regret."

I was frozen, taking in Rick's empathetic point of view, and knowing that everything he was saying was what had made me forgive Jake enough to let him back into my life as a friend.

"I say this because I did a few things I regretted when I was Jake's age. I hurt someone. I can't take that back. Neither can Jake. But if he's trying, then maybe you should at least give him the time to prove he means it. He'll either prove himself right or wrong, but in the end, you won't regret not giving him that shot."

I nodded. "I appreciate that. I do. However ... it's not really about giving him a shot. I've done that. I just ... it's too hard to now."

Understanding lit up Rick's eyes and his voice dropped. "You still ..."

I nodded again.

Before he could reply, my cell buzzed in my jeans. Since I hadn't heard from Claudia after I'd texted her that morning, I knew it was probably her. Quickly, thankful to escape our conversation, I dried my hands on Rick's dish towel and yanked my phone out of my ass pocket.

"Merry Christmas, Claud."

A lot of background noise hit my ears first and then Claudia's quiet voice. "Merry Christmas."

I didn't recognize her tone and I didn't like it. "Honey, where are you?" I frowned. "What's going on?"

"My dad and I got into a fight," her voice shook on the words. "He was drunk. He ... he's not my dad, Charley. He told me he's not my real father."

Shock winded me for a minute. "Wha ..."

"My oversharing assholes for parents told me they had an open relationship when they first got married. My mom was seeing an artist. When I was five, Dad didn't think I looked like him because neither of my parents has green eyes and that art guy did. My dad got a paternity test. They've known I'm not his for fifteen years."

"Oh God, Claudia." I closed my eyes, hating the pain in her voice and wishing I could just slam her self-absorbed parents' heads against the wall.

She laughed softly, the sound breaking on a sob. "Dad was so callous, you know, like what he just told me didn't matter. I guess it makes sense why he's been an indifferent asshole toward me my whole life. And Mom. Mom's walking around with these big guilty puppy dog eyes and I just couldn't be there anymore." She sniffled. "I'm at San Diego International. My flight leaves in half an hour."

I nodded. "What's your flight number? I'll pick you up."

"I'm sorry, Charley, I know it'll be late."

"It doesn't matter," I waved off her apology. "I'll be there."

She shot off the flight number and I hung up, a weight pressing on my chest for her. My solemn eyes hit Rick's questioning ones. "Claudia just had the Christmas from hell."

By the time Claud's flight got into O'Hare, it was almost two in the morning. I was jacked up on caffeine so I'd stay awake for the drive. Rick wanted to come with me, but I thought it was better that I collect Claudia myself. She didn't sound like she was in good shape and having someone around she didn't know that well might not be helpful.

Mom and Dad wanted me to stay at a hotel with her in Chicago but I just wanted to get her home to somewhere she felt loved and wanted.

When I saw her just inside the doors of the airport, I put my arms around her and she started to cry. I held onto her for a long time until she finally pulled back and gave me a wobbly smile. "Have I ever told you you're the bestest best friend ever?"

"You're my family," I told her quietly, pulling on her hand and leading her out to my car. "Nothing is more important, least of all sleep," I teased.

She laughed softly and got in the car while I loaded her suitcase into the trunk.

As we drove out of Chicago and back toward Indiana, she told me everything from start to finish. Before I'd thought her dad was an ass—now I thought he was scum. The guy really didn't seem to care that he'd completely destroyed his daughter. He thought it no big deal that finding out the man you thought was your father really *wasn't*.

He hadn't even called Claudia and she'd been missing for over six hours.

Scum.

After a while Claudia lapsed into silence and I glanced down to see her tearing at a piece of paper, her fingers working frantically, nervously. "It's going to be okay," I assured her.

She nodded but didn't answer.

How long would it take me to drive to California? I wondered if Rick could help me commit the perfect murder.

Claudia's phone ringing made us both jump. We held our breaths as she pulled it out of her bag. Her expression fell a little as she said, "It's Beck. I texted him while I was waiting for you, but I thought he'd be asleep."

"Answer it."

She did. "Hey. Did you have a nice Christmas?" she waited and then frowned. "What? No, I'll explain it later. I'm fine now, though, okay ... no, I'm fine ... Look, it was a pretty big blowout with my parents but I'm dealing ... I'm here, actually. Charley picked me up at O'Hare. We're driving back to her parents' house ... Well, because I didn't want to disturb you ... Beck, no, I'm fine ... it's nothing ... Okay, I promise ... yeah, I promise I'll call you next time ... I'll tell you about it later ... Yeah, my girl's got me ... I'm sure ... Oh? What happened? ... You're kidding me?" I felt her wide eyes on me. "Yeah. I'll let her know ... We'll talk later? ... Yeah ... You too."

My heart was pounding as she hung up, knowing that whatever Beck had said, it had something to do with me. Claudia exhaled heavily, her long dark hair falling in front of her face. She tucked it behind her ear and I felt her eyes on me. "He's pissed I didn't call him to come get me."

"Of course he is," I muttered, beginning to lose patience with Beck's behavior when it came to my best friend. All the caffeine, tiredness, Claudia's shock, and the fact that I knew *something* had happened probably didn't help my irritability much.

"Also ... Jake broke up with Melissa the day you guys arrived back in Chicago."

As though she'd stood on my chest instead of delivering news, I fought to breathe for a moment, my hands tightening around the steering wheel. I couldn't speak.

"Apparently he's been trying to contact you?"

Swallowing hard, I nodded.

"So ...?"

I glanced at her expectant face and shook my head, doing my best to shove the news of Jake's breakup and all the consequent questions to the back of my mind. "Now is not the time. You're more important. We're going to go home and drown your sorrows in chocolate pie. Okay?"

She continued to stare at me for a moment, her concern palpable, which was crazy considering what she'd just been through. Finally, my best friend let it drop. She nodded and settled more comfortably in the passenger seat. "Sounds good to me."

Chapter Twenty

Indiana, January 2013

The overbearing nosiness, teasing, and coddling of my family helped Claudia get through the rest of the winter vacation with me in Indiana, but the hurt and confusion in the back of her beautiful eyes never quite disappeared. When she finally told Beck what happened, the guy jumped on a bus to Indiana and spent the night on my parents' couch. To my surprise, my parents loved Beck. I'd thought he'd scare them off with his tats and his devotion to a guitar pick, but it turned out Beck was a lot like Jake. He could turn on the respectful charm in an instant.

After Beck took her for a walk around town to talk, Claudia came back with a glimmer behind her eyes. Whatever he'd said to her had her calling her parents as soon she returned. Dad was at work and Rick and Andie had gone back to Chicago, so Beck, Mom, and I sat in the sitting room pretending to ignore Claudia's raised voice as she yelled into the phone in the kitchen.

Twenty minutes later she stepped into the sitting room with a tight smile on her face. "Well, he didn't exactly apologize." She shrugged but I could see the hurt she was trying to conceal. I knew by the way Beck's fingers curled into fists that he could see that too.

"But he upped my credit card allowance and offered to book me and my friends on a vacation before we return for classes."

My mom looked horrified. "That's ... nice?"

Claudia rolled her eyes. "It's whatever ...but ..." She grinned at me. "I was thinking we've got four days before classes begin when we get back to Edinburgh. Why don't we all take a trip to the Highlands? I mean, we're in Scotland and we've barely stepped outside Edinburgh."

"All of us?"

I still hadn't answered Jake's attempts to contact me. Although I was dying to know why he broke it off with Melissa on the first day of Christmas vacation, I was also terrified to discover what he wanted from me. Confused as I was, I wasn't sure I could handle it if he still wanted to be "just friends." And yet I knew I wasn't sure I could handle being anything more. The original reason for me backing off was apparently no longer an issue, but still ... I was afraid to be around Jake. Me. Afraid? How crap was that?

Thus, I didn't really want to be stuck on a minivacation with him.

Claudia nodded and hurried over to where she'd dumped her laptop. "Like a cabin or a lodge somewhere."

Beck nodded. "I'm sure Lowe and the guys will be up for it."

"I was thinking us, Lowe, Matt, Denver, Rowena, and Jake. I'd invite Maggie, Lauren, and Gemma, but I really don't think we hang out enough for that not to be awkward. Plus, Maggie has a whopping big crush on Beck. It's a little irritating to be around."

"For who?" Beck smirked and relaxed into my dad's armchair. "Definitely not me."

The two of them bantered back and forth but I was too busy trying to control my racing heartbeat and the cold sweat prickling over my skin.

Okay, so I hadn't exactly told Claudia of my plans to avoid Jake. He'd texted a couple of times since her arrival and he'd called when I didn't reply to the texts. Claudia had been baking with my mom so she didn't know about those, but she knew I'd been avoiding contact with him. Gauging me well on the subject, and still in turmoil over her own *actual* drama, she hadn't badgered me about it.

Two hours later Claudia had found a lodge in a place called Fort William, a town on a loch about a five-hour train journey from Edinburgh. The lodge accommodated ten people and was in a place that did look beautiful and not too isolated, but I couldn't really appreciate the beauty of it. I was too busy trying to work out ways to get out of it, even though I knew in the end, I'd go along since the whole idea had put a spark back in Claudia's eyes.

"I'll call the guys," Beck said, ducking out of the room.

"You'll all be careful outside of the city?" my mom asked, worry creasing her forehead.

Claudia nodded. "Of course, Delia Mom. We can get a train from Edinburgh straight there and we'll get a taxi to the lodge. And we've got all the guys with us. We'll be fine."

Oh, yeah. We'd be freaking awesome.

I pretended to bury my nose in the site images so I didn't have to fake a smile both Claud and my mom would see right through.

Five minutes later Beck walked back into the room smiling. "Most of the guys are up for it. Denver is emailing Rowena to see if she wants to come with us but Jake said he's not sure."

Yes! There is a God!

Trying to hide my grin, and suddenly feeling very excited about our trip north, I shrugged casually. "That's cool. We'll still have fun without him."

I deliberately ignored Beck's burning gaze, sensing he was desperate to ask what my problem was. Thankfully Mom was there, so he didn't get his chance.

Beck returned home that night and Claudia successfully avoided talking about his sudden white-knight appearance for about two days, just as I successfully avoided talking about Jake.

We were lounging around the sitting room watching a Disney Pixar movie when my cell rang. It was on the floor near Claud and she lifted it absentmindedly to me. "It's Jake."

Feeling that unwelcome churn in my gut, I took it from her and hit the disconnect button.

Claudia glanced up at me over her shoulder. "You didn't answer? Again?"

I pinched my lips together and threw the phone beside me on the couch.

In response, she paused the movie and turned around. "You're ignoring him? Since when?"

"Since I got home. I didn't want to say anything because you're going through something serious. My drama with Jake and Melissa doesn't even matter."

"Of course it matters," she scowled at me. "And remember ... there is no longer a Jake and Melissa and I think we can all guess why. Don't you want to find out for sure?"

"I'm not ready to. I can't be his friend and I'm not sure I can be anything else. So ... for now, I'm happy with avoidance," I replied softly.

Claudia's eyes melted with concern. "You're a mess."

I nodded. "Yeah."

"So ... you're just ignoring him? You're not even going to talk to him about it?"

I shook my head. "What's the point? I don't want to have this big heart-to-heart with him. Look, I know I miss him, I know I still want him, I know that he can make me feel on top of the world and seconds later like shit. But I also know I don't trust him with my feelings. You're right. It's a mess." I closed my eyes. "Honestly, I think the best thing to do is walk away. Move on. A clean break." I shrugged. "And you know it might sound petty, but he left me last time with a crappy explanation and no closure. I don't owe him a chat. I don't owe him anything."

The expression in Claudia's eyes suggested she disagreed but she kept her mouth shut and just nodded.

"What about you and Beck?" I arched an eyebrow, trying to turn the spotlight off me. "He rushed all the way to Indiana to make sure you were okay. He took you for a walk and when you came back, you seemed better. A lot better. Not even I lifted your spirits the way he did."

As soon as her eyes dimmed, I kicked myself for bringing it up. "I'm just as confused as you are. We walked and he ... he just gets it, you know. His mom or whatever. My parents are never going to give me what I need emotionally, but Beck suggested I needed to tell them how much they hurt me, even if it didn't penetrate. He said I needed that closure. And he was right. They didn't say they were sorry or that they loved me, but they came as close to an apology as I'll ever get out of them—upping my credit card limit and sending me on vacation."

"Beck really cares about you."

"I know," she nodded, her eyebrows drawn together. "As much as he can care about me. I've accepted that. It took me a while, believe me. I kept fantasizing about it changing because of our attraction, but Beck is too messed up emotionally to go there.

Maybe in ten years when he's grown up a bit, but not now. You know, though, I'd rather have him as a friend than not have him at all."

"Claud, what's happening between me and Jake isn't the same. He's my first love and all that stuff is mixed together with a pretty ugly history. There's too much regret and hurt."

"I'm sorry, Charley," she whispered. "I'm sorry you can't see what the rest of us see."

"And what's that?"

"That no matter what happened in the past ... you guys are still meant to be together."

"Don't—"

"We all see it," she cut me off. "When you guys are together, it's like the whole world goes away. And ... Beck knows Jake better than anyone. He says he's never seen him as happy as he's been these last few months."

I felt that pressure on my chest again and breathed hard through it. "Claudia, I know you think you're helping but you're not. Please ... stop. Okay?"

"Okay, okay. I'll shut up." She sighed and turned around. "I just don't think you should give up on him just yet."

Saying goodbye to my parents for another four months didn't feel great, but I managed to hold in the tears. Claudia, on the other hand, was a mess. Mom and Dad had done such a good job of trying to make up for her parents' lack of affection that Claudia had bubbled and clung to Mom for a good five minutes at the airport, before I managed to pry her off.

When Claud had suggested I change my flight to the only flight she'd managed to get out of Chicago, rather than taking the same flight back as Jake and the guys, I'd jumped all over that. Avoiding Jake was almost turning into a game.

He'd called me three more times and left a voicemail the last time. I didn't listen to it.

I also deleted his messages on Facebook without reading them.

Returning to Edinburgh would prove the ultimate test, of course. It was going to be much more difficult to avoid Jake when he lived a two-minute walk from our apartment.

Milking her parents' guilt money for all she could, Claudia upgraded our flights to first class, so I enjoyed the luxury and tried to ignore the dilemma waiting for me when I arrived in Edinburgh. Technically, it wouldn't be a dilemma until I got back from Fort William. A day after we landed, we were catching a train to Fort William for our minivacation.

I could start worrying about dodging Jake after my brief stint in the Highlands.

Since everyone else had already arrived in Edinburgh a day earlier, Claud and I had just enough time to crash, sleep off the jetlag, and pack before we were to meet the guys on the Cowgate. We were walking to catch the train since Edinburgh Waverly Station was a less than a ten minute walk from the apartment.

"I do not feel awake enough for more traveling," I grumbled as I strolled into the kitchen with my small suitcase. Wrapped up in a sweater, a fleece-lined Regatta, my black Levi's, Uggs, cashmere scarf, and wooly floppy knit hat, I was ready to meet the winter Highlands. Or I would be once I woke the hell up.

"Um ..."

The "uh oh" expression on Claudia's face was like a shot of caffeine. "What is it?"

She winced. "Jake's coming."

"What!" Blood whooshed in my ears.

Throwing up her hands, Claudia gave me a helpless look. "He decided to come."

I felt sick. "This isn't happening. I was supposed to have four more avoidance days!"

"I'm sorry, Char."

I blinked rapidly, trying to think of a way out of this. I spent a good five minutes coming up with one lie after the other, each gaining in elaboration and entertainment.

Finally, I groaned. "Fuck it. I'm a grown-ass woman, I can cope with this."

Claudia was too busy typing really fast on her phone to answer me.

"What are you doing?"

"Asking Lowe to run interference."

Okay, now I was going to strangle her. Through clenched teeth, I asked, "Why are you asking Lowe to run interference?"

"Because you told me what he said at Frankenstein, so he seems like the best option. He knows what's going on and he's on your side. He'll keep you out of Jake's way. Not that I think you should stay out of Jake's way, but it's what you want so I'm helping you achieve it."

Musing over this, I eventually bobbed my head in reluctant agreement. "You might be right."

"Phew!" Claudia grinned cheekily. "Crisis averted. Now let's go conquer the Highlands." She sailed past me, her little pink suitcase following in her wake.

Chapter Twenty-One

Edinburgh, January 2013

The sight of Jake standing talking to the guys on the sidewalk of the corner of Blair Street, his hands stuffed into his black wool coat, his small duffel bag at his feet, made me feel like I was coming out of my skin. A rising wave of jittery nerves crashed against my stomach and I almost stumbled to a stop.

"You okay?" Claudia asked, her eyes pinned to the group.

Denver stood with a rainbow-colored Rowena at his side, Matt joked with Jake, and Beck and Lowe watched us approach.

"I'm fine," I lied. "Let's do this."

The wheels of our small suitcases rattled along the hard sidewalk and the sound drew everyone's stare.

Do not look at Jake, do not look at Jake.

With a single-minded determination, I focused entirely on Lowe.

"Hey," he grinned.

"Oh, finally, more girls," Rowena smiled. Her bright eyes settled on Claudia. "Thanks for inviting me. I love free trips."

"Who doesn't?" Beck smiled and then turned to Claudia, eyeing her carefully. "How's it going?"

"We're good." She smiled at everyone. "But late, so we better motor if we want to catch our train."

Feeling Jake's gaze burn into my cheeks, I was ever so thankful that Lowe fell quickly into step beside me as we walked up a very steep Blair Street. It stopped me from doing something foolish like desperately asking Jake if he was okay since his split with Melissa three weeks ago. It shouldn't bother me if he was or wasn't, but I still cared. I still cared enough to not want him to be hurting.

"Did you have a good Christmas?" Lowe asked softly.

"I did. Did you?"

"Yeah, it was cool. We decided on Chinese takeout this year. Very Christmassy."

"Please tell me you at least bought cake or a pie?"

"I bought beer."

I laughed. "At least tell me you used it to soak in some kind of sponge cake?"

"I'd like to say we were that inventive, but my brother and I are pretty low-key."

"Hmm. I think next year I'll box up some of my mom's Christmas desserts and send them your way. We always have a ton of leftovers."

Lowe snorted. "We're not poor."

"No, just lazy." I grinned so he'd know I was teasing.

"About food, yes. About other stuff ..." he shot me a wicked smile, "I've been known to work my ass off to get *things* done right."

"How is it possible that you made that sound dirty?"

"It's a gift."

I laughed and continued to banter with The Stolen's lead vocalist as we hauled our asses up onto The Royal Mile and then down the winding and bizarrely named Cockburn Street.

"Don't even say it," I said quickly, watching Lowe's eyes flicker up to the street sign.

His mouth twitched. "I wasn't going to say anything. It's not pronounced the way it looks."

"It's not?"

"Nope."

"Well, that's disappointing."

Lowe nodded, his eyes catching mine as he smiled affectionately. Concentrating on enjoying the comfortable camaraderie between us made it easier to ignore Jake's eyes scorching my back as he walked behind us.

When we arrived at the train station, it became clear that Claudia had indeed enrolled Lowe to play interference between me and Jake. Climbing onto the train, I felt him at my back. As soon as Beck scored us two tables, Lowe's heat pressed into mine as he shuffled me in across from Claudia and Beck and took the seat beside me. This left Jake to sit with Matt, Denver, and Rowena at the table across the small aisle. Lowe put my suitcase up on the overhead space and as he did, my gaze, with a will of its own, lifted and met Jake's.

The tightness in his jaw told me he was angry, but the look in his eyes was mostly questioning. It took everything in me to keep my own face blank and calm as I casually glanced away from him to smile at an excited Claudia.

For the first hour or so, we chatted about Christmas break and I pretended not to be hanging onto Jake's every word, even though I was. It turned out Lukas had won over the girl he'd met in his first semester at Boston and since she was also from Chicago, Jake and his parents had gotten to meet her over Christmas. According to Jake, Luke was totally gone for her and the girl, a bundle of energy, was more than a match for Jake's blunt-tongued Nana, and thus considered a member of the family.

No one mentioned Jake's breakup with Melissa.

Of course, if anyone asked I'd feign ignorance that I'd been listening closely enough to know any of that.

By the time the second hour was underway, we'd descended into silence, some of us watching the passing scenery outside while listening to music, others reading, and some of us (Matt) were even sleeping. As I watched Scotland pass before me, rolling green hills, sheep, and cows broke up suburban areas, the lush vastness closer to the images of Britain I'd seen on TV throughout my childhood. As we started to climb, the landscape became more rugged, the hills were higher, the greens darker, interspersed with black and gray rock. It was beautiful and wild, and only made more breathtaking by the sun-speckled lochs—placid and peaceful lakes in the valleys between.

I'd been staring out the window, my earbuds in, listening to Adele's "Don't You Remember," when I felt Lowe shift beside me. He said something to us, but I didn't hear what. I could only guess that he was going to the bathroom and I felt my heart flip a little at the sight of the vacant seat beside me. My eyes were definitely not on my side because they immediately sought out Jake who'd glanced over when Lowe had gotten up. Our eyes met and a thousand things passed between us before I swiftly looked back out my window.

The flippy thing my heart was doing turned into a full-on somersault as the seat beside me depressed and the smell of Jake's cologne hit me. His arm brushed mine and even though we were both wearing a sweater, I felt that brush take hold of my entire being. I froze, my muscles locked.

I felt the tug on my left earbud as Jake gently pulled it out, his knuckles brushing my jaw as his hand dropped.

"What?" I asked quietly, pretending to be unaffected by his questioning and hurt countenance. As I tried to ignore Beck's and

Claudia's enquiring gazes, I also attempted to ignore the call of Jake's soulful eyes.

He raised an eyebrow at my tone. "I just came over to say hey."

I took out my other earbud, suddenly not wanting to hear Adele's mournful tones begging me to remember. "Hey." And because I couldn't help myself. "Are you okay … I mean … I heard."

Jake shot Beck and Claudia a quick look and the two of them ducked their heads to watch the movie Claud had on her tablet. Jake switched his focus back to me. His voice was low as he bent his head toward me. Unfortunately this meant I was transfixed by his perfect mouth as he said, "It's been a rough couple of weeks, but it was the right thing to do. You I don't get, though. Why have you been avoiding me? Did I do something?"

"No."

"No? Then why haven't you answered my calls or my texts? Why haven't you spoken one word to me until now?" His brows puckered and I could read the genuine concern in his eyes. Now that I was faced with him, I suddenly felt very childish and cowardly for avoiding him.

I shrugged, looking away. "I guess I just needed some space."

Jake's strong hand slid up my thigh and I almost jumped out of my skin. "Space?"

Shocked, I looked at him and saw the pucker between his brows had deepened and the concern had changed to full-blown anxiety. I glanced down at the warm hand he'd placed intimately on my leg. Just like that, he quickly withdrew it.

One glance into his face and I could tell he hadn't even realized he'd put his hand on me.

"Space," I reiterated, my heartbeat doing this horrible jittery jumpy thing that I felt vibrating all the way up into the bottom of my throat.

"Space?" he repeated back.

As we stared at one another, I realized I was at once desperate for him to get away from me and yet desperate to know more. It occurred to me that much of the push and pull with Jake was because I'd never had a sense of closure. I never had closure because I still didn't fully understand why he'd broken up with me. Never mind Melissa. Me.

"But before space ..." I tilted my head. "Why? I really want to know why you broke up with me."

Jake glanced at Beck and Claudia again before inching even closer to me. "You want to talk about that now?"

"I need to know if you blamed me. You said you didn't ..."

He studied me for far longer than I liked, emotion I didn't understand crossing his expression. Finally he heaved a heavy sigh and nodded. "Okay. Yeah, I blamed you. It was irrational, and stupid, but I was angry. Mostly at myself for letting the shit with Brett go on for months like it did so that it culminated in the most stupid loss of life I've ever ..." He cursed under his breath, the color leaching from his cheeks as he went on. "There was too much angry in me. And being angry at myself did nothing to dispel it so ... I chose to be angry with you. I guess subconsciously, I thought because we were so close that once I was done being angry with you, you'd still be there and you'd forgive me." He glanced away from me, his jaw tight with tension. "Didn't work out that way," he muttered.

We sat for a minute in silence as I tried to process that. I think ... I think it helped. And yet it didn't. I don't know what I expected but I didn't expect to feel just as confused as I'd been a few minutes ago.

"Jake, man, you're in my seat."

We both jerked our heads up at the sight of Lowe standing with his arms crossed over his chest, a patient smile playing on his lips.

Jake waved at the seat across the aisle he'd vacated. "Take mine."

Lowe grimaced, "Well, see, I've spent a good couple of hours indenting my ass cheeks into that one for optimum ass comfort and I kind of don't want to go through the whole thing again."

Glowering, Jake's eyes held a definite note of suspicion as they swung between me and Lowe. With a grunt of annoyance, Jake slid out of the seat and let Lowe back in beside me.

My whole body breathed deep with relief.

The tense atmosphere between us pulled tight like a cord attached to my chest and lodged into his. Despite the people and the aisle between us, I felt it pulling painfully on me and for the next couple of hours, I watched in a daze as Scotland passed by, wondering how the hell I was going to survive the next three nights around Jake.

The worry buzzing around my brain was only momentarily halted when, what would turn out to be about thirty minutes outside of Fort William, Claudia gasped, "Oh my God."

"What?" I asked, frowning as I watched her eyes grow brighter and brighter as she stared outside at the deep valley below us.

"Oh my freaking God!" she shrieked.

I winced along with the rest of my friends and about half the passengers in the carriage. "What?"

Her head dipped to her tablet and she tapped away at the screen. Two seconds later she shrieked again.

"Jesus," Beck groaned, slapping a hand protectively over his ear.

"What the hell is going on?" I asked, suddenly worried she was going to get us kicked off the train.

Claudia just grinned at me like a kid. "We're on the Harry Potter viaduct that the Hogwarts Express takes!"

That wasn't at all what I'd been expecting, but the info had me almost slamming my head against the glass to see outside. My eyes took in the familiar scenery and I smiled, "This is so cool."

"Very," Lowe agreed, smiling along with me.

"Oh my God!" Claudia threw her hands out, her eyes wide and deadly serious. "Are they taking us to Hogwarts?"

We stared at her, processing her question in silence for a moment.

Laughter burst forth from us along with everyone in the vicinity who'd heard her. Realizing the improbability of her query, Claud blushed and a chuckling Beck put his arm around her and drew her into his side so he could kiss her forehead. "I get stupid when I'm excited," she mumbled, her lips curling up at the corner so we knew she was taking our teasing laughter in good fun.

By the time we pulled into Fort William, I'd almost forgotten the ache in my chest. But as we stepped onto the platform, breathing in the crisp, cold air, my eyes collided with Jake's and just like that, the ache was back again.

Claudia had given us a rundown on Fort William prior to our arrival. By the time we stepped into the town, we knew it was the largest in the Highlands, only smaller than the city of Inverness. We knew it was near the famous Ben Nevis, and we knew that it was settled on the shores of Loch Linnhe and Loch Eil. Despite being the largest town in the Highlands, it was still pretty freaking small, but I guess I wouldn't care about that if I lived in such beautiful surroundings.

The town center was quaint with cobbled streets and, a little like Edinburgh, really old buildings sitting next to more modern ones. When we got two taxis at the station to take us to the lodge, we discovered that our lodge was really just a house in among the homes built into the mountain, rising up away from the town center. Despite the snow-capped tops of the mountains around us, there was no snow on the roads as we wound our way through little suburbia.

To be honest, we weren't too disappointed when we discovered the "lodge" on a street next to residential homes. The view was unrivaled. Inside the main entrance, one set of stairs led up and another led down. Upstairs held the kitchen, a bathroom, two bedrooms, and a huge sitting room, and at the end of that room, patio doors led onto a balcony. Because we were so high up, we had a fantastic view of Fort William and the glistening loch below.

There were five bedrooms outfitted with twin beds. Beck and Jake took one of the upstairs rooms and Lowe and Matt took the other. Denver and Rowena got a bedroom each downstairs and Claudia and I took the bedroom with the French doors that lead out onto a private terraced garden. We had mountains all around us and no neighbors above. It was so unbelievably peaceful, I just wanted to lock myself out there and the rest of my friends inside.

Unfortunately, that wasn't the plan. Despite the five-hour train ride, Claudia let us have only two hours to freshen up before she called a couple of taxis to take us back down the hill into town for a pub dinner and drinks.

Wrapped up in my winter gear, I headed out with Claudia at my side and kept her there when our taxi driver dropped us off at a recommended pub. Inside, the heat from the roaring fire in the huge brickwork fireplace hit my cheeks and helped me relax. As did the fact that when we were seated at a table, Claudia was on my left, Lowe was on my right, and Rowena was opposite me. This made it much easier to avoid Jake.

After a while the excitement of being somewhere new and scenic set in and we were all laughing and joking, swapping Christmas break stories and bemoaning our academic fate when we returned to Edinburgh.

We were just finishing up dinner when my phone beeped. I pulled it out of my pocket to discover a text from a classmate asking me if I'd done the reading for our first week of classes. I smirked at her zeal and quickly text back that I hadn't.

"So you do know how to answer that thing after all," Jake observed somewhat caustically.

Our group stopped talking as I stuffed the phone back in my pocket, my face blank as I met Jake's stare. I was embarrassed he'd brought up our estrangement in front of everyone, even though it was obvious to them all. Still, I didn't want to ruin this trip for them and definitely not for Claudia because Jake had decided to corner me. The thing about cornering a confused, emotional woman is that she tends to unleash the claws in defense.

"Depends on *who* is trying to get in touch with me."

He raised his eyebrows at my answer and shook his head in hurt disbelief, looking away from me as he took a long gulp of his lager.

I ignored the choking feeling around my throat and slumped back against my chair.

"What was it, anyway?" Lowe asked me quietly as conversation between my friends picked up again. "Hot date?"

"With a reading list? Yes."

His eyes smiled as he dragged his teeth over his lip ring. My eyes dropped to it and he grinned. "Are you staring at my mouth?"

I glanced away, reaching for my pint. "You're the one who drew attention to it."

He laughed and I smiled up into his flirting gaze, ignoring the glower blasting my way from Jake's direction.

An hour later Jake was so wasted, Beck and Claudia took him back to the lodge. Guilt grabbed hold of me as I watched Beck help an inebriated Jake out of the pub. Inebriated Jake was a sad Jake, and I knew I was the cause of his sadness. It took every ounce of willpower I had to stay seated and not help him back to the lodge.

This evidence that he still cared perhaps a little too much was more proof that there was a huge possibility Jake had broken it off with Melissa because he could no longer be "just friends" with me, either.

Holy hell. What a clusterfuck.

I felt warm, strong fingers thread through mine and I looked up into Lowe's face.

"Don't," he told me quietly. "You're not doing anything wrong here, Charley. You're just trying to protect yourself and I don't blame you."

His assurance made me feel better and I relaxed into him, still holding his hand. We threw back a couple more beers so we were definitely buzzed a few hours later when the pub owner came over to throw us out because he was closing.

Rowena and Denver helped an almost-sleeping Matt into the taxi, and I climbed in beside Lowe, my hand still tight in his. Arriving back at the lodge, we discovered it was dark and silent so we tried our best to be quiet as we maneuvered Matt inside.

We stood in the hall, Lowe and Denver now holding up a passed-out Matt. "We'll put him downstairs with you, man," Lowe said to Denver. "It's easier to get him down there than upstairs."

Denver nodded and Rowena and I did our best to help them get Matt to bed quietly. Finally, I said goodnight to them all as Denver closed his door and Rowena disappeared into her room. I was just about to head to the room I shared with Claudia when Lowe grasped hold of my hand and tugged me gently toward him.

Not quite as coordinated as I was when sober, I collided with his strong chest. "Oops," I giggled, tilting my head back to meet his gaze.

He smirked down at me. "You're a pretty fucking cute drunk, you know that?"

I wrinkled my nose. "I'm not cute."

"What's wrong with cute?"

"It's so ... cute."

Lowe snorted. "Okay, you're a pretty fucking cute drunk but you also happen to be an incredibly sexy one too."

I considered that. "Okay. Bette—"

My answer was swallowed in Lowe's kiss. Shock blew my rationale to hell and ... I kissed him back.

"Come to my room," he murmured against my mouth.

"Oh God," I breathed.

"Charley?" His questioning eyes searched mine and he leaned back. "Do you not want to?"

My body definitely liked the idea ... but my head ...

"You're Jake's friend. If this was something more, it might be worth hurting him but ... not for just a quick ... whatever."

"Are you shitting me?"

"Not really."

"Charley ... Jake put you through hell last semester, never mind that he broke up with you. I might have been the only one who noticed how hard it's been for you watching him with Melissa, but it doesn't mean you didn't feel all that. Suddenly he breaks up with Melissa and what ... you're just supposed to run to him?"

Attempting to shake off my drunken fog, I frowned at Lowe. "You're not stupid, Lowe. You've got to have seen how he looks at us when we're hanging out."

"Yeah, like a jealous boyfriend. But he's not your boyfriend and he doesn't get to have his cake and eat it too."

"I've never understood that expression. A cake *is* for eating."

Lowe groaned. "Stop being cute when I'm trying to be serious." He grabbed my hand and because I knew his intent wasn't to seduce, I followed him as he dragged me upstairs and into his room.

With a sigh, I sat down on Matt's bed while Lowe lay down on his, kicking off his boots, his gaze questioning but patient. "I know you think I'm letting him dictate what I do but Lowe … he's your friend. I'm his ex. If you go there, he won't be happy. I wouldn't be happy if he went there with Claudia. As I said, if this was serious, then maybe, but we both know it isn't. You don't do serious, Lowe."

After a moment of contemplation, Lowe gave me a reluctant nod, his eyes darkening with sincerity. "If I were the kind of guy who did serious … you'd be it, Charley."

I smiled at him. "While I appreciate that, I think if I was 'it', you'd suddenly be the kind of guy who did serious."

"Like Jake did?"

The reminder of Jake's pursuit of me when we were younger cast a pall of sadness over me, but I nodded.

"His head is all messed up, Charley. I'm not saying he doesn't care about you. What I'm saying is that I care about you, and I don't want you to be the one who gets hurt again."

I took a deep, shaky breath. "That's why I need space. But I'm over being a child about it. I thought I could just avoid him and bury my head in the sand and it would all be okay."

"But it's not. You have to talk to him."

The thought sobered me. "Yeah."

We were quiet a while, each lost in our own thoughts. Finally, Lowe smiled tiredly. "You want to stay here?"

In answer I slid under the covers, turning on my side to stare at Lowe who was already lying back under the duvet on his bed. "You're a really good kisser."

"I know."

I snorted. "You definitely need to work on your confidence, though."

"I'm on it."

Smiling, I snuggled deeper against my cold pillow. "Lowe?"

"Yeah?"

"Thank you for being such a good friend."

He was silent so long, I didn't think he was going to answer, but then he replied quietly, "You make it easy."

I was almost drifting off to sleep with a small smile on my lips when Lowe whispered, "Charley?"

"Yeah?"

"If I didn't think it would get me hurt in the end ... I'd be the guy who got serious for you."

His confession hung in the air around us, making tears burn in my eyes. An overwhelming melancholy set over me.

Lowe was a great guy. The kind of guy I could really fall for. But he was right to guard himself against me, because no matter how many times I told myself otherwise, I still hadn't let go of Jake. I was beginning to fear that I'd lose every good thing that came into my life because I just couldn't set myself free of him.

Chapter Twenty-Two

Fort William, January 2013

Light streamed in from the thin curtains hanging at the small window in Lowe and Matt's room. My eyes rested on Lowe sprawled on his stomach, his arm dangling over the side of the twin bed, his graceful fingers almost touching the floor.

His face seemed so much softer in sleep, but it could be that after last night, I was feeling especially tender toward him.

Curled up on my side on Matt's bed, nerves bit into my empty stomach at the mere thought that my friends would assume Lowe and I had slept together if they discovered I wasn't in my room with Claudia. If I'd been a little more sober last night, I would've realized slipping into Matt's bed was a terrible idea.

At least Jake had gotten so drunk he'd passed out before realizing I'd disappeared into Lowe's room. The clock on Matt's bedside table told me it was just before seven in the morning. Nobody would be roaming around yet, so it seemed like a safe plan to get up now. Flipping back the covers, I quietly got out of bed, not bothering to fix my bed head or my wrinkled clothes as I tiptoed toward the door. Passing the mirror fixed to the wall, I saw I had sleep-smeared mascara around my eyes. I looked like I'd been up to no good.

Groaning under my breath, I pulled open the door as silently as I could, tiptoed out, and turned to click the door shut gently. Feeling a little hungover and a lot tired, I turned to head toward the kitchen for a glass of water and instead of meeting an empty hall, I met Jake.

Frozen, I stared at him numbly as his eyes glanced from Lowe's door to me, back to the door, and then back to me. His already pale face turned white and the glass of water in his hand trembled. His assumption settled as an unpleasant ache in my chest and before I could explain, he jerked like I'd shot him and quickly disappeared into the room he was sharing with Beck.

Panic suffused me and I stood there, stuck in the awful moment. My breathing was harsh as I leaned against the wall, cursing fate that I'd have to have crossed paths with Jake of all people as I snuck out of Lowe's room. Sliding down the wall, I buried my head in my hands, trying to talk myself off the ledge.

I hadn't cheated on Jake, for Christ's sake! I was barely even talking to him.

Why did it feel like a betrayal?

Why was I terrified Jake would hate me?

This was what I wanted. I wanted closure; I wanted Jake to let me go so I could move on. But I never wanted to move on like this, and I definitely didn't want to put a strain between him and Lowe.

If the horrified look on his face was any indication, I'd say Jake was not going to speak to me ever again.

And why did that thought burn in my throat so badly, when that's what I'd said I wanted all along?

Winter sun shone on us as we stood outside the lodge ready to trek down the hill to the center of the small town. There we'd decide where we were going to eat before we got taxis out to the Ben Nevis Whisky Distillery.

I was staring down at the beautiful sight of the sun glinting across Loch Linnhe, waiting on Claudia to declare us fit to go and worrying about Jake who'd told Beck he wasn't feeling up to leaving his bed. Ten minutes earlier I'd pulled Lowe aside and warned him about my encounter with Jake. His mouth had gotten tight but he'd given me a reassuring pat on the shoulder. I guessed that meant he would deal with it.

I didn't want him to have to deal with it.

This was so messed up.

"Jake?" Claudia suddenly asked and I whirled around to see Jake coming down the concrete porch steps toward us. "I thought you weren't coming with us."

His dark eyes were hard and brittle as he stuck his hands into his coat pockets and came to a standstill beside her and Beck. "Decided fresh air might do me good."

No one else seemed to notice that anything was wrong with him, perhaps putting his obvious bad mood down to being hungover, and Claudia continued on trying to explain to Matt why a bunch of novices couldn't, and definitely shouldn't, try to take on Ben Nevis.

"I'm just saying it's the kind of experience you want to tell your grandkids about," Matt said, his eyes wide with hope.

Lowe snorted. "And what grandkids will that be, Matt, considering you're probably going to die at the bottom of the highest mountain in Britain?"

He grimaced. "The highest?"

"I just told you that," Claudia frowned at him. "Don't you listen to me?"

"Honestly, when you talk I'm pretty much just staring at your mouth. Or your boobs."

Beck slapped him across the head.

"Dude," Matt rubbed the back of his skull. "I'm going to have brain damage before I have kids with the way you keep fucking smacking me around. Just have sex with her already and be done with it."

Claudia blushed while Beck took a menacing step toward Matt.

Lowe stepped in front of Matt protectively. "He's just messing with you," he grinned. "Give him a break. The guy is seriously hungover. He was wasted last night when we put him to bed."

"We?" Jake suddenly asked, his tone demanding.

Lowe stiffened, his hands curling into fists as he nodded. "Denver, Rowena, Char, and me."

Jake took a step toward him. "And then what happened?"

Oh fucking oh! My feet started walking toward them both with a mind of their own.

Lowe's eyes sharpened and he murmured silkily, tauntingly, "And then we went to *bed*."

Without another word Jake launched himself at Lowe with fierce aggression and punched him so hard in the face, Lowe stumbled back and lost his footing.

As a group we shouted a multitude of curses and cries of shock, and I propelled forward, putting myself between Jake and Lowe.

Shaking, I flinched when Lowe glanced up at me, his lips bloody and swelling, and gave me a sardonic shrug.

"Don't fucking look at her," Jake growled, trying to push past Beck. "Get up."

Lowe eyed him with arrogant insouciance but slowly stood.

"Whit is goin' on?" Rowena asked softly, worry dripping from the words as Denver now helped hold Jake back.

Lowe wiped his lip. "He thinks I fucked Charley."

Everyone hushed at that announcement. Even Jake grew still.

All eyes but Lowe's and Jake's turned to me.

I blanched. "He didn't!" I denied vehemently.

Jake jerked at the denial and whipped his head around to me. "He didn't?"

"No, I didn't," Lowe answered for me, his eyes fixed on Jake. "I kissed her. One kiss. We stopped. Decided it was a bad idea. But since you dumped Charley years ago and flaunted a new relationship in front of her for months, I'd like to know what business it is of yours who Charley fucks and why just the thought of some lucky guy going there stirs you into a blind rage?" His eyes narrowed now and suddenly it occurred to me that Lowe wasn't as unaffected or nonchalant as he let on. He was pissed at Jake. Big time. His voice was rough as he continued, "Sort your fucking head out, man, before you lose friends and worse ... hurt someone who definitely does not deserve to be hurt by you again."

After a few seconds of hard-faced death stares, Jake's shoulders slumped wearily and he scrubbed his hands over his face.

I felt sick.

Never did I want to be the girl who caused a fight between anyone, let alone friends, and I definitely didn't want to be the girl to put blood on Lowe's face and that look in Jake's eyes.

"Talk to him," Claudia whispered, coming to a stop beside me, her fingers squeezing mine. "We'll get Lowe cleaned up and head into town. You take Jake for a walk. You need to work this out before it implodes. No more avoiding."

Swallowing the nausea, I nodded at her and watched as she quietly and calmly herded everyone, except for Jake, back into the lodge.

Claudia gave me one last bolstering look and disappeared inside.

Jake looked over at me, a riot of emotions roiling in his dark eyes. I felt those emotions blast into me and take hold, pleading with me to go to him. Instead I turned in the opposite direction and began to stride away with the hope that he'd catch up to me.

He did.

Soon we were walking downhill, side by side, the atmosphere between us thick and exasperating and a little frightening. We'd always, always felt too much around each other. Jake punching Lowe was proof enough of that.

"The thought," he suddenly said, his voice raspy, gruff, "the thought of you being with him, with anybody ... I was sitting in there trying to get past it, trying to tell myself it wasn't my business, but it just ... it was eating at me and eating at me and I just had to get it out."

"By punching Lowe?"

"I wasn't thinking."

Taking a deep breath of crisp, clean air, my voice shook a little as I replied, "We're not together. Who I sleep with shouldn't matter."

"But it does."

"Jake ..."

"Did the thought of me being with Melissa bother you?"

The question hurt like a mother and I stopped so I could glare up at him in disgust. "You don't deserve an answer to that question."

Jake stared down at me sadly. "No, I don't. But I need it."

I didn't say anything for a while but slowly his anguished expression loosened the words until they fell onto my tongue and right out of my mouth. "Why do you think I started avoiding you? I need to move on from us, Jake, and I couldn't do that and be around you ... and Melissa. When I heard you broke up with her ... that didn't really change how I felt."

He hung his head, his fingers scrunching into his hair. "You put up a good front. I used to be able to read you but you seemed fine. I kept looking for some indication, something ..." He shrugged unhappily. "Then your dad's attitude at the airport ... I couldn't get the questions out of my head. What did it mean? Why was he still pissed on your behalf? Did you want me still?" He breathed softly. "It caused another huge argument between me and Melissa. We broke up in a fucking taxi," he sighed sadly.

Every word he said repeated in time with the hard thud of my heart. "Is she okay?"

He shook his head. "She wasn't at the time. But it's been almost a month so ... I don't know. I never meant to hurt her. Never. But I started to think maybe you weren't fine. That you were just lying to protect yourself. Then your question on the train ..." He looked up from under his eyelashes, studying me. "It gave me hope. Until you went back to avoiding me again."

My body jerked at the unexpected comment. "Hope?"

Jake nodded, shoving his nervous hands into his pockets. "I wasn't looking for anything from you. I never imagined you'd ever want me back. Not after what I did, how I acted." He turned now, starting to walk again and I found myself hurrying to catch up, my breathing shallow as Jake's confession became my whole world. "A few months after we moved back to Chicago, I still wasn't doing well. I wouldn't talk to my parents, my grades were slipping, I spent most of my time holed up in my room listening to crap music, and I was ... pretty good at pretending to be numb."

"What happened to Brett wasn't your fault, Jake," I reminded him quietly.

"I know that," he nodded, "I know that now. But back then, I couldn't get the what-ifs out of my head. For the most part, I did a good job of negatively associating you with it all." Jake's gaze was apologetic when he saw me flinch. "That didn't last long. Three months after we left Lanton, I was up in my room and I still had a lot of moving boxes lying around. My parents paid for a company to pack most of our stuff and transport it back to Chicago, so when I opened one of my boxes, I wasn't expecting to see you there. I'd forgotten about the tickets to Blind Side and that frame I had on my bedside table ..."

I hugged my arms around myself, remembering the photograph that Lukas had taken of me and Jake leaning against Hendrix. He had his arms around me, I had my hand on his stomach, and I was smiling up into his face. Jake wasn't smiling but the expression in his eyes told everyone who looked at that picture that he was in love with me.

I'd loved that photo. So had Jake.

Tears formed in the back of my eyes and I fought hard to restrain them.

"I pulled out that photograph and as I stared at it, it was just a floodtide. I remembered. I remembered how much I loved you. How happy you made me. How much you could surprise me. How hard you made me laugh. And what it felt like to feel you laughing against me. To hold you. To kiss you. To be inside you." He shot me a dark look and my breath caught. "I remembered what I said to you. I remembered every tear on your face when I broke up with you, and I couldn't believe I was the one who put them there. That's when it hit me: there was no going back. When I threw you away, somewhere deep down I think I believed it would be okay because we were us. We were solid. But reality set in after the fact. After what I did? There was no way I could win you back." He glanced warily at me. "I lost it. The blame, the guilt, the anger, the loss, it all just swallowed me whole. My parents heard me yelling and breaking things and by the time they got to my room, I'd trashed the place and I'd cut my hands on the picture frame glass." He shrugged sadly. "That makes me sound psycho, I know ... but think of it from my perspective. To me, in that moment, it was like you'd died too.

"My parents made me talk to someone and it helped with all the other stuff—Brett's death, his dad's campaign of hate, and my responsibility in it all, or lack thereof. I've accepted what happened wasn't my fault. I won't forget it, but I've gotten through it. You," Jake's smile was crooked, halfhearted, and rueful, "were harder to deal with. So I went back to my old ways instead."

Meaning he slept around a lot. I ignored the unpleasant clench in my stomach at that thought. "Then you met Melissa."

"You should know I applied to Edinburgh on the off chance you'd be here and I'd get to apologize, find some closure. Never, not once, did I ever believe I could get you back."

"So you'd given up and you moved on."

Jake stopped us again, his hand touching my elbow gently. "Baby, I don't think I ever moved on." He ducked his head, stepping forward into my space, his dark eyes mesmerizing as always. "And for the first time I'm allowing myself to hope that you haven't moved on, either."

My breath caught and I honestly felt my body teeter at his words. "Jake, I can't." I backed away from him.

Ignoring my silent plea for space, Jake moved so near, I had to tilt my head back. The smell of his cologne hit me and I had to rein myself in against the temptation to press my mouth to his strong throat. "These last few months have been torture, Charley. Getting to be close to you but not close enough. I will do anything to make this work."

"You broke up with Melissa for me?"

Guilt sharpened his expression as he replied, "For you. For me. For her."

My body remembered how beautiful it felt to be wrapped around Jake Caplin and it was pleading with me to throw caution to the wind.

"You want this as much as I do," Jake said gruffly.

I saw no point in denying what was so obvious between us, but just because I remembered how beautiful it was to be in love with Jake and have him love me back didn't mean I hadn't forgotten how ugly it was to have him tell me he didn't care anymore.

"I do," I admitted softly, "but that doesn't mean I want a relationship with you. I don't trust you, Jake, and I don't know if I'll ever trust you again. You shouldn't have thrown away a girl who trusted you implicitly for me."

"I care about Melissa, I do—"

"Last year you *loved* her. Now it's only care?"

"Yeah, I thought I loved her, but that's because for a while I let myself forget."

"Forget what?"

"What's it's like to love you." Jake reached for me, his fingers brushing my cheek tenderly.

I curled my hand around his wrist and closed my eyes, not sure if I was blocking out his confession or soaking it in.

"I've never stopped loving you. If I stayed with Melissa, it would've been a lie and she deserves better than that. And I know you deserve better too, but I'm just too selfish when it comes to you. I want you even though I don't deserve you."

"Jake ..."

"You save people. You save me. It's what you do. You even tried to save Brett and I'm so proud of you and of how you coped with that night. I missed out on getting to tell you that and I missed out on helping you deal with that too. Because it didn't just happen to me. It happened to us all.

"I wish I could go back to that scared-shitless kid and tell him to be brave like his girl. I can't take that back, though. All I can do is attempt to make up for it. I want you to give me that chance, but if you don't, I need you to know I never lied when I told you that you're extraordinary, Charley. Whatever your answer is, just know that I will always believe that, and I will always believe in you."

"Jake." I was panicking, panicking because I wanted to give in. The brave girl everyone thought me to be had fled down the cold Scottish hill. "No." Stupid, stupid tears slipped down my cheeks as I said it, my stomach flipping in protestation at the word.

"Charley," he whispered hoarsely, pleading, as he reached up to brush away my tears with his thumb. "Please. Please try because every time I look into your face, all I feel is ... so in love with you. Then two seconds later, every time without fail, it hits me like a sledgehammer in my gut that you're not mine. That I'm not allowed to reach out to you ... I thought I could accept that, I thought I'd come to terms with it, but I can't. We're not over." Tears shimmered in his beautiful eyes. "We *can't* be over."

The knowledge that he felt the same pain I felt every day, and the sight of his overwrought expression, beat away at my panic until all that was left was fear and stupid, stupid hope.

Hearing his breathing grow heavy with anticipation—and if the trembling in his hand was any indication, also fear—my eyes slowly opened. I stared up into his burning expression and leaned my cheek into his hand, my fingers flexing around his wrist. "I can't guarantee you anything. I know I haven't moved on from you, and I know I still care about you, but Jake, you have to know that I might never trust you again and if I don't trust you ... we're never going to work." I squeezed his wrist. "I might not be able to give you what you want."

Eyes blazing with relief and determination, Jake dipped his head close to mine so his words whispered across my lips. "I'm willing to risk it."

We stared at each other in silence until the tension between us became almost unbearable. My eyes dropped to his mouth and I had to physically restrain myself from reaching up and taking what I'd been dreaming about for months. When I raised my gaze back to his, Jake's eyes were heated and the muscle in his jaw flexed as if he was also struggling to hold himself back.

My chest rose and fell in rapid breaths as I fought to come to the right decision.

In the end I went with my gut and sighed into him. "Okay," I breathed.

Jake's grip on me tightened as his eyes widened. "Okay, okay?"

I nodded, shivering now with the decision. This could go horribly wrong after all.

But suddenly Jake was grinning, his eyes shining as he pulled me close and leaned his forehead against mine.

The shivering stopped. His warm breath fanned my face. "Thank you, baby."

My hands reached for him, gripping his coat at the waist. "Where do we go from here?"

"I need to get the next train back to Edinburgh."

A strange and unpleasant mix of guilt and jealousy washed over me. "To Melissa?"

"Not to Melissa but," he groaned, rubbing a hand through his hair, "if I stay here, I'm not going to be able to control myself and I think maybe we should take things slow. For us. And also out of respect. It's only been a few weeks ..." He quieted, seeming anxious about my reaction to his concern for Melissa.

In actuality, his concern convinced me that I should at least try to give this guy I once loved completely another shot. It would somehow feel callous to start a physical relationship only a month after their breakup.

And then remembering Melissa's words at Frankenstein, her description of her relationship with Jake, I suddenly felt a cold rush of uncertainty. "Jake ... she said she's one of your best friends. That she brings you peace. I don't know if I've ever given you peace ... Are you sure you're—"

"Stop," he whispered roughly. "Mel is one of my best friends and hurting her was awful. But as for peace ... I don't know what she said but I know what I know. Mel and me ... our relationship was comfortable, quiet. We rarely argued and she was supportive and kind." His expression grew more intense as he studied my features, as if they were the most important things he'd ever lay eyes on. "But peace ... that comes with feeling complete, and I haven't felt that way since I was seventeen and I walked away from a girl who could make me laugh harder, feel harder, and burn harder than any other person in my world. You gave me peace, Charley. *You* did. You *do*."

Swallowing hard, I felt my own guilt rise. "Melissa ... she knows, then?"

Jake pulled back, his expression uncomfortable. "We almost broke up after Halloween but I convinced myself that I could make it work with her, that being around you again was just confusing. The argument at the airport, in the cab, it was one of many lately. She knew, Charley. She also knew it would be worse for both of us if I'd gone on pretending."

Confused how his emotions could've switched so quickly, I let him go and jammed my hands in my pockets. "You really have fallen out of love with her?"

He took a moment before answering carefully. "I still love her. I'm just not *in* love with her. Charley," Jake shook his head, all the awe, affection, and tenderness I'd missed for years back in his eyes,

"I knew after weeks of meeting you that I was never going to love another girl like I love you. You're it for me. They write books about what we have. You felt it when we were sixteen—I know you did because you gave me everything, and I'm going to spend the next few weeks, months, years if needed, proving to you that when you gave everything to me, it wasn't because we all do 'stupid shit sometimes,'" his voice cracked as he told me he remembered the awful things he'd said to me, word for word, "it's because we're 'it.' What I did, losing you, it was the hardest lesson I've ever learned. Now nothing will get in my way of making you happy."

It sounded wonderful. It sounded like it had sounded before. A huge part of me wanted to pull him toward me and kiss the mouth that had spoken such beautiful things so they'd melt on my tongue and seep deep into me, but the broken part of me wasn't as persuaded.

Jake saw it and his eyes softened. "Baby, I'll earn it back. I promise I'll earn it back."

Chapter Twenty-Three

Fort William, January 2013

Before Jake left us, he caught up with Lowe to have a private word with him. Whatever passed between them, they returned more at peace with one another. Lowe even winked at me to let me know everything was all right between us.

I wasn't sure how everyone else would react to the news that Jake was going back to Edinburgh because we had no self-control.

A bundle of nerves, guilt, and excitement, I was quiet while Jake told the group he needed to go back to the city. When the taxi arrived and Jake climbed inside, I watched from the balcony, questioning over and over if I'd done the right thing.

"So tell us, Charley," Denver asked lazily, "is he going back to escape you or is he going back so he doesn't fuck you?"

I stiffened at the question and looked over my shoulder, my eyes resting on Claudia first. She looked back at me, her eyebrows drawn together in concern. I nodded slowly at her. "The latter."

My friends murmured to one another but I didn't hear what they were saying. I was too busy watching as Claudia marched toward me with purpose. Without a word she grabbed my hand and hauled me out of the sitting room and down the hall into Beck's room. She shut the door behind us and leaned against it, giving me a look that clearly said, "Go on …"

I shrugged helplessly. "He still loves me."

"Well, that's obvious. It has been for at least two months now."

Narrowing my eyes on her, I mirrored her stance.

"Well?" She threw up her hands, giving me a confused smile. "Tell me this is a good thing. Right? You're happy?"

"Yes. I mean, I'm scared and we have so much to work through and work out … but … it's four years later and I still feel … incomplete without him." I smiled sadly.

The romantic in her rose to the fore and she quickly blinked away tears. "So you're giving him a shot?"

I slumped down on the nearest bed, heaved a massive sigh, and flopped onto my back. "Yes. I told him I hadn't moved on but that I might never trust him again, but he wants to try. We've decided to take it slow for us and for Melissa. Apparently we have no self-control so he went back in case being in such close quarters proved too big a temptation." I rolled my head so I could watch her reaction.

Claudia bit her lip. "And Melissa? I was right? He doesn't love her?"

Just the thought of Jake loving Melissa felt like someone raking sharp nails across my insides. "He does. But it's not what we had, Claud. I let myself be convinced that all my memories of our relationship were somehow blown out of proportion, that I'd only imagined the intense connection between us. It's real. I haven't forgotten and neither has he. I can't describe what it feels like. It's just … like a rope binding us together." I sat up slowly and finished solemnly, "I have to give us one more chance or I might never move on."

My best friend walked quietly across the room and sat down beside me. With a small smile on her lips, she took my hand in hers. "Then I'm happy for you and I'm going to be there for you. It sucks about Melissa, but it's nobody's fault. It's just timing. Sometimes timing is a bitch."

I squeezed her hand and nudged her shoulder affectionately with mine. "You don't need this crap with everything that's going on with you."

"Nonsense. This is big, and no matter what's going on with me, I want you to always feel like you can talk to me. People can judge you and Jake and take sides with the whole Melissa thing but I'm not people. I'm your friend. I'm just here for you."

Feeling myself getting emotional, I drew in a shuddery breath. "I pretty much freaking love you."

She laughed softly. "I pretty much freaking love you too."

We sat for a while, holding onto one another until Claudia finally drew away. "I suppose we better face the music. Just so you know, Beck will be cool. Jake tells him everything and he drops hints to me every now and then. I didn't want to say anything because I didn't want to confuse you, especially when all I had was Beck's nonsensical hints and not facts, but looking back, I get the impression that Beck has known all along that Jake was in love with you. I think he's been rooting for you both. So you're golden there. Getting the best friend on your side is one of the biggest hurdles."

I grinned at her. "Thank you."

In answer she hauled me to my feet and I followed her back out into the sitting room. Everyone shut up when I walked back in and I instantly slid on my badass blank face so they'd assume I didn't give a crap what they thought.

If I was just getting back together with Jake, I wouldn't care. But the situation was complicated by Melissa and I did care about her getting hurt and I cared that my friends would see me as some kind of ogre because of it.

"About time," Matt grumbled sleepily. "The foreplay between you and Jake was killing me. I was starting to feel bad for Mel." He blinked rapidly. "Hey, do you think she'd go for me?"

"You're a douche," Lowe replied.

Matt thought about that for a second and then shrugged.

"Personally, I think it's naebody's business but Charley's, Jake's, and Melissa's," Rowena put in pointedly and stood. "So let's put Charley out of her misery and go tae this bloody distillery before it closes."

I knew I liked that girl for a reason.

The tour of the distillery was fun and Claudia definitely tried to take my mind off Jake by pushing whisky samples my way, but I couldn't get him out of my head.

It grew even harder when he called me three hours after his departure.

I wandered away from the group, stepping outside into the parking lot, and answered. "Hey," I said a little breathily, my nerves jumping all over the place.

"Hey." His deep voice rippled through me and I closed my eyes, knowing that despite all the confusion and complication, if he'd been there with me, I'd be on him in a second. "Just wanted to check in."

"Make sure I haven't changed my mind?" I teased, only half joking.

"Something like that."

"Well, I haven't."

"Good."

I sighed. "How are you?"

"Got to admit, baby, I'm not looking forward to arriving in Edinburgh when you're in Fort William. I wish you were here. I can't believe we decided to give things a shot again and I'm on a train five minutes later traveling hundreds of miles away from you."

"I know. But you were right. We need to take things one day at a time."

"Yeah." He sucked in a deep breath. "So are you at the distillery?"

"Yup. We got a tour and everything. But I barely remember a minute of it. My mind is kind of wandering …"

Jake was silent a moment before he told me quietly, "I feel like the biggest shit in the world right now because even though I'm sad about Melissa and I feel guilty as hell, I'm also pretty fucking excited we're getting back together."

"I know what you mean."

"Yeah?"

"Of course, Jake. I wouldn't have said yes to you otherwise."

"Good, baby. I'm glad."

"We still have a lot of things to talk about …"

"I know," he replied quietly. "For now just tell me that when you get back on Sunday, you'll meet me at Milk at nine o'clock so we can start over."

I smiled tremulously. "I can do that."

That night I lay in the bed next to Claudia's and stared at the ceiling. I tried counting sheep, I tried going over song lyrics in my head, and I tried making lists of things I needed to do in an effort to bore myself to sleep. Yet, sleep eluded me. In the end, all I could think about was Jake and if I'd acted too impulsively by agreeing to get back together with him.

"You can't sleep, can you?" Claudia's voice surprised me.

Startled, I turned to her. "Apparently you can't, either."

"It's because you're thinking so loud."

I grimaced. "I can't help it."

My friend flipped onto her side, tucking her hands beneath her pillow. "Do you want me to take your mind off it?"

"Uh, yes, please."

Claudia's expression was serious as she replied, "My mom called while you were taking a shower."

Sensing something big, I twisted around onto my side to face her so she'd know she had my full attention. "What did she say?"

"She told me my real father's name. She tracked him down for me."

I raised an eyebrow. "She did? Wow."

Claudia nodded, her mouth twisted in a little moue. "Apparently she's more of a human that I thought. It's the Botox— it confuses things. Anyway, his name is Dustin Tweedie."

I blinked. "I know that name. Why do I know that name?"

"Because he was a pretty famous artist but he retired ten years ago. Google him. His art was weird but rich people buy weird shit. I would know. I live with two of them."

It took a lot of self-restraint not to pick up my phone and put his name into Google. "Do you know anything else about him?"

"Just that he was brought up in England. Mom found out that he's still a bachelor and he lives in Barcelona now."

"My God, Claud. Are you okay?"

Her shoulder moved up to her ear. "I don't know. I'm thinking I should just forget about him. Move on. He doesn't know I exist and he lives in freaking Barcelona, so … it's stupid to … I don't even …"

Hearing her confusion and the crack in her voice, I slipped out from under my covers and darted across the room to her bed, my feet protesting against the icy cold floor. Claudia shimmied back, holding her duvet up, and I slipped in beside her. We faced each other and I reached for her hand. "Take your time thinking about what you want to do. Just know it's not stupid if you're thinking about reaching out to him. We'd all think about it if we were in your shoes."

She nodded, biting on her lip, tears shimmering in her eyes. "I'm just tired of feeling like I'm constantly looking for something I never had. I'm not a kid anymore, Charley. I need to grow up and just accept what hand I've been dealt."

"No." I shook my head. "Never accept what hand you've been dealt if it's not the hand you wanted. You deserve more than that. You deserve to win. Put all the other crap out of your head and just think about what you want."

Her grip on my hand tightened so much, it was almost painful. "Did you tell Beck?"

She shook her head. "He gets really mad about the whole thing—"

Because the idiot is in love with you!

"—and I didn't want to turn the evening bad. He's in a really good mood."

"Are you two still … platonic?" I asked carefully.

"Oh no," she shook her head, "you're not getting to play matchmaker just because you and Jake are on your way to sorting your shit out. No, no, no."

I laughed softly. "I just want you to be happy."

Claudia made a face and replied airily, "I'm always happy."

I squeezed her hand and whispered, "Not fake happy. Real happy."

"You know what," she whispered back, "I'm not *un*happy. I've got you and I've got Jim and Delia Mom and Andie, and yes, Beck and I may be completely dysfunctional, but I have him too. And maybe one day I'll have my own Jake. I'm not unhappy, Charley. I'm just trying to be hopeful and hoping that being hopeful doesn't make me a child."

"You're not a child, Claud. You're just human."

We snuggled close to each other, our heads resting against one another. "It's been some trip, huh?" she teased.

In answer I started to laugh until Claudia was giggling uncontrollably, our hilarity muffled by our pillows so we wouldn't wake our friends.

Chapter Twenty-Four

Edinburgh, January 2013

Truth be told, I felt like I was going on my very first date.

By some miracle, I'd gotten through the rest of our trip in Fort William. Honestly, because we weren't there to climb hills or do anything remotely relevant to the location, and because we didn't have a car so we could check out the surrounding areas, we were pretty bored by the end of our stay, ready to get back to the city. Me more so than anyone.

I'd gone back and forth, back and forth on my feelings until I realized that every time I even thought about picking up the phone to call Jake and tell him I'd made a mistake, my chest burned with denial. I was doing this. I had to suck it up and accept my decision.

Once I'd gotten that through my thick head, I was pretty excited about getting back to him. Yes, I was nervous, and yes, I had no idea what our future held, but that would be the same in any relationship.

We got back to Edinburgh around five o' clock. Lowe walked at my side as we ambled back to our apartments and as soon as we hit the Royal Mile, he grinned at me.

"What?" I frowned up at him.

"You. You're a bundle of energy. You're dying to get back to him."

"Am not," I grumbled petulantly.

Lowe laughed. "You are too. Did I tell you Jake Caplin is the luckiest son of a bitch I've ever met?"

"What am I now? Your soundboard for smooth talking? If I am, I'm giving you two big thumbs up on that one."

Chuckling, Lowe threw his arm around my shoulders. "So fucking cute."

I frowned. "You're going to keep calling me that because you know I hate it, right?"

"Oh yeah."

Despite growling at him in irritation, underneath the snarl I felt easier and more assured that Lowe was acting cool. We hadn't talked much the last two days and I was worried that I might've wrecked our friendship. There was no need to worry. With Lowe, what you saw, you got, and he meant it when he said he was rooting for me.

Claudia, Denver, Rowena, and I said goodbye to the guys on the Cowgate, my eyes darting up to their building before I hurried to follow my friends back to ours. I did not expect to be greeted by a wide-eyed Maggie as Claud and I strolled into the kitchen.

"Well, is it true?" Maggie asked, excitedly shoving the papers in front of her to the side. "Did Jake Caplin break up with Melissa Bouchard for you?"

I blinked rapidly, feeling the color leave my cheeks. How had news traveled that quickly?

"Oh my God, he did?" If it was possible her eyes widened even more. "Gemma is not going to be happy. You know she and Melissa are friends, right?"

Actually, I didn't know that. Fabulous. Now I'd have to live with Gemma giving me dirty looks for the next four months.

Blowing the breath out between my lips, I made a sad face at Claudia. "I need a drink."

Claudia tried not to laugh at my uncharacteristic pout and failed. "I think we have vodka somewhere."

"That'll do it."

The buzz from my two shots of vodka had worn off, which was probably why I was a nervous wreck by the time nine o'clock came along. It turned out that everyone was meeting at Milk because the guys were doing a set.

I followed Claudia past the bar toward the archway at the end of the room and shook out my hands, trying to fight off the churning in my stomach. I was not a nervous person by nature and I really hated it that Jake could get me into such a state.

However, as soon as our eyes met across the room, the nerves transformed into excited butterflies and Claudia smiled at me. We made our way through the cluttered room, dodging chairs and rounding tables, and the whole time my eyes never left Jake's. He stood when he saw us, and Denver, the only member of The Stolen not onstage setting up, followed his gaze at the same time Rowena did.

Everything and everyone but Jake disappeared as he moved around the table and came to a stop inches before me. I leaned back and gave him my best cocky smile. "So you're the mysterious guy I'm supposed to be meeting," I said, in reminiscence of the first thing he'd ever said to me.

Recognizing it, Jake's eyes glittered. "The mysterious newbie. Jake," he offered me his hand, his expression teasing.

I took it, feeling a sense of peace slide through me as we clasped hands. "Charley."

"I know. You're famous. Supergirl."

I laughed, forcing myself not to lean into him for a kiss. We were taking things slow, after all, and keeping our relationship a quieter affair in public for Melissa's sake. Looking deep into Jake's eyes, I knew he was feeling the pull too and he gave me a regretful little smile before nodding his head toward the table. "Sit. I'll get you a drink."

"Beer." I smiled back at him and headed around the table to sit in the empty seat beside the one he'd just vacated.

While Jake was at the bar, Denver joined the band just as the manager of Milk hopped up onto the stage and scratched his thick beard with an amused curl to his lip. "If ye don't know who these guys are by now, then ye're definitely no regulars. There has been a fair amount of women visiting Milk these last few months, which I think has more tae dae wi' the effect these guys have on their knickers than ma inexhaustible charm."

We laughed and I felt an immense amount of pride rush through me for The Stolen. My friends really were awesome and glancing over at Claudia sitting across the table grinning up at the stage, I knew she felt that pride too.

"Don't let their pretty boy façades fool ye. These guys are phenomenally talented. So without further ado, back from their trip home tae the States, Milk presents The Stolen."

We whooped and catcalled as the manager smiled at the guys and then bounced offstage. Matt hit the drums, leading them into one of my favorite upbeat tracks that Beck had co-written with Lowe. Listening to Lowe's smooth, deep voice, I was lost for a while until I sensed Jake's eyes on me. Turning my head ever so slightly, I met Jake's gaze as he approached with beers in hand. He carefully handed Claud hers, eyes still on me, and then he rounded the table. Jake sat down next to me and casually shifted his chair closer. He draped his arm around the back of my seat and just like that, I lost my focus, Lowe's voice becoming a muffled hum in my ears.

Jake wasn't even touching me and every single part of me was absolutely aware of every single part of him. We sat like that for four songs and then the guys stopped for a break.

By this point I was having difficulty breathing and when I chanced a look at Jake, his dark eyes were burning. Being close, knowing we both wanted to be closer, and doing our best to be respectful ... well, it was a sick kind of torment.

"The guys sound great tonight," I said loud enough for him to hear.

Jake nodded and leaned a little closer. "They always sound great." I gave him a teasing smile at his devotion and he shrugged. "I'm a groupie. You know ... without the sex."

"Well, that's a shame. They'd be lucky to have you."

He smirked. "That's true. And they do all want me. I've remained strictly friends with all of them so I don't upset their band dynamic. It's been particularly difficult for me. They're all very handsome."

Lips trembling with laughter, I nodded gravely. "Quite the temptation." I leaned closer. "But let me in on the secret. Who would you have chosen ... groupie."

Deadpan, Jake quirked an eyebrow. "I thought that would be obvious." He nodded to the stage where the guys were chatting and taking sips of water. "Matt. Look at him. That's all raw animal magnetism right there."

When I turned to look up at Matt, he was rubbing a hand towel under his sweaty pits.

I threw my head back in laughter and turned to Jake to find him smiling at me in that way—that way he used to. That way that said he adored me completely.

Terrified of that look melting every single one of my defenses, I turned back to the stage … and immediately frowned. Beck had jumped off the small platform to talk to a blond girl who'd approached the band. Beck said something with a flirtatious tilt to his mouth and the girl leaned her hand on his chest and laughed, stepping into his body. Eyes lit up Beck continued to chat with the girl, and his hand dropped to her hip to hold her close.

I looked at Claudia. Uneasiness moved through me at the sight of Claudia's pale cheeks and lowered gaze.

If I, a person on the outside of their bizarre relationship, thought that Claudia and Beck had only grown closer over the winter break, then it came as no surprise that Claudia must've been feeling that way too. Unfortunately, Beck was a tool, and I would never understand him. For a guy who seemed so concerned about Claud's feelings, he sure had a nice way of trampling all over them.

"She terrifies him," Jake's deep voice murmured in my ear and despite my anger at Beck, Jake still managed to make the hair on the back of my neck rise.

I turned sharply to him, frowning. "What?"

Jake nodded at Beck. "He cares about Claudia more than any girl. Ever. I know that for a fact. I also know he's pretty messed up when it comes to women. He doesn't mean to hurt her."

Shaking my head, I shot my friend another worried look. "She's going to have to walk away before he breaks her heart."

Strong, warm fingers threaded through mine and tightened. "I hope she gives him a chance first."

Staring up into Jake's sincere eyes, I knew then he wasn't just talking about Beck and Claudia. Swallowing past the lump of emotion in my throat, I nodded gently. "I know she'll try."

It became quickly apparent that Jake and I had very little self-control. Or at least we weren't good with temptation.

Our decision to take things slow meant we hung out with our friends like we had for the last few months. There was no kissing or cuddling or anything remotely sexual. Okay, not going to lie … there was a lot of eye-fucking going on.

The first week passed quickly and without incident. Kind of. We'd returned to classes and every day at the university, I'd dreaded bumping into Melissa. I knew from my roommate Gemma that Melissa was having a hard time. I knew this because Gemma hostilely informed me of her condition before endeavoring to treat me like Hester Prynne from *The Scarlet Letter*. If I walked into the kitchen and Gemma and one or both of the other girls were there, she'd cease talking as though I wasn't good enough to be privy to her conversations.

On campus I passed her between classes and she glared at me before murmuring something to her companions that made them wrinkle their nose at me, as if I smelled bad.

I ignored this bitchy, childish behavior because frankly, I couldn't give a shit what she thought. Unfortunately, I did care what Melissa thought, so when I turned down one of the book stacks on the third floor of the library and came face to face with her, I pretty much wished I were *anywhere* else in the world.

Our eyes met as Melissa looked up from her book. As I stared into her wounded, broken expression, I felt like she'd punched her fist into my chest and squeezed my heart.

Feeling sick, for the first time in as long as I could remember my bravado failed me, and I trembled a little as Melissa put the book back on the shelf and walked slowly toward me. Not once did I think about dropping my gaze. I owed her that much.

She halted in front of me and I stopped breathing as I took in the dark circles under her eyes, the sharpness in her cheekbones that hadn't been there before Christmas break.

It felt like forever we just stared at one another, the sounds of pages turning, computer mice clicking, hushed murmurings, and soft footsteps all seeming incredibly loud in the taut atmosphere.

Melissa blinked, the corners of her pretty mouth dipping. "I …" She shook her head, her eyes dim with pain as she continued softly, "I really want to hate you."

Remembering the days after my breakup with Jake, remembering the ache and needles of pain in every nerve, bone, and muscle, remembering the stifling feeling that came over me as I had to pay witness to Melissa's relationship with Jake, the only thing I could say was, "I know."

A tear slipped down her cheek at my response and before I could say anything else, she quickly swiped it away and brushed past me.

At her departure I sucked in a huge gulp of air and leaned back against the shelves, wishing life wasn't so goddamn complicated.

Later that night I told Jake about the encounter as we walked to the movies. The two of us were quiet all that night, and for the next week it was a little bit easier not to give into the temptation of one another.

That wasn't to say the pull wasn't still intense.

In order to somehow avoid the pull, Jake and I had actually stopped spending so much time together. It was three weeks after our return from Fort William, the end of January, and we'd decided to spend yet another date at the movies because it meant at least two hours of time where we could pretend not to be focused on one another.

We'd both fallen in love with this small art deco theater in an area called Morningside, about a thirty-minute walk from the university. The theater offered leather recliners and large, comfortable leather sofas as well as ordinary cinema seats. Jake and I usually got recliners so we weren't sitting too much in each other's space, but on the eventful night when we kicked off our five-day ban, we could only get a sofa together.

As soon as we sat on that small sofa, I knew it was a bad idea. We'd spent the last few weeks ignoring the sexual chemistry between us, which meant we'd pretty much been ignoring our relationship and continuing on as we'd done before the Christmas break. Claudia told me she got that we were trying to be kind to Melissa, but whether or not we were sleeping together wasn't going to change the fact that Melissa assumed we were.

Honestly, by this point I was with Claudia, but just as Jake was willing to prove himself to me, I was willing to respect the memory of his and Melissa's relationship for him.

That's why the sofa thing was such a bad idea.

The tension was so thick between us, it was like our attraction had physically manifested into a large elephant sitting on and crushing my chest so I couldn't breathe properly.

Our arms brushed and Jake's might as well have been a flame licking my skin. My cheeks blazed and I murmured, "Sorry."

When the lights went down for the movie, it was unbearable. I could hear Jake's shallow breathing racing to find rhythm with mine. In the dim light, I saw his hands flex into tight fists on top of his thighs. And because I was trying my best not to think about sex, all I could think about was sex with Jake and how good it had been and how much better it would probably be now.

I found myself beginning to sweat. My body was like a furnace.

"Fuck it," Jake suddenly whispered and turned to look at me as the light from the screen flickered over his face. "There's taking things slow and then there's taking things glacial."

My lip curled up at the corner. "Done with the glacial?"

His eyes burned in the dark. "I think we're doing a pretty good job of melting the glacial right out of us."

"You feel it too?"

"Fuck yeah," he leaned in close, his lips millimeters from mine. "Baby, I've been feeling it with you since I was sixteen."

He breached the gap between our mouths, his warm lips brushing over mine, tingles rushing south. He grazed his lips over mine once, twice, and then he nipped my bottom lip gently, before sweeping the tip of his tongue over the bite. I gasped, the erotic noise swallowed in his mouth as he closed it over mine. Jake slid his hand around my neck and into my hair, gently tugging me so I fell into his kiss, my hands resting on his chest.

His kiss was soft at first, almost hesitant, but as soon as I began moving my lips against his, telling him that I wanted this, the kiss changed. I felt his tongue flick lightly against mine and my fingers curled into his T-shirt in response. He teased me with those flicks until I was squirming in the dark for more, my arms sliding around his neck, my fingers tightening in his hair as I opened my mouth wider against his and licked his tongue in a deep, wet kiss that shattered what little thread of control he was holding onto.

Our kiss turned hard and hungry and Jake's arms slid around my waist so he could crush me against his chest.

The leather of the sofa creaked at our movement but I would've barely noticed it if it hadn't been for the harsh female voice from my left that whispered admonishingly, "This isn't a hotel room."

Jake and I pushed away from one another, our breathing heavy, my cheeks burning, as we gazed into each other's wide eyes.

We both knew then that we were so screwed.

Somehow we got through the movie and then Jake walked me back to my building. We didn't talk much and the entire time I was wondering if we were done with the whole moving slow thing and finally restarting our relationship. It occurred to me, now that I had a reminder of how combustible things were between us, I wasn't sure if that was what I wanted or not. Moving slow meant we didn't really discuss the things that mattered or the problems that still existed between us. If we finally entered into something serious and real again, it would mean opening myself up completely to Jake.

That was a worrying thought.

However, when we reached my apartment, Jake stopped and ran a shaky hand through his hair. "If we're going to keep up this whole taking-it-slow thing, maybe we shouldn't hang out alone for the next couple of days."

Part of me wanted to ask him why we were suddenly not just taking things slow but coming to an almost halt. At the cinema he'd seemed to be pretty adamant that glacial was bad.

I felt my brow pucker. He'd broken up with Melissa almost two months ago. Wasn't that a respectful amount of time already?

And yet ... the other part of me was almost relieved. It was a reprieve from having to let Jake in.

So I nodded, gave him a shaky smile, and walked up to my apartment feeling more confused than ever.

Chapter Twenty-Five

Edinburgh, February 2013

It all came to a head five days later.

The Stolen were playing at one of the student union venues—The Pleasance. It was a ten-minute walk down and then up from the Cowgate. Although I'd talked with Jake on the phone, I hadn't seen him in days. In a way, it was nice for me and Claudia to hang out uninterrupted from the boys for a while, but I had to admit, walking into the bar and seeing Jake laughing with Rowena while the band set up caused a flurry of excited nerves.

When I reached Jake, he grabbed my hand and pulled me into him. He bent down to murmur in my ear, "God, I've missed you."

I smiled and as I pulled back, I nodded to let him know I'd missed him too.

As the guys began to play, Jake put his arms around my waist and I leaned into him, my back to his chest. He rested his chin on my shoulder, tracing ticklish patterns with the tips of his finger on my stomach through my thin T-shirt. I was lost in the feel of him, of the scent of his cologne, of the sound of his voice vibrating through me as he sang softly along with Lowe. It was no wonder I didn't hear Rowena's warning at first, not until she was tugging Jake back from me saying loudly and edgily, "Guys, the door."

We jerked back from each other at the interruption, our breathing a little harried, and when we turned our heads toward the doorway, Jake instantly dropped my hand at the sight that greeted us.

Melissa.

She stood like a beacon in the crowd, flanked by two friends. The pain in her features made me want to crumple inside myself. I glanced up at Jake for direction but he was already making his way through the students toward his ex-girlfriend.

When he stopped beside her, she snapped at him, her eyes filling with tears as she gestured angrily toward me. Jake reached out to soothe her and she pulled on his shirt, her expression suddenly pleading. He ran a hand through his hair and nodded, nudging her toward the exit. Before he left with her, he mouthed an apology my way and held up his hand as if to say, "I'll be five minutes."

Just like that, our reunion was destroyed and all my happy was being eaten alive by guilt.

"Ye okay?" Rowena asked softly. She stood by Claudia's side and the two of them were gazing at me in concern.

I shrugged. "I'm fine. He'll be back soon."

Unfortunately, Jake wasn't back soon and I never got a text or a call as to why. By the time The Stolen's set was finished, I still hadn't heard anything from him and I was beginning to worry.

"I'll walk Claudia home," Denver offered as we were getting ready to leave the now-quiet bar. "You go back with the guys to their place. I'm sure he's there."

Deciding it was the best thing to do or I'd end up having another sleepless night, I followed Lowe, Beck, and Matt back to their apartment. Their common room was surprisingly clean considering a bunch of guys lived there, but then I remembered Beck telling me that Lowe was a bit of a clean freak.

Jake wasn't there in amongst all the clean.

Lowe shrugged and pulled a bottle of water out of the fridge and handed it to me. "Just hang out here with us until he gets back."

Feeling my annoyance building, I nodded but pulled out my phone and shot a text off to Jake asking him what was happening.

No reply.

The guys attempted to keep my mind off where they knew it was wandering—into irrational jealousy land where Jake was hooking up with his ex—but by one o'clock in the morning, I was starting to get pissed. And more worried. "Do you think something has happened to him?"

Beck frowned and shook his head. "Nah. They're probably just hashing shit out."

"They hashed shit out weeks ago. What else is there to say?" My shoulders slumped when they all looked anywhere but at me. "Look, I'm not a bitch, okay? The expression on Melissa's face tonight ... yeah. I hate that I'm a part of that. But we're not even together, barely, and he's already ..." *Shutting me out.* I waved my phone at them, not saying out loud the words I was thinking.

When it hit two o'clock, I'd gone past feeling bad about being angry and was just plain mad. What the hell was he doing with her at two o'clock in the morning?

I shot to my feet. "I'm going to go," I muttered, grabbing my coat.

"I'll walk you," Lowe insisted.

"No, it's fine. It's two minutes away."

"I don't care if it's five seconds away. I'm walking you."

Deciding to give into his chivalry, I was brittle as I marched out of the building. I couldn't believe how terrible the night had been, a night I'd been looking forward to all week. A month into our "relationship" and Jake was already letting me down.

We'd barely taken two steps onto the pavement when Jake appeared around the corner. He saw us coming out of his building and started hurrying toward us.

My eyes narrowed on him, hating that he looked so good flushed from the cold, his eyes soulful and searching as he approached me. "Baby—"

"Save it," I snapped, shaking my head and darting past him.

"I'll walk her home," Jake said sternly behind me.

I stopped and whirled around. "You will not. Lowe is walking me home."

Jake's eyes narrowed dangerously. "Unless you want me and Lowe to have problems, you'll let me see you home."

Lowe held up his hands in a surrender gesture. "Sorry, Charley, but I'm exhausted. I'll let Jake walk you home."

"Traitor," I grumbled to Lowe's back as he hurried inside. My eyes flicked to Jake and I pinned him with my darkest glare to cover up my hurt. With a grunt of annoyance, I spun back around and started down the Cowgate toward my building.

Jake rushed to catch up. "Charley, let me explain—"

"Explain how you disappeared with your ex-girlfriend until two in the morning? Well, this should be good."

"Don't be like that," he replied, a sharpness in his tone that told me he was pissed. "Mel's having a difficult time letting go. She was trying to talk me into getting back together with her. I couldn't leave her like that. It wasn't exactly comfortable."

Remembering the look on Melissa's face, my shoulders slumped. "I don't imagine it was," I replied wearily, "but until two in the morning? And I texted you. You never replied." I pushed open the door to my stairwell and started quickly up.

"I couldn't. She was a mess. I was trying to handle it."

"You were trying to be a good guy. I get it. But you broke up with her two months ago and if you'd been final like you said you were and explained everything like you said you did, Melissa wouldn't have appeared tonight begging you to take her back. Which leads me to believe that your breakup must've been a little lukewarm, and if it was a little lukewarm, then what the hell are we doing here ... taking it slow!" I hissed at him, shoving my key in the door.

I caught his glower before I pushed inside, hurrying down my hall to my bedroom. I wasn't quick enough as I unlocked it and strode in with the intention of shutting it in his face. Jake shoved his way in and slammed it behind him.

"I have roommates," I reminded him snippily.

"I couldn't give a shit right now," he growled. "Let's rewind to the part where you think I don't really want this with you."

"Fine. Let's do that."

"You know what I think?" He stepped menacingly close, the air between us thick with ire and something much more powerful. "I think tonight I hurt you again and you know I didn't mean to because you know I had to make sure that Melissa gets that we're over and that I do that in the kindest way possible. I don't think you're angry about any of that. I think for the few hours I was away, you let yourself start to panic that I'm going to hurt you a whole lot worse than tonight. You started to panic because you still don't trust me."

I couldn't say anything. I could barely catch my breath. Just like old times, Jake had read me, unbalanced me, and I didn't know whether to haul him close or throw him out.

"You know what? I know I've got a lot to prove, but I'm still pissed, because I thought for sure you knew one simple truth."

"And what's that?" I asked, my body vibrating with Jake's nearness.

"This." His mouth slammed down on mine, his kiss hard and brutal and bruising as he wrapped a hand around my neck and yanked me against his body.

The familiar taste of him rushed through me and my body instantly lit up for him.

As I kissed Jake back, his kiss grew softer but no less heated, no less hungry, and suddenly we were tearing at one another's clothes, desperate to meld skin to skin.

Our mouths broke apart as we tugged our sweaters off. Mine was barely gone when Jake's strong hands were on my waist, caressing me, molding me, as if memorizing the shape of me. I pulled him back to my lips, my fingers digging into the golden smooth skin of his broad shoulders, my tongue licking his, urging him to control the kiss, to deepen it.

He answered my silent plea, our kiss wet and frantic, driven by the pure need to taste one another as deeply as possible. I gasped into his mouth, trying to catch my breath as he unhooked my bra. It slid slowly down my arms to the floor.

Goosebumps covered my breasts, my nipples erect in the cold air. I shivered but when Jake leaned back to stare down at me, a heated flush crept quickly back over my skin. I watched him in a lusty haze as he scraped his lower lip with his teeth, his study of me so intense the atmosphere between us blistered.

Slowly he reached out his hands and cupped my breasts, squeezing gently before rubbing his thumbs over my nipples. They pebbled under his touch, arousal coursing through my belly and down between my legs. Remembering how sensitive I was, Jake ducked his head and closed his hot mouth over my left nipple. I moaned, bowing my back, my fingers sliding through his hair to grip him close.

I grew damp ... so ready for him.

My hips undulated against air as I whimpered his name.

Jake's control snapped.

His mouth was back on mine and his kiss was hard again, demanding, biting, almost punishing, and I gave him as good as I got, sucking hard on his tongue. Jake shuddered against me, muttering a curse against my lips as he shoved me roughly onto the bed, his fingers deftly unbuttoning my jeans. With a quick tug, he slid them down my legs along with my panties and then he got on the bed, nudging my thighs apart as he stared down into my face. I'd never seen him look at me like that before. Desperate, possessive, *needful.*

And since I was feeling exactly the same way, my body was frenzied to answer his need.

Parting my lips on a rushed sigh, I slid my arms above my head so my breasts arched up toward him.

In response, Jake leaned over me, his hands encircling my wrists as he pressed his jeans-covered erection against my naked body. "You're mine," he whispered hoarsely against my mouth. "Always."

"Jake," I groaned, wild for him.

His right hand left my wrist to draw down his zipper. He shoved his jeans low enough to release his dick and then returned his hand to my wrist to pin me to the bed. I felt him throb hot and hard against my inner thigh.

Then all thought was lost as he slammed inside me before I could draw another breath. I cried out on an exhalation at the pleasure-pain that surged through me.

My thighs gripped Jake's hips instinctively as he pulled back out only to thrust even harder. His rhythm was fast. It was definitely rougher than any sex we'd had before. Desperation to feel every inch of one another guided us. I *could* feel every inch of him and yet I gasped for more. "Jake, harder," I begged as he pounded into me, his features fierce and taut with lust.

INTO THE DEEP

The bed surged against the wall as Jake fucked me toward climax. As the orgasm tore through me, ripping me into little pieces, I cried out his name so loudly, I'm sure the whole building heard me.

Fluttering back to earth like confetti, I felt Jake's hips jerk against me. He threw his head back as he came and I watched him through lidded eyes, feeling my inner muscles contract in aftershocks around him as his climax drew out. Finally, he shuddered to a stop, his head dropping forward to my shoulder. His hands relaxed around my wrists as he kissed me and pressed a clammy cheek to my muggy skin. "Baby," he moaned. "What was that?"

I wrapped my arms around his shoulders. "That was a loss of control," I whispered, still languid and dazed.

Jake's fingers gripped my hip as lifted his head to look into my eyes, his own suddenly filled with remorse. "Did I hurt you?"

I shook my head, a small smile playing on my lips. "You exhausted me, but not hurt." I brushed a thumb tenderly over his mouth. "It was ... wow."

"Yeah," he agreed, seeming just as dazed. "I ... I've never wanted anyone the way I want you."

I smiled at him, shielding him from my inward wince as he pulled out of me. "I'm on the pill, by the way," I murmured casually since he'd obviously forgotten about protection in his determination to have me.

Jake groaned as I moved over to make space on the twin bed. "I'm a genius tonight."

"We're good," I assured him and he smiled as I yawned. "Sorry. You've tired me out."

He kissed me softly, the tip of his tongue just touching the tip of mine. "I'll let you sleep."

"Mmm, I guess we're done taking it slow."

He laughed softly, enfolding his arms around me. Jake snuggled me close and I decided for tonight not to think about anything too serious or too worrying and just delight in the languorous satisfaction of mind-blowing sex that had melted my limbs.

I was relaxed, at peace for the first time in a long time, when Jake pressed his mouth to my ear and whispered, "I love you, Charley Redford."

Stiffening at the confession, it took me a few seconds to get my breathing back under control. Fear shot through me, paralyzing me, and the words I was sure I felt, lodged in my throat.

I couldn't say it back.

I wasn't ready.

Instead, I snuggled deeper into him, hoping he'd understand my silence.

Jake's fingers brushed through my hair gently. "I can wait."

Chapter Twenty-Six

Edinburgh, February 2013

A heavy weight was settled on my back, foreign limbs tangled with mine, and I felt trapped against the mattress for a second as I tried to work out what was happening.

I pried my eyes open, wincing against the light filtering in through the thin curtains at my small window. The bleariness eventually cleared from my vision, and I caught sight of my hand on the mattress beside my head and realized masculine fingers were curled around my wrist.

The night before came flooding back to me and the memory of Jake surging inside of me had my lower belly clenching in lust. My wrist twitched in his hot grip and I felt and heard a masculine purr against my shoulder.

Jake was sleeping across my back, his face pressed to my skin, his torso half on me, half on the mattress and his knee bent between my legs.

He shifted, rousing from his contented sleep.

I'd never woken up with Jake after a night of sex and sleeping together. During our eight-month relationship, we'd been too young to have that moment. Feeling myself get stupidly weepy about it, I covered it by grumbling against my pillow, "If you're going to be settled heavily between my legs, I should at least get something good out of it."

His chuckle rumbled through his chest and moved against my back in a deliciously intimate way. "Morning to you too."

"Mmm, morning."

He let go of my wrist and coasted a hand down my side, his touch shivery soft, as he caressed my bottom and then gently slipped two fingers inside me. I groaned, widening my legs.

"Baby." Jake's dick hardened against my outer thigh. "You're wet already."

I curled my fingers into the sheets. "Don't stop."

He kept gliding in and out of me slowly, torturously building tension as his mouth scattered kisses all over my skin. Stopping his sensual assault, Jake eased off to turn me onto my back. His dark eyes glistened in the morning light as he teased strands of my wavy hair between his finger and thumb. "I missed your hair," he kissed it, dropping it to pick up my hand so he could press kisses along my knuckles. "I missed everything about you."

"I missed you too," I confessed quietly, smiling through the tears in my eyes. "Like a whole lot."

He smiled back at me before he turned his attention to kissing every inch of me. Spending more time between my legs than anywhere, his masterful use of his tongue on my clit had me breaking apart. Loudly. He levered himself up, bracing above me, and as my lower half still shuddered in climax, Jake moved inside me slowly. I sighed in pleasure, and my hands gripped his waist as he rocked into me gently. His head dipped to kiss me deeply, meaningfully, reassuringly.

That morning Jake spent a long time making me come, making me dazed, and making love to me. It was a stark contrast to our fast and furious sex the night before and far, far more beautifully scary.

We didn't come out of my room until early afternoon, waiting until we were sure my roommates had gone for the day. I'd been pretty loud and was almost a little embarrassed to face them. Especially Gemma, who probably wouldn't take too kindly to her roommate having loud sex with her friend's ex-boyfriend.

Pouring Jake a black coffee as he settled on the seats by the kitchen window, I winced as I remembered my attitude the night before. Taking the coffee over to him, I attempted to ignore the hot, satisfied look in his eyes as I approached. It would only distract me and we really needed to talk.

"I'm sorry about my attitude last night," I told him quietly, handing him the mug. "I know you were just trying to be a good guy."

Reaching over for the nearest chair, I was about to take a seat in the opposite corner when Jake pulled me onto his lap. It brought me close to him and my nostrils flared slightly at the scent of my perfume lingering on him.

Something primal and possessive rushed through me at the realization.

Jake was mine again.

The breath whooshed right out of me.

"You don't have to be sorry. No one does. It's a shitty situation," he assured me. "But I promise it's the last time I prioritize her over you. I just … felt I owed her last night. I owed it to be patient and kind with her. I owe you more, though, Charley. I promise it won't happen again."

I nodded in understanding. "Does Melissa finally get what's happening here?"

His eyes dimmed as he nodded. "She's still pretty broken up. She kept talking around in circles, trying to convince me ... I eventually had to just lay it out. I told her I was in love with you and I always would be. I told her I was sorry, but that nothing she said could change my mind."

I closed my eyes, remembering how awful it was to lose him. "I feel terrible for her."

He cupped the back of my head, just behind my ear, while his thumb pressed lightly against the pulse in my neck. My eyes popped open as he leaned his face into mine. "You have nothing to feel guilty about, okay? I won't have that on you."

A memory of the first time Jake held me like that—on the track at school back home—came to me only to be obliterated by the memory of him holding Melissa like that in the student union.

An ache I thought was gone cut through me and I jerked my head from his grip. "Don't."

He frowned, a flicker of unease passing through his eyes. "Don't what?"

Trying to understand my own reaction, I shook my head. My only guess ... I wasn't quite over what he'd had with Melissa. I'd had a relationship too, so it wasn't that (although we needed to discuss it and I wasn't particularly looking forward to telling Jake about the particulars). It was just that I'd never had closeness with anyone but Jake, and Jake ... well, he'd definitely been close to Melissa. Despite his declaration of love and my silence on the matter, I realized that deep down, I was worried I was always going to be that little bit more in love with Jake than he'd ever be with me. That didn't sit well. Not at all.

Shoving the ridiculous notion aside, I shrugged. "I don't like you holding my nape like that." I smirked at him, attempting to turn it into a joke. "It's so alpha male."

However, Jake didn't smile. He studied me, growing somewhat grim. "Char—"

The kitchen door swung open, cutting him off. Claudia walked in, chattering to Beck over her shoulder. Beck's gaze moved to us, drawing Claudia's attention.

For a moment she just blinked at us and then a sly grin spread across her mouth. "Thanks for the lack of sleep, guys."

I blushed, groaning into my hand as Jake laughed softly and wrapped an arm around my waist. He gently moved my body where he wanted it to be so I was tucked with my back against his chest, his chin resting on my shoulder.

Claudia shook her head, still smiling. "Look at them, sickeningly cute already."

I curled a hand around the thigh of Jake's bent leg, getting comfortable. "For someone who didn't get much sleep last night, you seem awful cheery."

She gave Beck a long look and he nodded at her. With a deep breath she turned to me, leaning against the kitchen counter. "I told Beck everything my mom told me about my real dad."

After the incident with the groupie girl at Milk that first night back, Claudia had cooled off toward Beck, not confiding in him, hanging out with him less. It drove him nuts and he wore her down until she started letting him in again. I didn't know which one of them I wanted to shake the sense into. All I did know was that I didn't like the idea of my friend letting a guy—no matter how kind he could be—continually walk all over her feelings. Claudia was a little defensive on the whole subject, so I'd decided to leave her to it and just be there for her when their relationship finally cracked.

Jake stiffened behind me and it suddenly occurred to me he didn't know anything about Claudia's family situation. It must've struck Claudia too because she informed him far more carelessly than she felt. "Oh, at Christmas my dad dropped the bombshell that he's not my real dad. Turns out my real dad is this retired artist, Dustin Tweedie. He lives in Barcelona."

"Shit," Jake muttered. "Merry fucking Christmas."

"Exactly," Claudia replied dryly. "Anyway, I told Beck and he helped me come to a decision. So I called my mom."

I raised an eyebrow, not knowing where she might be going with this. "Okay?"

She smiled but the smile was shaky, nervous, but excited too. "She's going to pay for me, you, Beck, and Jake to stay in Barcelona for spring break ... so I can meet my real father."

My mouth dropped open at the news. Jake gave me a reassuring squeeze when he felt my body grow tense against him. "Are you sure that's what you want?"

Claudia nodded jerkily. "I need to do it. Otherwise it's just going to eat at me. And I'd invite everyone, but I don't want everyone there. It's too personal. I just need you guys with me. If you're willing to come along with me, that is."

"Of course." I nodded

"I'm happy to come too," Jake answered softly as my eyes sought out Beck's. Not sure this was a good idea at all, I kind of blamed him for encouraging it.

I won't let anything happen to her, he promised me silently.

I narrowed my eyes. *That makes two of us.*

"Well," Claudia heaved a sigh, "that's good news. And it'll be fun too. I mean, Barcelona," she smiled, trying to cut the tension. "It's still a few months away. Something to look forward to. Your parents will be fine with it, right?"

At the mention of my parents, I tensed again. "Uh ... yeah."

Understanding my sudden discomfort, Claudia's eyes widened. "Oh, you haven't told your mom and dad about Jake. That should be fun," she grimaced.

Jake stilled behind me.

"Fuck," I murmured.

Jake had asked me a few times in the last month about my family and their reaction to us being back together. I'd been deliberately vague about the whole thing because … well … I hadn't told them. They knew something was up because I'd been somewhat cagey in our conversations, but I just hadn't been able to bring myself to discuss Jake with them.

The truth was I didn't know how to discuss it with them, to make them understand, when I was still trying to work out the whole thing for myself.

By the tightening of Jake's body against mine, I could tell he wasn't happy about the news. He'd told his family. Apparently they were delighted for him, for us.

Shit.

"Anyway," Claudia gave me an apologetic smile before continuing on, "Beck and I were just dropping by to grab my purse before we head to the movies."

"Movies?" I jumped on the idea, suddenly not wanting to be alone with Jake because I knew he was like a dog with a bone and would interrogate me about my family and then ask me about the whole "nape" thing again until I told him the truth.

Claud frowned. "You want to come?"

"Sure." I twisted around to smile at Jake. "Movies?"

He studied me carefully, and I knew he didn't like whatever he saw behind my eyes. But he let it go and nodded slowly.

I crawled out of his lap, ignoring the strain between us. Pulling playfully on his hand, I tugged him up off the seat. We filed out of the kitchen after Beck and Claudia, grabbing our coats as we went. Claudia and Beck stepped out into the building hallway and I was just about to follow when Jake's hand appeared above my head on the door and he slammed it closed.

Whirling around in surprise, I stared up at him as he pressed his body into mine. "What are you doing?"

There was a wary aspect in his eyes as he replied, "I don't really feel like a movie right now."

"Oh?"

"I have something far more active in mind."

Relieved that he didn't want to talk and also already turned on, I gave him a cocky once-over. "Do you think I'll find it satisfactorily entertaining?"

"I'm thinking mind-blowing."

"Mind-blowing?" I arched an eyebrow. "You'll have to work really hard for mind-blowing."

He smirked at me, his eyes lidded with desire. "I think I'm up for the challenge."

"It'll have to—"

He cut me off but I didn't care when he did it with such skill. His kiss was lush and earthy and so addictive. I held onto him for dear life as he kissed me breathless. When he eventually came up for air, I panted hard against his mouth. "Mind-blowing could definitely work for me."

Jake gave me a cocky smile and grabbed my hand, leading me back down the hall toward my bedroom. "Don't get too comfortable," he told me smoothly. "Sex first. Issues and answers later."

My grip tightened in his at his announcement and despite my fear of Jake discovering just how fragile my grasp on our relationship was, I followed him bravely inside.

I may not be ready to let Jake lead me back into the deep, but that didn't mean I wasn't willing to let him try …

To be continued ...

OUT OF THE SHALLOWS

(Into the Deep #2)
Coming 2014

Read on for Bonus Content
(Jake's P.O.V)

JAKE

Edinburgh, September 2012

Sitting in the Library Bar, picking nervously at the soft wood of the table he was leaning on, Jake glanced at the clock above the bar and wondered for the fifteenth time if Charley was actually going to turn up, or if this was a deliberate stand-up. A form of revenge.

For the first time in a very long time, his stomach churned with nerves.

He'd always hoped that he might come across Charley at Edinburgh University, that he'd finally get a chance to apologize for the shitty things he'd said and done, but to actually see her for the first time since Lanton was so much more overwhelming than he'd expected.

The sight of her across the room at Denver's party had knocked the breath right out of him, and everyone else, including his girlfriend, had disappeared. When Charley had run from him without even saying a word ... well, that stung. More than stung.

He'd been a moody bastard for the last couple of days, something that was not lost on Melissa, and she was smart enough to know why. It wasn't fair to her. He needed to talk this out with Charley, needed the closure so he could move on like she probably had and then make it up to Mel for being such a dick.

All thoughts of moving on were shoved forcefully out of his mind as Charley Redford finally stepped into the Library Bar. The first thing she did was share a flirtatious smile with the bartender. Jake felt a spike of possessive jealousy simmer in his blood. Scowling at the guy, it felt like it was three and a half years ago again—as though Charley was his and he was pissed off because she'd smiled at that idiot Alex Roster, who made it so obvious he was dying to get into her pants.

Jake mentally shook himself.

It wasn't three and a half years ago. It was now. She wasn't his to care who the fuck she smiled at.

Supposedly.

Swallowing hard, Jake watched her cross the room, a slight, natural swing in her hips that he didn't think she was even aware of. That was the thing about Charley. The girl knew she was smart, she was confident, and she was capable, but she had no fucking clue she was sexy. It only made all those things about her sexier.

What the hell was she wearing? Was she trying to kill him?

Her long, blond hair fell down her back in a riot of pale waves, dyed platinum now instead of her natural ash blond, still a constant reminder of amazing sex. She had bed hair. He'd loved her bed hair. Every day the sight of her hair had been a reminder that he had the distinct honor of knowing more about her than anyone else in the world.

Right now that hair was swinging against her back, leaving her perfect breasts unobstructed from all male view in her snug green Harley top that showed off a sliver of her flat stomach. Jake wasn't even going to get started on the tight black jeans and ankle boots.

His dick stirred in his jeans and he shifted uncomfortably, longing and guilt warring for control within him.

Guilt won and he focused on her face, reminding himself he was there to move on.

"Jake," she greeted him, her voice emotionless.

A sharp pang radiated in his chest at her indifference, and he had to stop himself from physically rubbing the pain away.

Finding his voice, he replied just as calmly, "Charley," then raised his hand for the ogling asshole of a bartender to serve them. They gave their orders to him as the guy focused on Charley like he wanted to eat her up. It took a lot of effort not to tell the guy to piss off.

A silence Jake didn't like fell between them as they waited for their drinks. They'd never had awkward silences between them. Never. He'd been able to sit in the most perfect quiet with Charley, neither of them saying a word because they didn't need to fill every minute with conversation. They'd never felt the need to prove to the other that they were interesting. They'd always just … fit.

Fuck. It suddenly occurred to Jake that being around Charley might be a bad idea, if only for his and Melissa's relationship, but when their coffees arrived and she glanced up at him with those spectacular hazel eyes, the same eyes that had drawn him in from the moment his had collided with them at a bonfire, Jake was a goner.

A contentment he hadn't felt in a long time began to settle over him and he relaxed in his seat, sipping his coffee. "Your hair is much lighter. It looks good."

She stared blankly back at him and he felt his chest tighten again.

When he first met Charley, it was her eyes he noticed, not just because they were physically striking but because of the way she looked right into you. If Charley caught your eye, you'd find it difficult to look away.

He'd never seen her eyes shut him out before. Not once.

When she wasn't smiling or laughing with him, her eyes were. If they weren't laughing, they were silently telling him she adored him, she'd do anything for him, he *was* everything to her. Even when they were arguing about something and there was a whole lot of fire in those eyes, the adoration never went away. An adoration and vulnerability made only more special because she didn't look at anyone else that way. Not ever. For her family, there was affection and love. For her friends, an easy loyalty. For Jake, all her doors were wide open.

To have that be gone and to know he was responsible hurt more than he was prepared for.

Jake cleared his throat, needing to apologize and explain. "I know I fucked up hugely."

Appearing instantly bored, Charley sighed. "Is that why I came here, Jake? To listen to you state the obvious?"

A panic clawed at Jake's throat as his worst fears and pained prediction were confirmed. She'd moved on. Wanted nothing to do with him. It's what he should've wanted. What he was sure he wanted for the both of them, and for him and Melissa, but now that Charley was sitting in front of him, he admitted to himself that he'd kill for her to smile at him. Absolutely kill for it. "I'm trying here. You used to admire honesty. Have you changed?"

"I'm meaner now. A lesson I learned from you."

Shit! Shit! Shit! Controlling his self-directed anger, Jake leaned closer, hoping she could see the sincerity in his eyes as he told her, "I was a dick to you. I can't take that back. But I can apologize. I can try to explain."

The slight nod she gave him unlocked the tension in his muscles.

"I was lost somewhere else inside my head when it happened, Charley. I couldn't see past that to anything or anyone. I was angry that it got that out of control and I blamed myself. You got caught up in it."

Still cool, seeming nothing more than curious, Charley replied, "I never turned my back on you, though. I don't understand why you blamed *me*."

Unable to admit the truth—that he had irrationally blamed her for what happened because he needed to be angry at someone other than himself—Jake fought through the surprising pain he felt at rehashing history with her. "I didn't blame you. I said things I didn't even mean. All I wanted was to get out of there and put the whole thing behind me. By the time I looked back, it was too late. I couldn't change what I'd done to you. I couldn't change what I'd destroyed. I thought it was better to just let you move on. We were just kids, Charley." He said it because he thought that's what she'd want to hear.

But it wasn't true. Not to Jake. Their age had nothing to do with it. They'd loved each other. And waking up out of his fog three months after leaving Lanton to realize he'd lost her forever had, along with the day of Brett's death, been the worst of his life. Luckily, he had parents who understood and helped him through it. A long time ago, his dad had let his work take over his life, neglecting his wife and young family. Jake's mom had left him. It scared the living crap out of Logan Caplin and he'd desperately fought to win her back. It meant Logan understood and he did his damnedest to get his son through it.

Jake was glad his dad had gotten his happy ending.

At least one of them had.

Watching Charley as she processed his apology, Jake studied every inch of her face. At first glance, someone might say she wasn't a knockout like her friend Claudia, but she was very pretty with delicate features. But when you looked again, there was something about Charley that took her beyond pretty, beyond beautiful. She was perfect to him, even when she wasn't.

Her brows puckered together as she asked quietly, "Move on from me? Or from there?"

Thoughts moving in the entirely wrong direction, Jake decided to answer honestly this time. "From there. From you too. You were a part of it, as much as I didn't want you to be."

For the first time since she'd sat down, Jake detected a hint of annoyance in her tone as she replied, "Then it's a good thing you didn't come back, if that's the way you still see it."

As much as he was glad to observe some emotional reaction from her, it was quickly becoming clear to him that he wanted to see her again and he couldn't see her again if he pissed her off. He guessed she'd only want to see him again if she still felt a modicum of something, anything, toward him.

At Denver's party her reaction had implied she wasn't unmoved by their situation, but her attitude the night before at Teviot and now again sitting across from him suggested she was. Confused, Jake hedged his words carefully to see if he could get her to admit one way or another how she felt. She definitely had been a lot easier to read when they were together. "Charley, all I remember now about you is the good stuff. I let all that other shit go. You were the best friend I ever had. I miss you. I've always missed you and regretted how I left it. But at the party ... the way you looked at me ... that was hard. I'd somehow convinced myself that you would be indifferent about it all. You quickly dissuaded me of that."

To his relief, Charley relaxed against her seat. "I know it wasn't easy for you and your family, Jake. I know that's the biggest understatement of the century ... I tried, though, I tried to understand, and as much as I want to, I can't excuse what you did to me because of what happened. That doesn't mean your apology doesn't help. It does. Thank you."

Tenderness toward her rose in him and he found himself smiling at her. For all her cockiness and smart-assery, Charley had always been one of the kindest people he'd ever met. She'd tried to be there for him so much after Brett died. God, she'd tried to be there for him when it was happening, and he'd been so proud of how she'd handled it. Even trying to save Brett's life. She was the one person in the world who hadn't deserved the shit he'd given her. Nothing could change what he'd done, or take away how badly he felt about it. However, he had the chance now to try to make it up to her as much as he could, to be a friend and prove to her that he wasn't the bad guy she thought he'd turned out to be.

He was still Jake.

Before he could stop himself or think of the consequences, he said abruptly, "I want us to be friends."

"What?"

Instead of using her disbelief at his suggestion to back out of something he knew Melissa would definitely have a hard time dealing with, Jake continued on in hope of persuading his ex to give him time to prove himself. "We're both here for the year. We were great friends once ..."

His hope was quickly dashed as Charley stood and threw money for her coffee on the table. "Look, Jake, I'm sorry I reacted that way to you at the party, and I promise that from now on, if I see you around I'll be polite. You don't deserve any more shit in your life. But it's been a while. We're different people now. Let's just leave it at that."

Before he could get another word out, she turned and strode away from him, unconsciously beautiful and consciously out of reach.

A fist of pure, unadulterated pain twisted in his chest and Jake sat back feeling breathless. Leaning his elbows on the table, his head in his hands, he fought to catch his breath.

Jesus.

He was still in love with her.

Hands shaking, Jake reached for the last of his coffee to soothe his suddenly parched throat.

He was still in love with her.

I'm still in love with her.

His insides felt suffocated. Jake didn't know how else to describe it.

It was a good thing she didn't want anything to do with him. Feeling this way about her wasn't fair to Melissa and in the end, it did neither of them any good.

Charley had done the right thing.

Exhaling heavily, Jake stood, pulling his wallet out and shoving a ten-pound note on the table, overtipping the irritating bartender and not even noticing. Instead he walked out of Teviot in a fog.

Next time he saw Charley, he'd just do as she wanted, leave her alone, and give her a polite nod hello.

Jake rubbed a hand through his hair, ignoring the knifelike pain in his chest at the thought, and knowing for certain that next time he saw Charley, he'd probably do everything in his power to persuade her that spending the next year of college in his company wasn't such a bad idea.

Cursing inwardly, Jake shoved his hands in his jeans and headed toward New Town where he was meeting up with Melissa. Melissa, his girlfriend. A sweet girl, a kind girl, a cute girl, and his friend whom he loved.

It had taken him a while to come to the decision to start dating her seriously, but he'd finally made that decision under the realization that he was never going to fall *in* love with a girl the way he'd fallen for Charley. If he couldn't have Charley, he'd have to settle for attraction and affection.

He'd battled with that decision because he thought Mel deserved better, but she'd convinced him she wanted to be with him, no matter what.

They both hadn't factored in the consequences of Charley's reappearance in his life. For a while, he'd let himself forget what it was like to be around her.

It was peace. It was war. It was excitement. It was contentment. It was exhilaration. It was soothing. It was heat. It was calm.

It was everything.

Thoughts betraying his girlfriend, Jake gritted his teeth, wishing he had it in him to let go of Charley once and for all. But as he passed her building, he glanced up at the windows and wished away his last wish on wishing for the chance to spend more time with her.

For as it turned out, Jake Caplin was a bit of a masochist.

Or maybe, no matter how much the evidence told him otherwise, Jake just couldn't give up on the idea that there would always be a Jake and Charley.

Acknowledgements

Jake and Charley's story hit me like a freight train one day, and their connection was so epic I had to drop everything to write it down on paper. I want to thank my mum for listening to me prattle incessantly about their story, and for giving me much needed feedback on the first draft.

A huge thank you to my agent Lauren Abramo, for not only always working incredibly hard for me and my work, but for also providing me with valued creative advice regarding *Into the Deep*. Your support and enthusiasm never fails to blow me away, Lauren.

The final edition of this book wouldn't be nearly so polished if it wasn't for the eagle eye of my immensely talented editor Jennifer Sommersby Young. Jenn, thank you! You put up with my obsession with adverbs so patiently, and your input into shaping this work was invaluable. You rock my wordy world!

I'd also like to thank my Hellcats, not only for their constant support, but for their opinions when I was playing around with font for this cover. You are so patient and kind and I love all your guts!

I always like to thank at least one blogger. I mean, I thank you all because you're all phenomenal, however, I'd especially like to thank Natasha Tomic of Natasha is a Book Junkie. Natasha, you go above and beyond, and your enthusiasm and support really means everything to us authors. Thank you.

And finally to my readers, thank you for everything. I love your guts, too.

About the Author

Samantha Young is a New York Times and USA Today bestselling author from Stirlingshire, Scotland. She's been nominated for the Goodreads Choice Award for Best Author and Best Romance for her international bestselling novel ON DUBLIN STREET.

For more info on Samantha's adult fiction visit
http://www.ondublinstreet.com

For info on her young adult fiction visit
www.samanthayoungbooks.com

Made in the USA
Lexington, KY
08 September 2014